The Abandoned

The *Abandoned*

Kyp Harness

NIGHTWOOD EDITIONS

Nightwood Editions
P.O. Box 1779
Gibsons, BC VON 1VO
Canada
www.nightwoodeditions.com

COVER DESIGN & TYPOGRAPHY: Carleton Wilson
Cover designed from a photograph by Ivan Lisenkov (Wikimedia Commons)

Canada

 Canada Council **Conseil des Arts**
for the Arts du Canada

 BRITISH COLUMBIA
ARTS COUNCIL
An agency of the Province of British Columbia

Nightwood Editions acknowledges the support of the Canada Council for the Arts, which last year invested $153 million to bring the arts to Canadians throughout the country. We also gratefully acknowledge financial support from the Government of Canada and from the Province of British Columbia through the BC Arts Council and the Book Publishing Tax Credit.

This book has been produced on 100% post-consumer recycled, ancient-forest-free paper, processed chlorine-free and printed with vegetable-based dyes.

Printed and bound in Canada.

CIP data available from Library and Archives Canada.

ISBN 978-0-88971-345-1

Contents

Book One: Winger

Book Two: The Bridge

Book One:

Winger

1. Trillium

ANDREW HAS WATER COMING OUT OF HIS MOUTH. I ASKED Mom why Andrew has water coming out of his mouth, but she didn't answer. He sits beside me on the bus going to school and he has a big long coat and he speaks differently, which seems to have something to do with the water coming out of his mouth. Certain words he doesn't seem to be able to say, and his lips twist weirdly and the clear, shining water—spit, I guess—comes streaming from his mouth as he tries to talk, but mostly he doesn't talk he just sits there, which I like because I can hold my fingers up before my eyes and wriggle them around and when I do that, I can see Mickey Mouse and Goofy, and I can see all the scenes that I imagine, like in the Walt Disney films where everything goes wrong at once, and the colours and the hilarity and funniness all shimmer and agitate, and my heart beats quicker.

Most kids I sit with on the bus I won't do it beside, but Andrew never seems to notice, or if he does notice he doesn't care, or maybe even accepts it, where the other kids make fun of me and put me down, and my dad sure doesn't like it, he gets mad and yells at me, and of all the things I do he acts like it's the worst, so I do it in my room where he can't see, or before he comes home from work in the living room, where I do it instead of watching TV, and I look forward to it all day at school, and with Andrew beside me I don't have to wait until I get home to do it, I can do it on the bus on the way home from school, and when I do it, it seems like the long bus ride doesn't take long at all, it seems I just start doing it and then when I next look up I'm home and the bus driver is saying it's my stop, and I don't know where all the time went, just like when I go in the house and sit in the chair in the living room and do it, and I don't know what's on TV anymore, and I don't know where the time goes, or even what's going on around me, and my dad comes home from work and I don't notice, till he stands at the door to the living room and slams his hand against the side of the door and it shocks me out of doing it. I jerk with an awful feeling as the visions of Mickey Mouse blast apart, and all I see is my dad's angry face shouting at me: "Tim! Stop that!"

A hard, sparking feeling goes through my body and turns to dread at my dad's anger, though it's better than at other times when he just looks at me and shakes his head disappointedly. Or the time when I was sitting in the chair by the front window and he drove in the laneway and got out of his car, and he got out and just stood there staring at me through the window, which I didn't notice until some feeling told me and I looked away from my fingers, from my "diddling" as he calls it, and saw him standing outside staring at me with an angry, sad expression on his face, that would have been bad if it was just angry, or just sad, but with the two of them together it was worse, and when he came in and asked me what I was doing and I said, "Diddling, I guess," and he said, "Oh, I thought you were waving at me, or something," almost joking—that was worse than if he had been angry and mad and shouting.

But Andrew doesn't take any notice, he mostly just looks out the window at the fields and forests drifting by, with the water on his lower lip and sometimes on his chin, glistening and shining in the sunlight coming through the window. He has shoes with strips on them called Velcro which stick together and keep them on instead of shoelaces, and I say to Mom I wish I could have those kind of shoes like Andrew and she says, "You don't want them," and I say yes, I do, because when I try to tie my shoelaces they don't stay tied and people get mad, and when I try again my fingers get nervous because people are watching me, because I think I can't do it and will never be able to do it, and the strings won't do what my fumbling fingers want, like they're making fun of me, like they're escaping me, and my eyes fill with tears and I feel cold sweat at the top of my forehead, and I want shoes like Andrew has, I ask my mom why can't I have them. She says I want them so I don't have to learn to tie my shoes, and it's true, but also because I don't think I ever will learn to tie my shoes, and it doesn't make sense when I could just slip my shoes on if I had shoes like Andrew has, and press the fuzzy, sticky bands over the front to put them on, and I wouldn't have to want to cry. But Mom says, "You'll learn to tie your shoes," and I can tell she's about to say something else, about Andrew, but she says, "You'll learn to tie your shoes," again like she didn't say it the first time, so I know I have to live with my fingers fumbling with the strings again, or people laughing at me when I walk around with them untied, adults saying, "You'll trip over that lace," but I never do.

But no one ever says that to Andrew because he has no laces, and even if he did they probably wouldn't say it, at least the adults, because none of them talk to him very much anyway. It's the other kids who laugh and poke fun at him, but that doesn't matter because he never talks back to them or gets upset by them, and just keeps walking in that slow way, and he's much bigger than all the other kids, and I'm one of the smallest kids in class, so I like hanging with him because he's almost like an adult, a quiet, slow, accepting adult, and I get upset when they laugh at me, when they call out rude names and say they're going to hurt me. But beside Andrew I don't get so upset or scared, it feels like he takes in all the bad words and the rude making-fun and it makes no difference to him so it should make no difference to me, or maybe he really is taking it into his big, slow body, pulling it in like a sponge or a shield, so it can't hit or hurt me, it goes all into him and none at me, like now he sits beside me on the bus so I can diddle, and he just sits at the window, the sun going down gleaming on the water on his chin.

At school Andrew has to leave every afternoon for a couple of hours, with a couple other kids for a special class, and sometimes I wish I could go too in the same way I wish I could have his Velcro shoes. He goes out the door with Sally, a thin girl with bright butter-coloured hair, and Jerry Passingmore, who has really short black hair cut close to his skull, and little white spots in his skin along his skinny jawbone. I remember on Valentine's Day when we all made little mailboxes for our valentines out of big orange envelopes that we taped up on the chalk ledge at the bottom of the chalkboard that went all around the room, and Jerry Passingmore didn't get one Valentine in his envelope and later when we sat at our desks waiting for the bell to ring to get on the bus, we smelled this weird bad smell, and looked at each other, and then we all looked at Jerry Passingmore.

He sat there staring down at the top of his desk, his face getting redder and making the white dots on his jaw stand out more, because the sickly sweet, heavy, warm, almost touchable smell told us all that he'd pooped his pants. Though kids smiled and laughed at each other, and some of the kids would later make fun of Jerry for pooping his pants, it was one of those things that you almost didn't want to make fun of or talk about, each of us imagining a log of poop in a toilet bowl, or more so the log emerging from Jerry's bum, and crumpling, folding over into itself in his underwear and filling it, stretching it with its pulp between his bum and the hard seat of his chair under it. You didn't really want to mention it because it was like death, a dead squirrel by the side of the road, or some other terrible thing.

Though it did make me think of when I had to pee, and I had it in my head that I didn't want to ask the teacher because I kept thinking I could hold it till the end of the class, and I kept feeling its tightness, that crackly, spidery feeling at the end of my penis until I was really fighting just to keep it in, till I was straining like when you're running and you can't run anymore, then you think you'll run to the next tree, and after that, you think you'll run just to the next pole, and so

I thought if I can just hold it in until... and then maybe I thought I could just let a little bit out, and I did whatever you do in your mind to let a few drops out, and when those drops came out it wasn't like just a few drops coming out, but they were a fact, a fact that pulled more drops of pee out of the end of my penis, and aside from the fact, their coming out was one of the most wonderful feelings I ever felt, they were a fact that pulled the rest of the pee out of me and I couldn't stop it, still thinking as the warm almost-hot liquid spread across the crotch of my pants that maybe no one would notice, the beauty and the relief of the sensation overwhelming me, pulling all of me from my head and all the other parts of my body down to my penis and through it, and the lovely warm flow overtaking the entirety of my lower torso and out onto the indented plastic seat of my chair, and then overflowing the seat, and then I feel and hear the urine splattering over the edge, dripping over the sides of the seat and pattering on the floor below. I hear it and do not dare to look down, knowing if I do what I'll see, the shining pool of pale yellow over the linoleum tiles composed of white and grey little stones and dots I often think of as planets when I stare down at them during boring math.

Now I knew they would be floating serenely under the reflective pool of pee, just as I knew kids were looking at me, that the spattering against the floor had got their attention, and I could feel their eyes on me and also see them from the corners of my eyes, and I dared not look at them just as I dared not look down at the pool I knew was growing on the floor beneath me, as the pee was not stopping, as I didn't know the volume of pee from a normal pee, or maybe I did know but my body fooled me that it wouldn't be so much, or wouldn't be noticeable by the others if I let some out, or if I let some out the rest wouldn't want to follow, or I wouldn't want the rest to follow, or I would be able to control or resist letting the rest go as it was now coming in a fast, vicious river of hot urgency, sending its rain rushing over all the sides of the seat, splashing and splattering on the hard floor below, and I knew and saw all eyes around me now focused, alerted by the sound, seeing the insidious glinting of the industrious seeping of the pool, and the darkening blackening stain of my pants now extending to my thighs, the pee on the floor widening till I have to move my shoes to escape the warm smelly wetness.

And when the teacher asks if I have to go to the washroom, then asks over the intercom if they can send Mr. Morton down, I get up, still not looking around at the kids, including Toby Norton who I know is grinning at me with sneering eyes, and the girls who I know are more sympathetic, but somehow that makes it all the worse. I meet Mr. Morton coming in with his mop and pail, and he doesn't look at me, not because he's mad or angry but more like he knows it's me that's done what I've done and it's no big deal, it's what he's used to or what he expects because he's the one who cleans up all the kids' messes, like when a kid gets sick he comes and sprinkles the white powder over the throw-up, which I don't know if it makes it easier to clean up or makes the smell go away, the smell that's so awful and inescapable that you can't smell anything else, and so strong it makes you want to throw up, almost like the throw-up on the floor is calling to the throw-up inside of you and is making it come out, making you gag to pull the throw-up out of you almost like the other throw-up is lonely, just like the first few drops of pee you think you can let out with no problem call to the rest of the pee and soon your seat is full of pee, the floor is full of pee, your pants are black with pee and you're walking to the washroom, your shoes squeaking with the pee and as horrible as the attention of the whole classroom is, it was wonderful to feel the flow, wonderful to feel the warmth, now going worriedly cool.

Some say that Andrew wears diapers, along with his Velcro-banded shoes, and the special classes he goes to, but what Andrew does best is carry snow. At recess we build forts and I take charge directing the other kids, Walter and Rachel Safer, to roll up the massive balls of snow and then carry them and set the other balls of snow to build a wall, for we are the kids who have no other friends, and the other kids build snow forts too, but ours is the best for we have Andrew and Rachel who is almost as big as Andrew to lift the giant balls of snow onto the others to make the walls bigger, and Andrew is the best at it. I tell him what to do and it seems he isn't listening, he just stands there, poised, not looking at me, the water dripping down his chin, but then he goes and does exactly what I tell him, rolling up a massive ball then lifting it and carrying it like it is a big beach ball filled with air, and he takes it even though he can't do a lot of things like tie his shoes or print or fold paper, he puts the snowball right in the right place in the wall, although I have to smooth it down and mould it in so it stays. He works away like one of those big machines, or like an animal, a horse that gives itself to help people, or an elephant that works with its small blinking peaceful eyes, never asking for anything, just eager to do what's required though with no particular urgency or stress—he walks carrying the boulders of snow as if he has always done it, a million times before, or as if he always will do it, forever.

But just like with the Velcro shoes, when I ask Mom if he can come to my birthday party she says, "Are you sure you really want him to come to your birthday party?" with the look like she had when I asked for the giant Mickey Mouse doll at Zellers, or when I said I wanted a dollhouse to play with, and maybe it's because the teacher said on my report card that I have trouble folding paper, or the gym teacher said my coordination was bad and asked my mom and dad to come in for a special meeting, or when I play sports at school and no one wants me on their team so when the captains are picking teams everyone gets picked and I'm left there on my own at the end, with both sides picked and the captains arguing about which one will have to pick me.

Maybe because of all that, and the diddling too, they think I'm like Andrew or Andrew's like me, since I heard Dad say that Andrew was "off," and I asked what that meant and he said Andrew "isn't normal," and it made me want to ask if I was normal but I didn't because I didn't know what he would answer, but it was like Andrew was some other thing, another thing that doesn't seem right, like a raccoon that lay beside the edge of the schoolyard and its body wasn't there anymore, all that was there was these shiny, bright things moving around constantly—maggots—and I said they were gross, and another boy said they were eating its body and I said they were gross again, and he said, "Why do you keep looking at them then?" And the truth was that I couldn't help looking at them, that my eyes and attention were sucked in horribly and totally by them, just like they sucked at the dead body of the raccoon, and I wanted, needed, to look at them, as though if I could take them in completely I'd have no need ever again to be horrified by them. I had to come back to them till they horrified me no longer, but at the same time I knew there was no end to their ability to horrify and that in itself was more horrifying and infinitely fascinating too, a deep dark bottomless well of horrification that was inexhaustible, that made all your bones feel hollow, and made you catch your breath painfully in your throat, yet was tremendously exciting at the same time, or something you knew that was not right but you had to go there anyway, you were impelled to cross the line because somehow if you didn't you might as well have never lived that day, you might as well have just gone back to bed and done nothing, like with the fluffy white kitten we got, Sally, and they said don't be rough with the kitten, and when I was alone with her in the living room I could hear them talking in the kitchen, and I picked up the kitten by the tail, and slowly began to swing her in a circle around me, and as she swung around at the end of the length of my arms and of her tail, her panicked eyes wide, as the lamp and the sofa and the TV all revolved around her like a merry-go-round, her body softly dipping and coasting in the graceful wind, an almost unbearable excitement and horror surged in me, and it was bad, and it was "off," and I let go of the tail and the kitten soared through the air, through the living room, and plopped into the curtains over the big picture window, then fell and plopped against the floor.

Just after that happened with the kitten my dad walked into the room, and he didn't know and never knew what happened and that made me think, as he went and turned on the TV then went and laid down on the couch like he did every night to watch it, that anything could happen the minute before a person walked into a room, and they would never know it, so that it was, for them, as if it had never happened at all, and so with this, the only person to know it happened was me (and the kitten, who was now padding dizzily out from behind a chair) so that it really was as if it never happened at all, except to me, who knew, but there was something desperate and awful, like a knife blade about it, something shameful and unpleasant, a piece of poop you suddenly find on your finger after wiping yourself, or those things your parents talk about in low voices and when you ask them what they're talking about they just stop talking about it, and look at each other and don't answer: Is Andrew like that and are they afraid I'm like that and is that why they don't want Andrew at my birthday because if he's there I'll become more like Andrew the same way more pee wants to come out when you start peeing, or the way throw-up wants to come out of your stomach when you see throw-up on the floor? Just like if they got me the special Velcro shoes I wanted then I wouldn't have to learn to tie my shoes, then I might have to go to special classes and wear diapers, and have water come out of my mouth like Andrew?

Or maybe it was like the trillium flower I saw back in the bush behind our house, when my dad pointed at it and said, "That's a trillium flower, but don't ever pick it." I asked why and he said, "Because that's a trillium flower. It's the official flower of our province and it's against the law to pick it."

It was a white, almost impossibly white flower whose petals were like a whole bunch of triangles, or the folded-up paper things that girls make at school that they move around with their fingers and ask you what your favourite colour is, and it glowed there amongst the indiscriminate weeds and brush and decayed wood and I said, "If you pick it will they put you in jail?" and my dad chuckled, "Maybe, little buddy—more 'n likely they'll give you a fine—but don't pick it, I don't wanna be payin' any fines," and we walked on and I looked back at the trillium glowing in the brush, and I knew I never would pick it but at the same time I wondered how anyone'd know if I did, whether they had police or inspectors going through the bush, or whether if I picked it someday men would just arrive at our door and ask for me without any of us knowing why, but mostly knowing that if I picked it my dad would know, and that was good enough for me.

Maybe Andrew was more like that trillium for me. He was like a secret, and if he came to my birthday party, or if I argued for him to come, they wouldn't allow me to be friends with him anymore, so I needed to let the trillium stay in the forest, and keep the secret of the cat swung around the living room, just like I needed to keep the secret of picking my nose and eating it, because it tasted good and salty, just like the sleepers in my eyes tasted good and salty, as the Plasticine at school tasted good and salty, like the white glue tasted tangy and salty, almost like mayonnaise, and the yellow glue from the tiny clear plastic bottles with the red, mouth-like applicators you could suck it out of tasted vinegar-like and sweet, though the stuff you picked out of your ears didn't taste that pleasant at all, and had a far less enjoyable, waxy consistency.

I suppose I knew I wasn't like Andrew just like they knew I wasn't, because I could talk, and I didn't have water coming out of my mouth like he did, and I didn't have to go to special classes like he did, and it's not like I wanted to be like him, but I didn't want to be like the other kids, or rather I didn't understand them, like the boy who stood behind me on the very first day of school and kept pushing at my back, and I turned around and asked him to stop, but then when I turned back around he kept on doing it, and I turned around and asked him why he kept doing it after I asked him to stop and he didn't answer, just smiled, and I didn't understand and I still don't understand, but Andrew would never do that, mostly because he of course doesn't talk at all, but also Andrew only does one thing, and only is one way, not lots of different ways like everybody else.

But also if not tying my shoes makes me more like Andrew and not like everyone else, that's my way of showing Andrew is my friend and I didn't care if I was like Andrew if that was the case, because I was uncoordinated and because I diddled, and because I didn't play with the ball mitt that my dad got the night I was born from his friend Fred Scott, as he always said, "The night you were born I went out drinkin', you know, celebratin' with my friends, and my friend Fred Scott, he said, 'Hey Dirk, you got a brand new son, hey?' and he left the club and came back with this ball mitt and said, 'Here, this is for your son, we'll make a pitcher or a left fielder outta him,'" and my dad would hold up the mitt when he told the story, the mitt that was born the same day I was, and I felt bad because I didn't play baseball, like I had broken some law of God by not playing with the mitt that had come into being at the same moment I had, but I just had no interest like I had no interest in hockey or football or any of the sports my dad had played, and even when my dad would say, "Whyn't you go play with the ball mitt—Fred Scott was in the other day and said 'How's your boy doin' with that ball mitt, is he a left fielder yet?'" I never had any interest in the ball mitt so maybe that's why they thought I might be like Andrew, or would become like Andrew through hanging around with him.

But anyway I had my birthday party, with all the kids coming to it bringing notes for the bus driver so he'd drop them off at my house instead of theirs at the end of the day, and Mom had a box full of little toys, each with a string tied around them that dangled out of the box and she brought it out, holding it up and letting the kids pull at the strings to get the surprise toy, and when my mom was getting it ready before the party I saw that one of the toys was a Mickey Mouse figurine that I wanted, so she put a little mark on the string attached to it with a red magic marker so I knew which string to pull, and also when she brought it around at the party she held that side of the box where the string was towards me, so I got the Mickey Mouse figurine and none of the other kids knew. Big Michelle from across the road was helping with the party and when it came time for the birthday spanking she held me across her lap where she sat on the floor, and let all the kids spank me for my birthday and when it was her turn to spank me she hit hard and it really hurt, and then she did a "pinch to grow an inch" and that really hurt, and tears came into my eyes from the pain and also from the anger that she would do this on my birthday—and for the rest of my birthday my backside smarted and I was mad.

That was in the house before the bush in which the trillium glowed, down a gravel side road from Highway 7, beside the creek the side road bridged across, though a lot of the time it seemed the bridge was out, and the creek ran up the side of where we lived, and then there was a pond back a ways. On one Easter the Easter Bunny brought me and my brother plastic colourful bug catchers, and after we unwrapped them and Mom and Dad went back to bed, me and my brother went to use the bug catchers where we knew there were lots of bugs, at the pond, where the bulrushes grew up high, and the tall grass, and the pussy willows and cattails, the strange milkweed plants that had pouches you open up that are filled with milk like you might get from an animal, like the white glue you get at school, or the pussy willows just like the paw of a cat, or the furry rabbit foot you got for a keychain (and Dad shot rabbits with the twenty-two gun he told you to never go near, and he cut up the rabbit in the kitchen sink) and the weird weeds that gave off little yellow pellets, or white ones, and the green thistles whose greenness seemed to add to their evil, as they waited for you to step on them to cause you pain.

Down in the pond was the seemingly powdery green stuff that gathered on its surface, making it seem almost solid, and all around the pond the earth was nearly liquid and the tall grass and the reeds hid it so there was no clear line where the pond ended and where the land began, it was all muddy and deceptive and most of all there were bugs flitting all around, the butterflies and also their more nondescript cousins, the moths and other bugs that whipped around but with wings only of white or grey or black, and the simple common flies that joined along, but with maybe a strip of electric blue or purple or green, the shining grasshoppers that leapt up suddenly from who knows where to throw themselves suddenly across your eyes, the mosquitoes that plagued every summer, the tiny almost-nothings inflicting their petty damage who were almost benign compared to the bees and the hornets—the bees which I hated because everyone told me they wouldn't sting you if you left them alone and didn't bother them, and once when I saw a bee I stood stock-still so as not to bother him, and he landed on my temple beside my eye, and he sat there and I felt and heard him buzzing, and I felt him moving around, his horrible buzzing like the turning over of an evil motor. I held my breath and willed myself into paralysis, as my insides crawled with the awful feeling moving at my temples like a cat pawing at its bed, until I knew that him moving around was just to get a decent grip from which to sting me as I felt the sharp stinger pierce into my temple with the fierce terrible buzzing seemingly gaining in volume and I cried with the pain but also with the feeling of betrayal from all those who said that if I left the bee alone he wouldn't bother me.

At least with the bees you got the satisfaction of knowing they gave their lives to sting you, because their stingers had rough edges so they couldn't pull them out without pulling their guts out and dying. It wasn't that way with hornets who, as my dad said, had long slick stingers that could go in and out like a needle on a sewing machine over and over again, as my brother found out when he went into my dad's old abandoned Jeep by the laneway and a whole swarm of hornets come out at him, like a long piece of black fabric unwrapping and flapping in the wind the swarm came, chasing his small boy body across the yard and stinging him over and over, so he got taken to the doctor who said now he was allergic to hornet stings and if he ever got stung by a bee or a hornet again he could die and my dad said, "I told you to stay out of that Jeep!"

All this was on our minds as we crept through the weeds to the pond on Easter morning with our bug catchers, and we heard the trilling all around that we always heard in the summer which I always used to associate with my mother's cigarette smoke and the way it smelled outside, but when I heard the buzzing trilling when she wasn't around I thought it must be the engine of summer keeping the summer going, or the sound made by the golden spidery rays of the sun that you saw when you half-closed your eyes and looked at it, for the sound sounded like the gold spidery rays looked, as though they shone so bright they became sound. Our excitement made our hearts beat faster as we came to the pond, and there above the pale green powdery growth on the surface of the pond, we saw the flittering, jiggling bugs of every description, some adding their sound to the buzzing trilling of spring, the insects coming at us from every direction and we rushed forth with our bug catchers thinking there wasn't a better place for their use in all the world, there beneath the blue Sunday morning sky, there in this perfect pond hidden from the world by its natural protective fence of weed and reed, and tall grass and pussy willows.

Running forward through the muck at the periphery of the pond, the tall grass bending down before us, we reached out with our bug catchers and I told my brother Jason to wait a bit behind, and we heard the low murmur of frogs and heard but did not see them plopping into the water at our arrival, and my feet in boots now splashing, now sinking with a sucking noise down into the muck which reached up to grab at my boots as we saw the most rare dragonfly seeming as big and stationary as a hummingbird hovering before us, its long tail we knew not to be a stinger but somehow very scary nonetheless, its grey bombardier body seeming weirdly big and its wings vibrating in a blur like an optical illusion looking weirdly unnatural and untrustworthy as I felt my feet go deeper into the muck, like a hand at the bottom of the green speckled pond was grasping them, and I tried to lift my feet, but found the sucking, squishing, sticking muck unseen would not relinquish and in fact seemed to pull my legs deeper like the quicksand we'd seen in cartoons and *Gilligan's Island.*

I clutched the bug catcher as I looked at the dragonfly and its whirring wings now abandoning its space in air as it turned and flitted, zooming like an untraceable shadow through the bright clear air, and then my attention turned to my feet ever sinking, and the water coming in over my boots, and my panic rising as I realized I was powerless over the earth which had now taken a notion to suck me into its innards. I reached out to my brother at the shore where the tall grasses grew and I called to him, "I'm stuck!" and he with his bug catcher just stared at me for a moment until I cried with my panic making me almost rigid for I'd realized that the more I moved the more the muck pulled me in, any movement increasing the gravity sinking me, and I called to my brother, "Get Mom and Dad. Tell them I'm stuck!"

He raced back through the tall grasses, and down along the creek back to our house where Mom and Dad were lying in bed and he called, "Tim's in the pond and he can't get out!" and they sparked into action: Mom in her nighty and Dad in his pajama bottoms, right out of bed and down the hall and out the door, through the bush that was our backyard, the bare feet going over the sticks and twigs and thistles, whipping back the branches, my dad's bare chest scratched by the thorns, for in both their minds was the pond, and me lying in the pond, face down beneath the green powdery sediment, stuck in the pond and unable to get out because I had drowned and was dead and nothing could be done but to pull my pulpy, rubbery body from the water, spiritlessly try resuscitation, then break at the point where past and future ended.

But no, they saw me from a distance as the weeds and reeds parted before them, my lower legs submerged, bug catcher in my hand, and the bugs still zipping and flitting around me, the jiggling flies and moths, butterflies and dragonflies unaffected by my cries of panic as the dark mud below and out of sight stubbornly and determinedly pulled, and Dad splashed into the pond, the look on his face a fear I'd never seen before but which I felt turning to anger in his arm clamping around me and lifting me from the sucking scum, up against his chest and to the bank of the pond my mother crying, and my brother too, almost too young to know what was going on, and Dad telling us we should have never gone down there alone, struggling to get his breath back as I saw the drops of water glimmering on the hairs of his heaving chest as we all sat there for a minute in the weeds by the pond on the almost indecently bright Easter Sunday morning.

That was in the house before the bush where the trillium was, when we could play on a fallen tree that was half propped up against another tree so we could pretend it was a bridge by the creek where you could fish, and when your fishing pole came apart and fell in the creek your visiting grandfather could wade in and get it back, and you could catch catfish and put them in a pail where they swam around. That's the house my dad built himself after work while we lived in a trailer, and he called in all his favours, and the workers all came and worked with him building the house that he'd designed, and he always told the story of one of the workers up on top of the roof nailing in the shingles, when he said to the guy, "You putting in four nails a shingle?" and the guy said, "Yep!" and Dad went in the house and looked up at the ceiling and only saw three nails coming through for each shingle, and he said, "Bullshit! I want four nails a shingle!" and he went back in and saw four nails come through for each shingle and never less than four nails ever again.

Local kids would come at night and vandalize the half-finished house, so he started sleeping there on the bare floor in his sleeping bag with his twenty-two but the police said he could be charged if he shot the vandals in the back as they were running away, so make sure to shoot them in the front. When the big front picture window was installed they came and scratched it up, so that he had it tinted blue so that the scratches wouldn't show so much, because he couldn't afford a new window. He worked on building the house at nights after his job and got so tired that he fell asleep while driving over the Bluewater Bridge one night and smashed into the toll booth on the other side.

That was the house with the fireplace in the basement and two sinks in the bathroom, with a front yard that was a sea of weeds—the house that was down a long laneway from the gravel road and one time when they had a party the lane was so mucky no cars could drive in so people parked at the road and Dad drove back and forth in the Jeep ferrying them from the road to the house, and after eating chicken we'd throw the bones into the ditch because he said the bones splinter and can choke dogs if they chew on them, but it's okay to throw them in the ditch because then the foxes would chew on them and choke and die.

When Mom and Dad went to work my little brother Jason and I were looked after by the Simpson family at their pig farm on the highway and I always felt bad because they liked Jason better than me, and they laughed and imitated him when he invented a pig sound to make, and said it was cute and asked him to do it again, but when I invented a frog sound they didn't pay any attention. Even at home I'd lie in bed and hear Mom and Dad playing with Jason and I'd feel bad and wish he had never been born. When we drove in Dad's car he'd always make us yell "Contact!" when he started his engine and driving down the sideroad the steady grinding of the engine always made me think I heard music in it, and when I thought of a song it seemed like the engine was singing the song too.

That was before we saw the men with orange bands over their chests taking pictures around our yard, or it seemed like they were taking pictures with tripods they would set up in the fields of weeds and even in the shadows of the bush you would see them, stretching long strings from one tripod to another, and at first there were just a few of them, but then there were more and they were all around until Mom said they were from the government and that Highway 401 was being built, and the way they planned it, it was going right through where our living room was, where the blue-tinted front window was, and we would have to move. They'd give us money for the property and a big sign got put up that they were auctioning off our house, and we'd have to pack up everything and leave.

Someone bought the house and put it on a trailer and towed it away somewhere else, and trucks and cranes and backhoes came, and far into the future there was only a highway, and the gravel side-road that had led to our house only came to a dead end with room to turn your car around and head back, and there was no creek and no pond and no bush with the trillium in it, and there was no Andrew, there was only the highway and everything else existed only in your mind if you could even still remember it.

2. Diddler

THE NEW SCHOOL WAS CLOSER TO THE CITY AND NEAR A MALL and a Kentucky Fried Chicken where the kids would go sometimes at lunch and get the box lunch, and there were older kids who walked around the back field at lunch and I saw some of them smoking and I told my dad and he said I should follow them and get some of the cigarette butts and bring them home after they were done so he could look at them because they could be smoking bad things. When I asked what kind of bad things he said, "Dope," and he said some of those guys who hang around his barbershop did dope, and he said to one of those guys when he was shaving him, if he ever heard of him selling either of his boys dope the next time the guy came into his barbershop to get a shave Dad would use his straight razor to cut his throat, wouldn't even say a word, the guy would just be dead.

I never did gather up any butts to show him but I often did hang around with the older kids when I first started because I didn't know anyone and they seemed to like me when I did my falls and acted stupid, for that was my favourite thing to do. I would clown around and pretend to fall with my legs going up in the air like I saw old comedians do on TV, and the kids would laugh, and oftentimes when I diddled I would imagine that I was the star of my own TV show, and pictured myself dressed in a grey jacket and hat like Jed Clampett from *The Beverly Hillbillies* and I would picture the image of me with my family, me making a goofy face while above the picture it

29

would say *The Tim Hendricks Show* and below it would say *will be back soon...* like shows did before they went to a commercial, and when I diddled I thought of how I would be the star of my own comedy show, and it was so obvious to me how great a thing it would be when I grew up that I couldn't help but think all other kids felt the same way and I feared the competition there would be when we all grew up and wanted our own TV shows. I'd imagine the show and the storylines and the gags, and it was almost like the show was already happening, that I was creating the show and broadcasting it as I diddled on the bus home and in my chair in the living room after school.

On the bus was an older boy named Tom Such, who didn't mind me diddling beside him on the bus, just like Andrew didn't mind, he just sat there and looked out the window, but he didn't have water on his mouth like Andrew, he had thick glasses and the kind of skin where he had round patches of pink on each of his cheeks and he had no trouble talking and didn't have to go to special classes at school like Andrew did, and I would sit beside him and diddle and imagine I was broadcasting my comedy show to my audience, sometimes even explaining to them what happened in the last episode.

Dad didn't like me doing the comedy. When he saw me doing it in front of my cousins at a family gathering, he said it was "acting stupid" and his angry face told me that "people should laugh with you not at you," which I didn't understand because he made people laugh at his jokes all the time in his barbershop, and I thought what was the difference, and I know the men would laugh with genuineness at his jokes and the look of happy surprise before their laughter actually started. Then it would come out with heavy dark sounds from their stomachs, but still my dad's laugh would ring out as loud and longer like a string of tin cans rattling out after his joke, and he would gaze around at all the men laughing with his comb in one hand and his scissors in the other. I thought: they are laughing at his joke but also maybe laughing at him laughing, made to laugh even more by his laughing, and if so are they laughing *at* him rather than laughing *with* him?

Some of the clowning around I did for the older kids at the school was just to get their attention, like when they asked me to kiss the bottoms of their shoes and I did it, until one time I met a big, fat boy named Pete Sanders and he asked me why I kissed the bottoms of their shoes and he said that was a silly thing to do and he became my friend like Andrew was, though he didn't have water on his mouth like Andrew did, though Pete didn't do well at school either, which he didn't care about because he was going to be a trucker like his dad, and I hung with Pete and a squat girl named Kim Hoswell. The older kids we spent our recesses with out at the wooden steps by the fence would laugh and say she was my girlfriend, and say we should kiss in front of them, and sometimes we did, and I'd recoil and do a funny fall on the ground, and sometimes they asked me to put my arm around her and touch her, and they'd laugh, but I wondered what a girlfriend meant, was it a girl who was a friend, or something else, and did it have something to do with the way my dad and the other men would look at each other and make a noise when girls would walk past the front window of his barbershop?

It was even better for my diddling on the school bus when my mom, who was worried about me now having to cross a busy paved road that was almost like a highway in front of our house when the school bus dropped me off, asked if possibly the bus could drop me off when it was coming the other way, so that I wouldn't have to cross the road to get to our house. In order to do that I had to travel and wait till all the other kids on the route were dropped off, and then the empty bus turned around and went back to the city so I was the only one on the bus for a long time, and I could sit and diddle, and then I would creep up the bus to the front where the driver Mrs. Harrington sat and talk with her as the only passenger she was driving, and she'd ask me questions about my day, and I looked out at the winter snowscape as the sun was going down and told her the clouds looked like mashed potatoes, and one time I told her I hated the national anthem and she said, "You can't hate the national anthem!" and I said I did because at night when my dad fell asleep on the couch in front of the TV I was always awakened by the national anthem playing louder than anything else that came on and it scared me, blaring out marching and warlike, and I would leap out of bed and run down the hall to where the national anthem blared as images of fighter jets streaking through the sky filled the bright screen.

I'd race across the carpet in my bare feet to the TV, panic rising in me, because as much as I was horrified by the booming noise of the national anthem, and the images of fighter jets and marching soldiers that accompanied it, even worse was afterwards when the images would disappear and the screen would break apart into chaotic white roiling insanity, the imageless video storm and the accompanying crackling, cackling hiss and ripping sound of interference and white noise opening a hollow, whistling void at the centre of me. I was always too late it seemed to shut it off before the anthem ended and the witless static madness began, the crumbling busy devastation that sounded like a thousand angry hornets' nests—and a voice signalled the end of another day of broadcasting, which seemed to me to also signal the end of the world and all creation. "No," said Mrs. Harrington. "You can't hate the national anthem, you have to be proud of your country," and she said the one that began, "O say can you see..." was the American anthem anyway, and I agreed, while in truth I hated the Canadian one too, which came on exactly after the American one, and was the one I was always racing to stop before the end of the world.

Mrs. Harrington dropped me off at my house, the sky now darkening because the longer ride made me get home so much later, and I walked up the shorter lane to the house my mom and dad had to do so much work on, and it was Monday, my dad's day off, so they were both at home painting the kitchen because the house needed a lot of work, and it was by a farmer's field on the outskirts of the city, across a field from where the train tracks were, and you could see the stacks of oil and chemical refineries on the other side of the tracks, and on some days you could smell an acrid fart odour from the refineries, and at night you could hear the trains as they crashed and uncoupled in the railyard, and at night you could also see an orange glow from the stacks, particularly from one that had an angry flame burning from the top of it all the time, and some of the others looked almost pretty, like the gathering of several of them that seemed to glow with purple light through a mist that I could see from my bedroom window that I fantasized looked like the castle at Walt Disney World.

Dad had to work hard at the house, fixing it up after he got off work at the barbershop, and for a while we ate every night at a picnic table in the kitchen while the walls were being stripped down and then painted, and it was on Mrs. Harrington's bus that I saw, scratched into the metal back of one of the seats, the words EAT MY MEAT, which I thought to be the most hilarious sentence I had ever read. The idea of someone offering another person the meat off their bones to eat was one of the most delightfully, insanely ghoulish concepts that was possible to be thought of, and I went into hysterical laughter each time I thought of it, the rhyming of the phrase making it seem almost casual and therefore all the more bizarre, and I repeated it over and over again, and I even made a little song that went, "You can eat the fruit that grows on my tree, you can eat the meat that grows on me!" and I sang it to my friends and to the older kids at school who were always trying to get me and Kim Hoswell to kiss, and I would sing it to our babysitter and then Mom told me it wasn't a nice thing to sing, and I didn't understand. Nobody was upset about the idea of eating the meat of an animal, not even the meat of a pig at a pig roast where the pig was on a pole and you could see where they were cutting your meat off the pig's body, so why was it so offensive to laugh about the idea of eating human meat, which was so ridiculous that it was funny?

It was like when I heard the older kids at school say *cocksucker*, which seemed to me the funniest thing I'd heard because I knew that *cock* meant *penis* and the idea that anyone could or would suck on your penis was the most ridiculous thing I'd heard, the image of one guy sucking on another guy's penis was so silly that I started calling my brother a cocksucker and he started calling me it back. One morning when we were supposed to be getting ready for school and we were wrestling on the floor, my mom told us not to use that word and we asked why, and she said our dad would tell us when he got home that night. That night after school and work Dad sat down at the dinner table and told us that sucking on another's penis was something a woman could do to a man but it was a private thing between them and rude to talk about. We asked why and he said because it was private. We asked did it being private make it bad and he said no, but we still didn't understand, so he said *cock* was a bad word. So we asked if we could say *penis sucker* and he said no in a way that made us not ask anymore questions.

Sometimes I stayed home from school when I was sick though I wasn't really sick. It seemed to happen every couple months that I woke up in the morning and knew I couldn't go to school that day. In general, I didn't like school. The only happiness I got was from making the kids laugh at recess and the rest of the time it was boring and then also kids would pick on me which I would try to defuse by clowning around, even to the point of letting them hit me, and reacting in a clownish way so that they'd hopefully stop hitting me. When I played sick I always had to remember to put in a little acting as the day went on, so that when 3:30 rolled around my dad wouldn't say, "You don't seem so sick now!" because when my brother or I stayed home from school we had to get taken to work by either my mom or my dad.

This one time I got taken to work by my dad, so I sat at the back of the barbershop drawing pictures. At the back of the shop there was a room that my dad rented out but he was re-modelling, so I would also sometimes go back and play with the tools. At one point my dad was in the bathroom for a while and a bunch of men were waiting for their haircut so I went in the backroom and got a saw in order to entertain them. I got up in a barber chair and made like I was playing it, bending back the blade and acting like it was hitting me in the face, and I thought some of them thought that was funny, so then I went out on the street in front of the big front window and did an act in which I pulled down my pants and tripped on them, falling over onto the street. When Dad came out of the washroom and saw me, he went straight through the barbershop, picked me up from the sidewalk under his arm with my pants still down around my ankles, strode back through the shop to the back room, pulled down my underwear and slap-spanked me across my bum till I cried. Then he went out to motion to the man next in line to come to the barber chair and started cutting his hair.

I stayed in the back room the rest of the day, or at least until the men who were there when I was spanked left. My bum felt like it was burning but just as much or maybe more so there was a burning inside of me that made me cry, something that was both burning and broken that made hot tears flood my eyes as I tried to distract myself by playing with some nuts and washers and bolts on a table in the back room, my mouth straining as I tried to hide both the sound of my sobbing and the compulsion or need to sob, as I looked down at the blurry nuts and washers.

But as bad as it was, it was better than those times that my dad got mad at me, or my brother and me, and we didn't know whether he was going to spank us or not, and the anticipation and dread of the spanking was just as bad as the spanking itself, if the spanking happened. We did something wrong and we could see it first in his eyes, in the way he looked at us, and we both knew. It was an anger that flashed in his eyes then turned dead, like there was death in his eyes, like burning molten steel poured into a form that then dries and solidifies into something harder than can be imagined, and sometimes his hand would even go up to his belt at his waist for a particularly hair-raising supplement to the dread he had sparked in us, and then in a hard voice he would ask a baffling and unanswerable question like "You want a lickin'?" or "You want a lickin' eh?"

which further frightened and confused me because it seemed to me these questions were riddles, that they were trick questions that had no right answers, and the air gathered round and pressured me till I felt I couldn't breathe, as though I couldn't get the air into my lungs to float the answer out on, and in a way there was no right answer since it seemed it would all end in a lickin' anyway, but still maybe if I had the right answer there was the tiniest chance the lickin' could be evaded so my mind raced in a confused frenzy which of course made it more impossible to come up with any kind of answer, for what was the answer to "You want a lickin'?" but to say "No"?

But that was so obvious there had to be a trick somewhere. For a while my confusion about the meanings of *yes* and *no* extended into other areas, not really sure what to answer if someone asked if I wanted some lemonade. If you said you didn't want a lickin' and got it anyway, what did the question mean? Obviously you did want a lickin' if you acted in a way you knew would make your dad give you a lickin'—even if the real truth was that you'd hoped to act that way undetected. "Tim knows, he can see it in my eyes," I heard him say to his friends. "He knows—he knows when there's a lickin' comin'." And it was true: if there came a time when my brother and I got in trouble, I would immediately start pleading. I would go down on my knees at his feet and start crying and begging him not to give us a lickin'—while my brother Jason just stood there. Sometimes we would hear the dreaded question, another unanswerable puzzle, as he would ask us right out of the gate, "Alright—who wants it first?"

Who wants it first? Was it better to get it over with and run from the room, or was it better to wait until maybe his hand would get tired from spanking the one who went first, or maybe the sight and sound of the first spanking only served to increase the panic and dread of being spanked, and sometimes you let your brother say he would go first just to put off your spanking, on maybe the slightest sliver of a chance that something might happen that would cancel your lickin', but really, you were just looking to stall it, to have just a few more moments unlicked, knowing it was coming anyway, knowing that the panic and dread of watching your brother get a lickin' was almost as bad as getting the lickin' yourself, if not worse, but not caring, because whatever the dread and panic, getting a lickin' was getting a lickin' and not getting a lickin' was not getting a lickin', and not getting a lickin' was better than getting a lickin', however many milliseconds the reprieve was before you got the lickin'.

It seemed always to me that my brother got it worse anyway, as when he and I were wrestling and yelling and making a lot of noise in our room and our dad came in and without saying a word to either of us lifted Jason by his arm and tossed him across the room, plopping him against the sliding door of our closet which caused it to clatter in its runner. Jason slid down to the floor and just lay there crying softly for a while unbeknownst to my dad as he'd turned and left the room right after the tossing. Or the other time when after school my brother and I got a bunch of grocery-store brand cans of ginger ale from the cupboard at the back of house and we shook them up and sprayed them at each other and all over the place, then seeing the mess, tried hurriedly to mop it all up, but the shining glaze of the drying ginger ale on the wooden cupboards and on the floor and on the ceiling escaped our notice, and Dad came home later, not after work, but later than that, and he had the look in his eyes which was made worse by what I was gradually identifying as different mannerisms he would have when he came home from a day of curling or golfing on a Sunday afternoon, which seemed to happen more often since we'd been in the new house, and he'd come in walking slower with a swagger that made him angle with one shoulder after another into a room, and his mouth would be downturned, and his right eye squinted up like he was looking through a telescope with the other one, and he talked in a low, sarcastic, mean-sounding grunt, carefully saying his words with a strange emphasis, like he was talking around some piece of food that was hot on his tongue, and he came up to us and said, "Did you guys spray that ginger ale all over the laundry room?"

At first we said "No," since we thought we'd cleaned it up so good, and he repeated in a low, gravelly, animal voice without any joking niceness you could sometimes get even from his angriest words when he was in another mood or state, and then he said the dreaded words: "Alright," he said, his hand moving to his belt and beginning to unbuckle it, "who wants it first?" doubly mad now since we'd lied to him, and this time I didn't even bother to fling myself at his feet and beg for mercy because the anger and the immediacy was too big. It wasn't a question of if the lickin' was going to happen but when, and the answer to that was right now, the belt was practically whistling through the air already, and we were in our parents' room, and without even knowing how it happened, my brother volunteered himself.

The pants came down and he laid across the corner of my parents' bed as my mother stood in the doorway, and if the downside of being the second in line for a lickin' was that you had to endure the painful yelps of the sufferer before you, it was of no consequence here as my brother just laid and took the lickin' without making a sound, the belt slapping across his bum cheeks, and then just as soundlessly when the lickin' was done, getting up, pulling his pants up and running from the room, and then it was my turn and I cried and yelped as I was spanked and found out later that one of the upsides of being second in line, the idea that the spanker would wear out some of his energy and passion and anger on the first lickin', was proven true when after a few days my mom said to my dad that my brother still had black streaks across his backside from where the black had come off his belt.

During this time my dad more often than not came home in the mood of having his right eye squinted up, and he would argue with Mom and she would shout back about his drinking which I never understood since everybody drank, we all had to drink in order to live, then later recognized it was drinking a particular thing that made him act differently, that gave him a particular smell, that I tried to identify so I could be aware of how he changed and how I should act so I wouldn't get in trouble with him. On the Sunday afternoons after he went to golf early in the morning we'd wait for him to come home and the hours slowly floated by till most of the day was gone, and then his car would drive unnaturally slowly down the driveway, and another identifying characteristic was he would smoke a different brand of cigarette than he would on every other day. One time he came home and sat under a tree in the front yard smoking his weird brand of cigarettes, and another time he went around hammering nails into the trees in the front yard, and later in the week he started giving hell to my brother, thinking he was the one who hammered nails into the trees. My brother said, "I didn't put those nails there Dad, you did!" and then I overheard him telling a bunch of his friends in the barbershop, "And I thought, by Jesus, maybe I did, all pissed up out there on a Sunday afternoon!"

The way he'd act when he was drunk was so far different from the way he'd act other times that they were like two different planets that had nothing to do with each other, no common language or even a knowledge that the other existed. One day he'd look at you with hatred, his voice and words stabbing out from an understanding that all is hell and that you are to blame for all being hell, yet the next day he'd come home from work and greet you with a broad smile, like the way he greets his customers in his barbershop, and say, "How y'doin', partner?" Yet sometimes his behaviour was good for me when he'd been drinking, when he would come home with a friend and then shuffle down the hall to my room and ask to have some of my drawings to show to his friend because I'd been getting some attention at school for my drawings, and my dad would take the pictures out and show his friend in the living room.

"Look at that! In grade two and he's in the newsletter for the whole damn school," and from my room I'd peek down the hall and see him leaning from his Laz-Z-Boy to his friend, showing him a drawing, pointing at it and saying, "Look at the detail there—now the average person might not see that, that kinda detail there, and he put that in," and he was praising and appreciative as he was at no other time with my brother or me, and I would pull my head back in from the hall, feeling the warmth of his praise, feeling it pull at the muscles in my face, and my mother would notice and say, "Now you know he's just saying that because he's been drinkin'. You know he's not going to be talking that way tomorrow," which made me feel weird because if I felt scared and disturbed, panicked by the way he acted when he was drinking and mean, why couldn't I feel warm and happy when he was drinking and complimentary?

Was the good untrue in a way the bad was not? Or did they both mean nothing, happening in a dream that you were powerless to change or affect but which settled all around you and comprised your reality totally, for the entire time he was in your presence or in the house, and not a moment more or a moment less, no matter what you thought or felt, or what you did or didn't say or do? So to feel warm at being praised was wrong in such a circumstance, like being comforted by lies, or eating poisoned fruit, yet being panicked or disturbed or hurt by his meanness wasn't wrong or right, but simply *was*, in a way you couldn't help, so thoroughly did it infiltrate your heart and stomach, you had no choice but to adjust your animal instincts to the temperature of his moods.

Yet my drawings drew genuine admiration from my classmates as they sometimes gathered around my desk, and one of the students even said out loud to the teacher, "Why can't I draw like Tim does?" and the teacher said, "Well, Tim can't play soccer like you do," and the kid said, "That's right, we get out on the field and he won't even take the ball—he lets the other team have it!"

"You see?" said the teacher. "We all have our strengths—it all evens out." Still the older kids would pick on me, and I would take a hit rather than run away, trying to make the kids laugh so they wouldn't bother me anymore. But with some kids that would piss them off even more. When he started school that fall, Jason saw the kids picking on me and me letting them push me around. He ran in to defend me and got a punch in the nose that made it bleed, and the teacher on recess duty had to take him to the school nurse.

Recesses were problems for me because of the kids picking on me so the alternative to that was to hang out with Kim Hoswell, the short, squat girl who the other kids would say was my girlfriend, or else sometimes I would hang with my friend Carl Plympton who shared my interest in cartooning, but he also was interested in playing sports like all the rest of the boys so often he wanted to do that instead of hang with me, or to talk about sports, or to trade hockey cards in the endless ritual of the winter months, which I didn't do, so my task was to convince him to be with me and do what I called walk-and-talk, which consisted of walking around the fence of the schoolyard and talking for the whole recess, which is what I wanted to do, but which he only wanted to do, or could be convinced to do, sometimes.

Mostly I was stuck back with Kim Hoswell, as she was another kid that most other kids didn't want to hang with. She wasn't as fat as Gabby Ferguson who literally was as wide as she was tall, and whom teachers nonetheless made do the kilometre run with the rest of the class even though she couldn't run in any real sense, her ball-like rotundity causing her to rotate her body one side at a time to put her short, stumpy legs one ahead of the other, her shoulders likewise taking turns swinging ahead and her long straight hair swinging side to side like a cantering horse's tail, all while she wore an inexplicable, eager-to-please smile. She persevered far, far behind the rest of the class till you could barely see her behind us as we ran the circumference of the field and the teacher called back to her across the chasm, "Come on now, Gabby, pick up some speed. You can do it!" and later when everyone came in panting back to the classroom, there would always be a ten-minute interval before Gabby came in, panting and sweating, slipping behind her desk, still smiling her eager-to-please smile.

Kim wasn't as heavy as her or as separated from everybody else like Gabby was, just as I wasn't separated from everyone else the way that some other boys were. But whenever Kim asked for an indoor recess because she said she wasn't feeling well, I asked for one too. That was the kind of recess I preferred anyway, the empty silent classroom and the other kids visible out the window, laughing and running and playing in the field, and me glad to see them out there and doubly glad I wasn't with them, maybe in my heart feeling superior to their childhood outdoor raucousness as I sat at my desk and drew pictures.

In addition to Kim Hoswell during one indoor recess there was Mary Hiemstra, a girl who I thought really was sick and sat doing her homework at her desk in her dress, for she was of that religion where the girls had to wear dresses and keep their hair long down their backs all the time, and the boys had to wear real shirts with collars all the time, and pants that weren't jeans, and had to keep their hair really short all the time. Sometime toward the end of the recess Mary came by to look at my drawings and asked why I drew all the time, and as a joke she took one of my drawings and ran through the room, and I chased her laughing and Kim came too, and somehow we ended up on the floor in the cubby beneath our teacher's desk and Mary asked me to show her mine, and I was nervous, looking over at the door when she offered to show me hers, and she pulled up her dress and I began to see her underwear, and Kim, laughing, undid her jeans, so I decided it must be alright, so I pulled down my pants, and from the front of my underwear I let out my penis, and both the girls giggled nervously, but also in their eyes was something still and interested and serious, and shaking myself I made my penis jump around a bit, and then in a jarring blast somehow there was a figure standing at the side of the desk, a figure that was a shadow that then resolved itself into Mr. Goodearle who'd been walking down the hall and heard us, then came into the classroom to the side of the desk, and called out, "Tim!"

And then hastily fumbling my penis back into my underwear, and then the horror-filled instant when we were all marched by Mr. Goodearle out of the classroom and down the hall to the principal's office, me feeling sick as we approached, thinking of how everyone would now know that I pulled out my penis, thinking of my dad and how he was so mad that I pulled down my pants at the barbershop, and the huge door of the principal's office loomed before me, the principal's office where the lickin's took place, where we'd heard there was a wooden case of various leather straps increasing in length and size and thickness in order to fit the appropriate punishment to the crime, and this principal in particular, it was said, had the unique habit of pulling a hair from your head before the administering of a punishment, of laying it across the palm of your hand, then lifting the leather strap and bringing it whipping down upon the hair on the palm of your hand so that there was a precise slit-like bleeding cut across your palm exactly where the hair had been, and we came into the office ushered by Mr. Goodearle to where the principal sat behind his desk, looking up impossibly placidly as we shivered and Mr. Goodearle told him what we'd done.

The principal's face frowned with severity as he looked at us, then looked at me in particular and said, "Tim, why did you take your privates out of your pants?" I pointed at Mary Hiemstra and said, "Because she told me to," and Mary Hiemstra looked at me and said, "If I told you to jump off the Bluewater Bridge would you do that, too?" because the Bluewater Bridge was the nearby bridge over the river to the US and one of the highest bridges in the world. The principal looked at me with what I thought was the smallest hint of a smile and at the same time with the smallest flicker of his eyes over to Mr. Goodearle said, "Well, Tim, if anyone ever tells you to do that again, you come and tell me, alright?" the tiny smile of which panicked me for I thought its ridicule was directed at my lame and cowardly attempt to blame Mary Hiemstra.

"But try not to do it again," the principal said, and dismissed us and we went down the hall and back to our classroom, Mary acting mad since I said she told me to do it, but she did tell me to do it, and in my relief, and in all our relief at not being given the strap, I felt the gathering dread that the principal was going to phone our parents, that in particular my dad would find out about me showing my penis and he would be enraged as he was at my pulling my pants

43

down on the street, or at my diddling, or at me not wanting to play with the ball mitt Fred Scott gave him when I was born, or at me for acting stupid and playing the clown and making myself someone who people laughed at rather than with, and it would be another thing where I wasn't normal enough—like Andrew—and I wasn't boy-like enough and he would be embarrassed by me being his son.

But when I got home, let off by Mrs. Harrison to tread up the laneway, and my mom came home from work a short time later, she gave no sign of knowing about that moment in the cubby. She was only tired and asking the same questions she asked every night as she sat in the La-Z-Boy smoking her cigarette and my brother and I watched *Three Stooges* and *The Flintstones* and *The Brady Bunch* in the living room, then she went to start to make supper, and later my dad came home and drank the beer he drank before supper, and then one with supper because he didn't have to drink milk like we had to, because he said, "Only women and children need to drink milk." The same way I'd search the expressions of his face to see if he was drinking and how I should act, I searched him every minute for any indication he'd heard from the principal, and even after supper, when he went out to lie on the couch in front of the TV and fall asleep the way he did every night, I waited in that interval because that's when sometimes he'd talk to us about serious stuff like when he told us not to say *cocksucker*, but still he acted in his usual calm, tired, kind of grumpy way, and I was a little relieved, but when I got in bed I thought he could still find out, that once something happened, anything happened, anyone could find out at any time, if not now, next week, or a year, or twenty years from now, and the only way for someone never to find out something happened is for it never to have happened in the first place, I thought in the darkness of my room as I heard the trains rumble and crash in the yard across the field across from my house.

It was still on my mind a couple weeks from then when Parents Night would be happening at the school, and as the day grew closer I got uneasy because surely Mrs. Robbins, my teacher, had been told by the principal and Mr. Goodearle what had happened, and maybe she'd be obligated to share it with my parents, and though my dread had lessened the further we got away from it, I was still hyper-aware as we strode to my class in the impossibly bright lights that shine in classrooms at night, and we went up to the very desk I'd shown my penis under, and Mrs. Robbins gave a rundown on my progress that year to date, and my brother stood looking wide-eyed at the classroom since he was only used to the different-looking classroom of kindergarten, and Mrs. Robbins suggested some exercises we could do at home to help me to learn to tie my shoes—like letting me practise on a larger, adult-sized shoe—since I was still lagging behind the other students in that regard, and then she said at different moments when the class has quiet time she notices that Tim sits at his desk and moves his fingers in a strange manner in front of his face, and she accompanied her observation with an acting out of the movement, her hands rising to wriggle her fingers in front of her eyes, and did he do such a thing at home, she asked them, was it something they too had noticed?

Mom said that was something they'd noticed, yes, and Dad looked over at me with an angry look because I'd failed to stop this habit—that I continued on with it purposely, it seemed, to embarrass him and to make myself abnormal, making myself into what would never be a man, and his eyes shamed me and I'd embarrassed him, embarrassed them, again, though Mrs. Robbins said that in every other respect I was doing very well, particularly with my drawing, I just needed to focus on neatness and tying my shoes, and concluding the meeting, we went down the aisle and there was Paul Roughton without his parents for some reason, standing in his plaid shirt with his hands in his pockets, and a cowlick of jet black hair darting down over his forehead and shadowing his freckled nose.

He looked up at my parents as they approached and he said, "So you're Tim's mom and dad, huh?" in his hoarse voice that seemed more like a teenager's or an adult's than a little boy's. I had always avoided him because he was derisive toward me. He wasn't the kind to physically bully but would sneer sentences that seemed to have unpleasant meanings. I never knew just what was supposed to be meant—I only knew that it was negative, insulting and mean. He always wore a contemptuously amused smile that caused his eyelids to half-drop over his eyes and it was with these eyes and that smile that Paul Roughton looked up at my mother and father and volunteered in a strangely weary and dry, croaking voice, "Yeah, Tim's doin' pretty good, havin' a pretty good year," he rasped, with a cock of his head that silently added, *all things considered.* "Only thing, though," he continued, "is that sometimes we notice him sittin' at his desk, doin' this." He raised his hands to his face and flapped them around grotesquely. "Dunno why he does that," Paul Roughton shrugged. "Other than that, he's doin' fine."

"I'll bet you do real good in school too, don't ya?" my dad asked him.

"I'm doin' alright…" Paul Roughton began, his odd, adult-like confidence in his small body preparing to continue—

"Yeah, I'll bet you're the type who really keeps outta trouble—a real genius student," my dad blurted, his dismissive bitterness vanquishing that of the comparatively inexperienced young boy's as he brushed past him and led us out of the room.

On our way home and later at my house my dad didn't look at me or speak to me, but when I went to bed my mom came into my room and said she knew Paul Roughton was being a smart aleck because she'd gone to school with his father and he was a smart aleck too, and as a matter of fact all the Roughtons were smart alecks, and they were tough, hard people, and she thought it was mean of him to try to embarrass me in front of her and my dad, but maybe I didn't have to do that diddling thing when I was at school in class, and then she turned out the light and left the room and I lay there waiting for sleep, thinking of Mrs. Robbins raising her fingers to her eyes and asking my parents if they were aware I did this, which was bad but still not as bad as it would've been if she'd told them I showed Mary

Hiemstra my penis in the cubby beneath her desk. Then shadows clouded around the image of my teacher and I fell asleep.

Dad still had to work hard on the house. It needed a lot of repairing, and so one weekend Mom and my brother and I took a train to visit some friends of Mom and Dad's who lived in a city a couple of hours away, so Dad could get a lot of work done while we were gone. Don Regnier was an old friend of Dad's and his wife was a friend of Mom's and they had four kids that my brother and I played with. Don and his wife had a waterbed that I would secretly go and lay down on, but we weren't allowed to sleep there, and I slept with my brother in a spare room down the hall and in the night, in my sleep, I saw myself and my brother and my father in our kitchen back home, and I was fighting with my brother, and I bit him on the arm, and my brother cried to my dad, and Dad came over to me angrily and his mouth opened, and it kept on opening as the blackness within it engulfed me entirely, and I felt the massive jaws closing around my head as if to say, "You bit him and so I'll bite your head off," and in an instant I was awake in a foreign bed as if blasted by an electrical shock to find I was already crying, howling and screaming in the strange room till Don Regnier came through the darkness from the waterbed in the next room and said with sleepy-eyed alarm, "Hey, hey, hey, what's the matter?" and I was sobbing too hard to speak, yet even when I could speak I couldn't tell him because he was Dad's friend and I didn't want to tell him I'd dreamed of Dad biting my head off, and he kept saying, "Jeepers creepers, what's the matter? You're gonna wake the whole house up," and he hugged me to try and get me to quiet down and after a while I did.

The next day Dad was coming to pick us all up and drive us back home, but we were all surprised when he came not in our usual car but in a small sports car he only used occasionally because it didn't have any back seats but only a space for me and my brother to crouch, and also because it was a Triumph Sprite and was always breaking down and needing parts that were hard to get. When we asked him where our other car was, he said he'd been driving late at night across a bridge and all of a sudden a deer came into his path, so he was forced to steer the car off the bridge and it sank into a creek.

As we rode home, my brother and I wedged in and crouched behind the bucket seats, and he told the story again and I imagined the deer suddenly appearing in the silvery ray of the headlights out of the blackness of the night. I imagined the slivery ray suddenly swerving into further darkness, the low guardrail providing no barrier to the car as it tilted into the creek, but as much as I could see this, I couldn't help but imagine there was never a deer at all, that something else had happened to our car, or that yes, maybe it had gone off the road and over the guardrail and into the water, but a deer had nothing to do with it, and the thought seemed inescapable, though each time I entertained it the guiltier I felt, at doubting my father, and also diverging from the story that everyone agreed was true. Something down deep in me knew that my suspicion wasn't just a nasty reinterpretation of events, but was itself reality—and what claimed to be reality was a play-acting performance by the rest of the family to make themselves and each other feel happy or simply okay.

Yet my dad did get a lot of work done on the house, and in the work that he did he seemed to take more pleasure and pride than in the hair-cutting during the day, though it took him a long time because he wanted it perfect, and we had two bathrooms and one of them would inevitably be out of service most of the time, and I was allowed to decorate the unfinished wall of the kitchen with a long parade of Disney characters I drew on a roll of paper Mom got at her work. He also liked to cook, using the Mondays he took off work to make elaborate dinners for the family when we got home, and sometimes apple and rhubarb pies, and when he called you out to the kitchen and got you to taste something he was cooking, he'd watch you intently as you ate it, and when you gave the reaction he wanted he'd respond with a high-pitched, hooting laugh and I noticed the fingers at the ends of his arms when he laughed, and they'd wriggle excitedly as his body shook with laughter, as they sometimes did when he laughed after telling jokes in his barbershop, and I'd think maybe he was feeling some of the same excitement I felt when I diddled, and maybe that's why he got mad when I diddled, because he was scared of his own diddling, which only came out sometimes.

Those times he cooked, Mom would say he cooked so good that he should open up a restaurant, and I would get excited about the idea, imagining my dad working in the kitchen, people sitting at the tables we'd set up in the living room and dining room, and my brother and I bringing the meals out to them from the kitchen, their cars parked out in the laneway and on the lawn. As much as I enjoyed the idea of our house being transformed into a restaurant, I enjoyed even more the idea of my father doing something he loved and got pleasure from, picturing him proudly bringing out some of the pies he made for his favoured customers, because it seemed to me the reason he was not coming home nights and staying out, or not coming home at all, so that I got up and went to check and see if my dad was beside my mom in their bed in the mornings, the more often he would stay out longer on Sundays, golfing and coming home angry with his right eye squinted up to have a fight with Mom, was because he didn't like his job, because he always came home from it depressed, to drink a couple of beers and go to sleep in front of the TV.

I wished somehow a sudden gust of inspiration would lift and compel my parents to turn our living room into a restaurant, though I knew it would never happen, still the thought was so appealing I couldn't help but hold out the tiniest hope they would choose to leave their uninspired lives behind to start a dream where the man who watched you tasting his food—looking with anticipation to see the expected response of delight—was my father, not the man who lay defeated on the couch. But I knew that it would never, could never happen, that the sun-dappled living room restaurant was only a dream.

Dad was coming home later on the Sundays, as he did on the day he promised to take us to the Point Edward Ex-Servicemen's

Club Picnic that was put on by the club he went to drink cheap beer most Saturday nights. This event was the one time these old, chunky, ruddy-faced gentlemen emerged from their mottle-floored clubhouse to commune with their respective family members at a gathering in Canatara Park and set up their picnic tables to serve their traditional delicacy of turkey burgers, taking turns to man the immense vats of shredded turkey on the gas burners, plopping the hot turkey on hamburger buns for the kids and the wives, as a little old man dressed as Popeye wandered the grounds handing out candies and suckers "for the kids."

Yet as the day wore on it seemed Dad wouldn't get home in time to take us to the Ex-Servicemen's Picnic, and about mid-afternoon Mom said, "Well, it looks like he's not gonna get home in time to take ya," which was too bad because our cousin Chris was with us, Chris who still lived out of town on a farm and with whom we shared many weeks of our summers, us going out to his place for a week, sleeping in the rooms at the top of the old farmhouse which still had a hole going through the ceilings and floors for the pipe of the now-absent old stove, then us running through each day in games of war in the hay mow where we built forts with the bales and swung out on a rope from the high window over the cow pen.

But now Chris was staying at our place and we'd told him about the picnic and the turkey burgers, and we sat in the desolate hum of the waning afternoon till suddenly our new car came edging up the driveway and we jumped up and shouted, but Mom said, "Don't get too excited, he'll be in no shape to take you," and the sight of my dad getting out of his car with his slow, disgusted gait and his looking around with his right eye squinted up like a mean and merciless stranger made me realize she was right, and he came in the door and Mom said, "You promised these boys," and he said huskily, hoarsely, "Well, alright... Let's go!" Jason and Chris and I got up excitedly even though I saw Dad wasn't in the best type of mood to take us, but I so much wanted to go to the picnic, riding on the enthusiasm of the two other boys, that I ignored the warning signs as maybe they did, though they seemed to have nothing but excitement as he scoffed to my mom, "We're still gonna go—come on, let's go!"

We ran to the door and she cried, "You're in no shape to take them!" but out the door and down the short sidewalk we went to the driveway where we all got into the front seat and my dad got in behind the wheel and for a moment he just sat there with his hands on the wheel, staring down, and then he got up out of the car, walked swiftly back into the house and after a moment emerged with a beer in his hand. As he walked to the car my mom appeared at the door calling, "Oh, yes! Don't forget to take your beer! Always got to have your beer!" and Dad gunned the engine, pulling out around our curved driveway, making the gravel jump and click as we zoomed out onto the road at a speed that made Chris and Jason and me tumble into the footwell at the bottom of our seat as we cruised into the city, my brother laughing and my dad looking at him with a wicked, ecstatic face as the speed made a hopeless wind sweep through the heart, at which point I tried to laugh too even as I felt compelled to clutch at the mats on the footwell of the car in search of solidity and stability as we whisked past all the other cars and trucks on the avenue, their roofs and hoods passing unnaturally fast at a cockeyed angle from where we huddled on the car's floor, and then we eased for a while into a normal speed, only to have my dad hit the gas again, so we lurched suddenly into a higher speed and my brother who had been laughing suddenly began crying with no apparent transition as my dad, whose face was against the side window and its whizzing landscape, looked at us with both eyes squinted up, the corners of his mouth lifted in a smiling laugh that wasn't sinister so much as beyond all concept of sinister and innocence, and in fact seemed to have no human feeling in it whatsoever as he laughed at us clutching each other and huddling together on the car's floor.

We got to the park where the picnic was just as the turkey burgers were shutting down for the day and Dad made sure we got the last ones. We also got to see Popeye, who seemed in a less than energetic mood, passing out his candies and suckers with exhausted sullenness. After we ate the turkey burgers in the fading sun as Dad sat on a picnic table and smoked a cigarette, we got back into the car and he seemed to fall into a different, quieter mood, driving us down unfamiliar streets without gunning the engine. We asked him where we were going but he didn't answer, and we pulled up to a neat little house that I recognized but my brother and of course my cousin didn't, and Dad led the three of us up to the door of his brother's house, where we never went, even though we lived in the same town, and only in the dimmest memory could I remember us being there before, and the handful of words my uncle ever spoke to me.

I remembered my uncle's wife only as a nervous person who worried about my brother and I touching things in her house, or dirtying them or breaking them, with big fat cats that she didn't want us to bother. This time she came out the side door with the green garden hose reeled on the wall beside the door and we were led down into the basement rec room where my dad's brother sat watching TV from his easy chair, and my dad sat down on a couch with us three boys sitting down beside him, and he asked pointedly for a beer, and his brother went and got one, and my dad sat there silently drinking his beer and smoking a cigarette on the couch as everyone looked at the sports on TV, and every so often my dad would look over at me or one of the other boys and make a face mocking his brother and his brother's wife, and the whole situation, and he'd blow out a gust of smoke disdainfully as if to say, "Well, isn't all of this pathetic and stupid, isn't this proof positive of what a miserable farce this whole thing is?" and after a silence I could feel as a tightening vice in my chest, we got up to leave, following my father after—and only after—he'd entirely finished his beer with a satisfying smack of his lips from the bottle as he sucked out its final drops then laid it on the coffee table and made his way up the stairs of the shadowed rec room to the evening still illuminated by the sun as we got back in the car, leaving as wordlessly as we'd arrived.

But just as it wasn't every Saturday night he would go straight from work to the Ex-Servicemen's Club without calling, leaving my mom worrying and waiting for supper, on Sunday he didn't always go golfing and curling and drinking away most of the day. Sometimes he would just get up and laze around the house, or on one Sunday we all went to Green Valley Trailer Park, for that's where Kim Hoswell lived, and we'd found that Kim Hoswell's dad and my dad were old friends, and though I worried my dad would find out from Kim Hoswell's dad that I had showed my penis to her and Mary Hiemstra, I wasn't entirely worried, since for Kim Hoswell to tell her dad she'd have to admit that she got into trouble and had to go down to the office too. We had gone over to Green Valley Trailer Park to use their pool, and my dad leapt in from the diving board so it made the water jump up over the sides, then he shot across the pool with slashing strokes from one end to the other—because he'd grown up by the water, by the river and the lake, and spent his whole summers in a bathing suit, he said, and made money from jumping into the lake and retrieving coins flung from travellers on the old ss *Hamonic* cruise ship.

And when he came out of the pool after his swift swim—for adults didn't stay playing in the pool all afternoon like kids did—he sat with the other adults in their lawn chairs with their beers and they joked about me and Kim, about us kissing and holding hands at school, and at one point Dad said, "Yeah, Tim does pretty good at school, but he's got this habit—you ever see him doing this, Kim? He lifts up his hands and starts flappin' them around in front of his face…" He paused to demonstrate the action. "Looks like he's got a mental problem or somethin'—you ever see anything like that?"

Shame mixed with a surprising blast of anger shot through me and grasped my stomach. "What're you doing?" Mom asked him. "Why do you say that in front of all these people here like that? You're embarrassing him," she said as my face was growing hot and Kim and all other kids of the trailer park were looking at me and the beer-drinking adults were gazing at me with impersonal curiosity.

"Maybe he should be embarrassed," my dad said. "Nothing else works to get him to stop—maybe he won't do it anymore if he's embarrassed to do it." Later in the afternoon he went in the pool again, and Jason leapt in with him, and they were swimming around the deep end and my dad called out to me to get in, but I didn't want to, and he called me in a more stern, commanding voice, swimming to the edge of the pool and glaring at me, so I walked to the edge of the pool, and he treaded water in the deep end, holding out his arms to me and said, "Come on! Jump in!" and I stood there, and even though my little brother was in with him and smiling up at me, and though I knew my dad could swim as good as anyone I knew, and had even saved my life in a pool once, I couldn't make my body jump into his open arms over the pool's glistening surface, for there beneath it, and beneath him, were the darkening untold depths of the water which had no safeguard or escape clause. There were my father's arms and his increasingly angry face, and his increasingly harsh voice beckoning, demanding that I jump.

I froze on the pool's edge and tears began gathering in my eyes, the same kind that gathered when I tried to tie my shoes and couldn't, or tried to solve a math problem and couldn't, or tried to do some commonplace task that everyone else could do but couldn't, and he would stand there sighing, the frustration coming off him in waves as he looked down at my fingers fumbling, failing and trying again, my panic dooming my efforts once again. And now shivering with my arms folded around me on the side of the pool, I felt the same again with the tears starting in my eyes and my dad hissing through his teeth "Don't cry... DON'T cry..." and all the people of the trailer park, Kim Hoswell and all the other kids, and Kim Hoswell's father and Dad's other friends, all looking as Dad treaded water with his arms stretched out saying, "Come on! Jump in!" his face and head and shoulders welcoming me above the water's surface, his legs pedalling down below, and the more he demanded and *needed* his son to jump into his arms in the pool in front of the other adults, the more impossible it became for me to entertain the idea of doing so, and finally he gave up, shaking his head and floating away with the same expression he had when he talked about me never using the ball mitt

Fred Scott gave him for me when I was born. He whooshed away in the pool as though departing some small, undignified, ignominious death.

I put on my shirt and joined Kim Hoswell and the other kids who were now playing outside the pool enclosure around a picnic table. Before long, Kim began telling the story of how I pulled down my pants and showed my penis to her and Mary Hiemstra at school. I wasn't worried or embarrassed, though, because the adults were far away and the other kids seemed to think it was really funny, so afterwards I was encouraged to provide a repeat performance, and there on the top of the picnic table it was easy enough to pull down my bathing suit and show my privates, and do a little dance to make them bounce around, and it was then that my dad came around the corner with a towel around his shoulders and saw me and the smile disappeared from my lips and all the light drained out of his eyes as he strode towards me, lifted me from the top of the picnic table with one sweep of his arm, plucking me from the centre of the kids and transporting me with calm swiftness into our car, and we departed from the Green Valley Trailer Park immediately.

It was a week after that that I woke up one morning before school and went down the hall to see if my dad was in bed. When he was there, I always tried to figure out if my parents had an argument the night before. I figured if I found them both sleeping turned away from each other they must've had a fight just before going to sleep, or if my mom was turned away from my father, yet he was turned towards her, it meant she had been mad at him, but he had been imploring her to reconsider when they went to sleep. Or if my dad was turned away, and my mom faced him, they had gone to sleep with her begging his forgiveness. But of course, if I found them both turned towards the other then there was nothing to worry about.

This morning the bed was empty, and I walked out to the kitchen where my mom was making me and my brother sandwiches for our school lunch, and I asked where Dad was and she said he was in the hospital. He had a bad pain last night, so Howard his partner at the barbershop came over to pick him up and take him to the hospital, and there they told him that he'd had a heart attack. Then they said he'd had another heart attack once they got to the hospital, and I asked when he was coming home and she said they couldn't say, and as she put the sandwiches together her bottom lip was shaking like it did when it looked like she was about to cry, and then she bit the inside of her lip at the side of her mouth which she did at times like this, I guess, to stop from crying, and that made me not want to ask her any more questions. I walked back down the hall to look at my parents' unmade bed, to look particularly at my dad's side of it. Then my brother got up and I told him what happened, and my mom told him, and then we got ready and went to school. For show and tell, I got up and told the class my dad had two heart attacks last night.

The Simpsons' older daughter was there to look after me and my brother when we got home after school so that Mom could go visit Dad in the hospital after she finished work. Jason and I weren't allowed to see him because kids couldn't go, and for a while they didn't know how long he'd be in there, then they said it would be three months, and as the days went by I would go into my parents' room and look at their wedding pictures, and remind myself of the way his face looked, and try to think of how his voice sounded as I looked at his younger face in the pictures.

The older Simpson girl sometimes stayed overnight as she helped look after Jason and me, but I didn't like her, the way she told us what to do as though she was taking over for both Mom and Dad. I didn't like or trust the food she made for us, or the way she barked like a seal in her laughter at *The Brady Bunch* or other shows that weren't funny, and especially at shows Dad didn't think were funny. I kept asking my mom for the Simpson girl to leave but she said she couldn't leave, and she told me to behave and stop mak-ing trouble, but still my brother and I would get into these terrible fights, and one night after school my mom said she would take us to the new McDonald's that had just opened up and even on that night, in the car ride over, my brother and I got into a kicking fight in the back seat so that my mother, just as she was turning the car into the parking lot, backed up, turned around and headed home, giving us a clear lesson that she wasn't going to tolerate the acting up we did when our dad was away, even at the very threshold of McDonald's.

Mom kept saying Dad might be moving into a different room where my brother and I could visit him. Sometimes Dad would send home little slips of paper that had the meal ingredients for his new diet with no salt and no butter, or he'd send home the little Styrofoam suction cups they used on the machine to test his heart, and we'd play with them. But as the weeks went by and I kept going into the bedroom to look at the pictures of him, his voice grew fainter in my mind, and the features of what he looked like now were harder to grasp and make out. One night Mom took us and the Simpson girl up to the hospital, and my brother and I stood on the lawn waving up to my dad's window, where we could see his tiny figure, almost impossible to make out, wave down at us from above.

Don Regnier and his wife and their three children came to stay with us for a week to help Mom as she was going back and forth to visit Dad, and I didn't like the way they invaded the house, and the way the oldest girl got peanut butter on my Snoopy plush doll, and the way Don Regnier's wife told me what to do, and I didn't like the way Don Regnier sat at the head of the table during suppertime. But Don Regnier helped out by completing some of the work Dad had started on the renovation, and he even installed a light fixture in my parents' bedroom that they had picked out: a fixture of two globes hanging on chains suspended from the ceiling over their bed, the chains looping through rings on the ceiling then draping back to connect to a medallion on the wall above the centre of their headboard.

Mom took advantage of their being there to go back and forth from the hospital more and I'd have to watch different shows with the Regnier kids who like the Simpson girl laughed at different and stupid things, and on the Sunday before they were leaving we were all having a big meal in the kitchen, and that was the day a phone was installed in Dad's room for the first time, and he made his first call during supper, and Mom passed the phone to Don Regnier and my brother and then to me and his voice came with all the familiarity I had forgotten existed until I heard it, the feeling of something fitting into a space which conformed to its every dimension and shape: "How y'doin' partner?"

And the strange shock of his voice down the line mixed somehow with my anger at the Regniers and the Simpson girl so that my throat suddenly ached, and I couldn't talk right away.

"Partner? How y'doin'?"

Finally I said, "Good," my voice catching and my eyes smarting, but I wanted to tell him I wasn't good at all, that Don Regnier was here sitting at the head of the table where he shouldn't have been, eating off our dishes and shoving our forks into his mouth, and his whiny mean kids were here, and his wife was telling me what to do in a voice you don't use on a friend's kid but the one you use for your own kid when you're really mad at him, and all of a sudden there were hot tears in my eyes, and I turned from all the people in the kitchen though I couldn't leave the room because the phone was mounted on the kitchen wall. I hunched up my shoulders to try to hide my crying, and I tried to control my voice to answer when he said, "Try and help your mother out now—just another month, the doctors say."

I ached with rage as I wanted to tell him that Don Regnier hung the light fixture over his and Mom's bed, and I wanted to tell him that Don Regnier shouldn't have been there, it wasn't right, he was in a place he shouldn't have been, doing something he shouldn't have been doing, but also conscious of having to hide my tears I felt even further away from him than when I couldn't hear his voice or talk to him, or hear him talk to me as his voice came down the line, saying: "Alright, partner, you be good now," and he clicked off.

3. Mrs. Hell

MRS. WINCHELL AT THE NEW SCHOOL WE WENT TO AFTER THE
other one got shut down had black hair that was like a helmet on her
head, and her black-framed glasses came out from the helmet like
goggles on a Halloween mask of a race car driver, and her mouth
had wrinkles around it, not the wrinkles you got from smoking like
my mom said you get, going straight up and down over your upper
lip like the folds in a curtain, but wrinkles at the side of your mouth
that say you're not smiling even if you are smiling, or the wrinkles
that grow and get deeper when you're frowning and show a mood of
angry disapproval even deeper than that which you're feeling.

She never laughed except without amusement, with a skeptical
small suspiciousness. To her the only realities were the unanswerable laws of mathematics and science—all else was suspect, to be
approached as if it were shameful and wrong, and potentially leading
to the ultimate ruination of everything. I found this out early in the
year when she was giving a talk on what to expect and I was listening
while drawing an elaborate picture on the inside of my Hillier notebook. When she concluded her talk she marched straight down the
aisle to my desk, leaned over, and using a ruler as a guide, tore the
back cover neatly from my notebook. "There'll be no drawing while
I'm talking to the class," she said as she marched off, though I didn't
know what was wrong since I'd listened to everything she'd said.

I had to tell Mom and Dad about it and Dad was mad, saying
she had no right to ruin the notebook, and he'd be damned if he

was going to buy another one, but Mom just got out some construction paper and scissors and made a new cover. Mrs. Winchell would become furious with my disinterest in math and science, and when I was confused I knew not to ask her, for her face said to me that she disliked me in a basic and powerful way that there was nothing I could do to change or alter, the same way I felt some other kids at school didn't like me. When we did math I just got more confused, for when one bit goes by and you're afraid to ask questions, and then another bit comes it makes it that much the worse, because it was built on the bit before, until you fear ever being able to understand the figures and symbols that are grasped so easily by others. Every minute your confusion deepens until the entirety of life seems hopeless and you are completely set apart from it as one who doesn't understand, who can't understand, and tears pour from your eyes as you stare down at the book on your desk, so that a classmate puts up her hand and says, "Mrs. Winchell—Tim's crying because he doesn't understand the math," so that you're exposed to the whole class as one who doesn't understand, can't understand, will never understand, even though your classmate calls out with real empathy and the desire to help—it then doesn't make it any better when Mrs. Winchell says, "Tim shouldn't be here if he doesn't understand it. He should be going to a special school."

My ability to draw didn't help me as Mrs. Winchell had no time for art. Although she had to teach it as part of the curriculum, she did it only in the most grudging way. When I made my science fair project about the technology used to make animated films and how the persistence of vision was used to create the illusion of movement, using my drawings to show how scenes from Walt Disney films were animated, she let her gaze fall over my presentation and asked, "You like that sort of thing, do you?"

Something that was strange was that her husband was the head of the Gideon society that brought little bibles to us with red leather covers and a place at the front to write our names and addresses, and also there was a picture of a Canadian flag and also the words to the national anthem. As he stood before us, Mr. Winchell, who looked a lot older than Mrs. Winchell, told us about Gideon from the Bible, and why his society left bibles in hotel rooms and gave them to kids in schools, telling us that in these books was all the wisdom of the ages, and the answer to all our questions, and that in our times of need and sadness, all we had to do was consult these books and be strengthened by God's word, so that these bibles could be our life's greatest companions.

I looked over at Mrs. Winchell watching him as he made his long speech and she looked a bit nervous and shy but also proud in that she believed in all of what her husband was saying, though it was sometimes hard to tell because in addition to the wrinkles by her mouth which always made her seem frowning and disapproving, the flesh of her face seemed frozen, like a mask placed over her real face, and the muscles were supposed to match up to the expressions she wore under her mask, but they were never entirely synchronized. When we lined up at the door to go out for recess, for the benefit of my classmates I'd put my hand over the first four letters of her name on the nameplate on her door so that it read *Mrs. Hell.*

Dad was let out of the hospital after three months. We went down to pick him up, and Jason and I hugged him in the hospital lobby where there was a statue of an angel. He wasn't supposed to work so he laid down on the couch for some time, and then he started going to a night class at the local college for interior decorating to learn how to decorate our house when we got finished renovating it. He also applied to be a member of the Masons and that required him to study a little black book that he said nobody else was allowed to look at, though I did look and couldn't make any sense out of it or see anything that was so secret. A couple of men had to come to our house to inspect it and see if he was suitable to be a member of the Masons, and Mom and Jason and me all had to stay in the kitchen with the door closed all night and we couldn't watch TV as he was entertaining the men in the living room, and we were only brought out to them one time to be introduced to the two men as they drank their beer, and then we had to go back in the kitchen and stay there until it was time to go to bed.

When my dad became a Mason he'd get regular newsletters in the mail which he said I also couldn't read, and which I did anyway, and he started going to meetings every week. He also got an apron decorated with flashy jewels that he wore to the meetings, which he kept in a leather case that I wasn't supposed to fool with, and when he started working again he'd take the case with the apron in it to work so he could leave for the meeting right after. One night we were at the barbershop after he'd turned the CLOSED sign over and was getting ready to go, and Mom jokingly held up the apron to Howard, my dad's partner in the barbershop, saying maybe he'd look nice in one of them. After Howard left, my dad got really mad at her, saying non-Masons were never to be allowed to wear those aprons, even in fun, and she had no business holding it up to Howard like that. I wondered whether they wore the aprons over their clothes at the meetings or whether they just wore the aprons and nothing else.

Meanwhile at school, if Mrs. Winchell wasn't impressed with my drawings the other kids were, as each day I made drawings of jokes and gags on the backs of exercise sheets that would get passed around the class. Carl Plympton, who came with me from the other school, drew too, and he liked the Disney characters as I did but was unable to draw them unless they were smiling. This didn't really work for most of the gags he depicted, especially when the gags themselves were so lame—he would draw Goofy pulling the trigger of a gun aimed at his own face, smiling all the while, and often the gags he used were stolen from my own drawings to such a degree that I referred to him behind his back as Xerox. I was glad, though, that for the most part the kids in the class could figure out that my drawings of the Disney characters were better, not to mention had more expressions, while I always couldn't help but regret that some others couldn't tell the difference between Carl's drawings and my own and happily enjoyed both as if they were equal.

A boy named Garry Lewis began championing me and my drawings and would get mad on my behalf at anyone who claimed Carl Plympton was my equal. With his encouragement I started a weekly newspaper called *The Homely Gazette*, which featured such stories as a soccer player missing the ball when going for a big kick and getting his foot wedged in his own mouth, and a man falling out of a window into a pile of rotten Kentucky Fried Chicken. I put the paper together at home, giving my brother Jason the credit for being "chief pencil sharpener," for he did race back and forth to my room, providing me with freshly sharpened pencils, and I gave it to my mom to Xerox some copies at her secretary job. I took the copies to school and sold them for fifteen cents apiece and Garry Lewis promoted them and strong-armed kids into buying copies.

At the same time it was Garry Lewis who, without meaning to, was the cause of the end of *The Homely Gazette*. In his class down the hall he was reading the paper as his teacher was trying to teach a lesson, so she grabbed it from him and marched off with it, as Garry told me one recess. "She didn't seem too happy looking at it," Garry said. "Sorry—I hope you don't get in trouble." That afternoon our principal Mr. Gosland arrived at the door of our class and asked, "May I borrow Tim for a moment please?" Anyone's first impression of Mr. Gosland would have been overwhelmed entirely by the sight of his large bald head which was ringed by a fringe of red curly hair, earning him the nickname of "Miner, miner, forty-niner" because the light that bounced off his shiny dome was so bright it made it seem as though he was wearing a miner's hat with a light on the front of it.

He took great joy in his job, and when teaching about the moon he would enter the classroom in a space suit that he made himself, and in teaching about Vikings, he would gather the kids in the gym and sit them on benches as if on a Viking ship while he stood before them dressed as a Viking captain and serving them cut-up hot dog as the meat of the dragon they'd killed, and in teaching about First Nations he would enter the classroom in a headdress. He also kept a chipmunk in his office in a glass box. He now stood in the hall waiting for me with *The Homely Gazette* in his hand.

I looked up at his serious features, usually so mild and amiable but now stern and disapproving, his eyes seeming insect-like the way people's eyes always do behind glasses. I could see the pores in his nose, and a slight white rash around the strands of his red moustache. "One thing I really respect is talent," he was saying, his tenor voice sounding as earnest and reasonable as ever, broadcasting, it seemed, from his sober, industrious heart that desired nothing more than to meet another like itself, whose tone rang with unanswerable logic, making it even more unsettling that this same voice was expressing disappointed dismay, though I could not figure out why, for to my mind there was nothing bad about my paper. "But one thing I hate to see is a misuse of talent," he said, indicating *The Homely Gazette*. "And this is a misuse of talent," he said.

I didn't see why, since Garry Lewis and all the other kids liked it. Was it because Garry Lewis was reading it when the teacher was talking? Did that make it a misuse of talent, and if that was so, didn't that apply to anything anyone was reading during class?

"So I'm going to ask you to stop doing this. Instead, we'd like you to do the drawings for the school newsletter each month it comes out," he said, finishing with a slight smile. I knew he wanted me to be pleased, so I acted pleased, and I was, but at the same time I'd liked making *The Homely Gazette* and would miss making it.

Garry Lewis was mad when he found out. "Miner Forty-niner don't have any right to tell you to stop making it!" he said, and at recess he saw Mr. Gosland outside doing recess duty and went up to him and asked him, "Why'd you tell Tim to stop making his paper?" Mr. Gosland's eyes narrowed and he asked, "Whose boy scout are you?"

"Ha-ha! Tim got in trouble for his paper!" my brother Jason said at supper that night.

"What're you laughin' about?" my dad said. "You're in trouble, too. You're in there as Chief Pencil Sharpener!"

"Yeah, that's right!" I said.

"Oh, you think it's okay if you go down, just so long as you take the other guy with ya, huh?" Dad said, turning on me.

The problem with doing the drawing for the school newsletter, though, was that I would submit the drawings suggested by Mr. Gosland relating to the subject matter of the newsletter, which he would advise me of when he took me into his office each month, and the drawing would be taken by the school's secretary and traced onto carbon by which the newsletter was reproduced. Her tracings, I found to my anger when the first newsletter was printed, often left out lines that I considered essential, making some parts of the drawings appear as blobs, or leaving out mouths or eyes on some of the figures. It didn't seem to make any difference to anyone else, but to me they didn't have any of the feel or spirit I'd drawn them with, and I asked Mr. Gosland if I could trace them onto the carbon myself, and he said that wasn't necessary because Mrs. Brennan did that job "very handily." I would try to say that my drawings didn't look as good when she traced them, but he chuckled and asked me if I wanted to see his chipmunk in the terrarium.

"Now for this month I had the idea that you could draw something relating to the maple sugar trip the grade ones went on when the class was told that to get sap they had to 'tap' the trees, and one of the children..." here Mr. Gosland paused to chuckle, "one of the children spoke up and asked if 'tapping the trees' meant putting water taps on them like they had at home. So I thought you could draw the trees with water taps on them."

At home my dad started going into work again. One night at my aunt's house on my mother's side of the family, I heard him telling Aunt Maxine and Uncle Elmer the story: "They said to me, you've had a heart attack and I said, 'Bull—*shit*! I didn't have no heart attack!' I didn't have any pain in my heart, it was my arm that hurt

65

like a bitch! And they said that's where it hits ya, and then by Jesus, I started feelin' terrible again and they told me I had another heart attack! And I wake up and this one over here..." I pictured him pointing at my mom, since I was in the next room playing with my brother and my cousins, "this one over here is sittin' there cryin' her eyes out! Jesus Christ! So I said, 'What's the matter with you? I'm the one that had the heart attack!' and she says she's worried about me. 'Well, Jesus, how is your sittin' there cryin' gonna help me?' I says to her."

Meanwhile, my cousin and my brother and I had found some old boxing gloves that we brought into the room where the adults were talking and when Dad saw them he started talking about how he'd boxed in the Navy. My cousin was Uncle Elmer's grandson, and his dad was there too. Since my cousin was the same age and size as Jason, they decided the two boys would put on the gloves and spar a bit so we moved out to Uncle Elmer's front room, and the men who'd been drinking some beers showed the boys the right way to lace up the gloves, and Dad prodded Jason while Uncle Elmer and his son-in-law coached our cousin, and as they faced off against each other, at first the two boys were smiling but something in the men's faces became tense and impatient as they stood behind the boys with their beers, my dad drawing fitfully on his cigarette.

"Hey, that ain't the way ya do it—ya gotta get in and under," he said to Jason, bending to show him how it was done, while Uncle Elmer and his son-in-law fussed with our cousin, getting him to hold his gloves up in the right way, and they all surrounded the two boys, the fight all of a sudden becoming serious:

"Hey—don't let him get ya like that!"

"Block him!"

"Uppercut!"

Something terrible came into the eyes of my father, his right eye squinting up, and on the other side, Uncle Elmer and his son-in-law becoming more hungrily brutish in a way I'd never seen before— until I remembered when I'd heard about my uncle going to secret cockfights in drive sheds in the country where they made roosters fight each other to the death, and the dark eyes of the men fed on the two boys fighting, pushing them together, seeming almost angry like there was a poison they needed to ooze out of themselves and the only way they could get at it was to have the two boys fight, and my brother and my cousin starting out laughing, now serious, now doing their best to stand up before the prodding of the men whose voices were getting more guttural and careless, and the boys finally began crying, tears spilling from their eyes and down over their contorted mouths and onto their gloves, and the men going, "Aw come on now, what's th' matter with ya?" and the little boys bawling, their faces red and hot with shame, and the women coming in from the kitchen, my mother, Aunt Maxine, her daughter-in-law: "Now what's going on here? What the hell are you doing to them?"

"Jus' a little boxin' lesson…" Dad said and shrugged, smirking at the other men, turning back to the women with amused and diminishing contempt.

For a while it seemed like Dad had not been drinking and then he was. Certainly I had heard him tell the stories of when his pals sneaked him beers into the hospital and he even bragged that the doctor told him one beer a day was good for him. "Just down a couple beds from me was Rob, you know, the guy who owns the funeral home in town, and he says, 'By God, I'll get you yet, Dirk!'"

He still had to go to a lot of doctor's appointments and after one of them as me and my brother sat in the back seat of the car I heard my parents talking in hushed voices about something I couldn't hear, though I thought it had something to do with what they sometimes did on Sunday afternoons when they asked us to go out and play, and they went into their room which they usually never did in the afternoon, and so we tried the bedroom door and found it locked, so we went outside and looked in through the window and in the dim shadows of the bedroom we would only see the shape of Dad on Mom, and could specifically make out only the sight of Mom's feet dangling over the edge of the bed with her panties draping from her toes, and later when she asked us what we saw, that's what we said, and now as they talked in the front of the car, their voices implying more than they said, with spaces in their sentences to be filled in by what was in their minds, all the words circling around the question of When? I knew somehow they talked of what made the panties drape from Mom's toes.

As he returned to work and to the Point Edward Ex-Servicemen's Club, my dad would call my mom to pick him up after an afternoon when he didn't come home, and I'd say to Mom, "Well, at least he calls now," and me and her and Jason would drive down to the club and get him, and he'd come sauntering out and get into the car, and once as he sat there numb and dumb, looking around with bewildered squint-eyed sadness, I asked him, "Why do you drink, Dad?" and he scowled and shrugged as my brother at my side shushed me and shook his head disapprovingly at me for asking the question but Dad just sat there looking down for a while as Mom drove, and then he said, "Well, drinking's a drug just like any other," and lifted his cigarette and stared at it. "This is a drug, too... a very, very, mild drug. But it's a drug, too." He took a drag and let the smoke curl out of his mouth as he looked out the window to the landscape passing by.

Dad began returning to his habit of not coming home after work, or sometimes not coming home at all, so I would check his bed when I got up in the morning to see if he was there, and sometimes at night I'd hear him come in, get into a fight with Mom, and then say he was going out again, and my mom would say, "Oh, you're going to walk out again? Do you think the kids respect you when you do that?" and I heard her go into another room, maybe the kitchen, and after that I pictured my dad sitting on the couch in the living room, and then I heard his quick footsteps and then the screen door opening and swinging then slowly coming shut.

Another night I was awakened by their fighting, a sound even more horrifying than the war-like national anthem surrendering to crackling static chaos, and my mother crying, "What the hell's the matter with you, do you want to have another heart attack?" and then my dad in frenzied mockery calling out, "I'm havin' one now! I'm havin' one now!" as he put his hand over his heart then fell to the ground. I heard the clatter and thud against the floor and my mother's voice sounding like shattered glass in hysterical fury as she picked up the phone yelling, "I'm calling the hospital! I'm calling the ambulance! Get up or I'm calling the ambulance!"

Slowly the work on the house continued somehow, with my dad's knowledge of interior decorating from his college course informing his choices as to paint and wallpaper for the walls. Sometimes he'd use his new expertise garnered from the course to tell other people how their colours clashed and were incorrect according to the experts.

But unfortunately the worst thing we found that year was that a developer had bought all the land around our house and was going to build a subdivision, and when they asked Dad if he wanted to sell he of course said no since we'd just moved in, but it wasn't long before the surveyors wearing the orange bands came around again, and the orchard on one side of us and the cornfield on the other, and even the old barn behind us where when we first moved in, two old men named Morris and Arthur sat every day, the dust at their feet littered with the many matches they used to light their pipes. All was uprooted, upended, and mowed down, the bulldozers and the backhoes came in, and the barn was demolished, collapsed into an isle of shattered wood and stale straw around which a moat of liquefied manure shone in the sun, sending packs of rats scurrying toward our home, and my brother and I watched the workmen perched on their bulldozers, nosing their way through the orchards of apple and pear trees and flattening them, and we knew them to be our mortal enemies, and one day one of the men with a large bush of red hair whom my brother and I derisively called, "Orange Root Beer Head," came sweating to our door and asked us for a glass of water, and we fixed him a cup of water with dishwashing soap in it to punish him for knocking down the orchard. We told Dad what we were doing and he leapt off the couch, "Christ, don't do that! If I asked for a glass of water and you gave me that I'd punch you right in the mouth! Go get the guy a nice glass of water!"

Mom and Dad had started bowling with a league once a week and one night they had a rare party after bowling, when a bunch of adults came to our house and stood around and drank alcohol. Dad was standing in the kitchen near a woman who leaned on the counter where the coffee maker was. "Hey Tim! Go get your brother!" he called to me, so I sprinted down the hall and told Jason that Dad wanted him. "Hey buddy, take a look at these!" Dad said to Jason as we approached, and Dad pointed, smiling, to the breasts of the woman beside him. She smiled indulgently at us. "You're always lookin' at Howard's magazines—check out the size of these," he said, and it was true, when we were in the barbershop and Dad's partner wasn't there, we would go look in the bottom drawer of Howard's barber counter and see the *Hustler* and *Penthouse* magazines, and my brother in particular would pore over the forbidden pictures of flesh before our dad would say, "Hey, come on, that's Howard's stuff! Leave it alone!"

Although the appeal of the pictures partly baffled me, it was true my brother looked long and hard over the women's chests portrayed in the magazines, and now he stood in shock as his father indicated the woman beside him and said, "Now these are what you call boobs! No doubt about that! She's sure got 'em, don't ya think, Jason?" The woman smiled benignly down at the boy, who recovered from his shock, turned on his heel, and sped down the hallway. "Jason? Jason!" Dad called after him in increasingly angry puzzlement. A storm crossed his face and he trudged down the hall after his son. Jason was under his bed in his darkened room. "What the hell's the matter with you?" Dad was asking, standing at the door. "Come out of there! Get out of there right now!"

Jason wouldn't come out or speak. I tried to tell Dad I thought he was embarrassed. "Embarrassed about what? I was just showin' him a woman that was really built!" Dad argued. "Get outta there!" he called under the bed. "Come on!" He finally gave up and left the room disgusted. Since Jason seemed to have turned in for the night, I put on my pajamas and got into my bed, listening to the voices of the adults talking down the hall. The voices grew fewer as the front door on the other side of the wall from my room opened and shut.

I heard a body trudge down the hallway that I could tell from its footfall was my dad. I heard the trickle of him in the bathroom and shortly after, his shadow appeared in my door, framed by the hallway light. "What's the matter with Jason?" he demanded. "Why won't he talk to me?"

"He's embarrassed," I said.

"About what? You know as well as I do that he can't get enough of the pictures in those magazines of Howard's!"

"Yeah, but it's different when it's a picture and when it's a real person."

"Well, Jesus," he grunted as he came into the room and sat on my bed. "I wasn't tryin' to piss him off, for Chrissake!"

"He just got scared," I said, realizing he never would understand. He lay down beside me on the bed.

"You and Jason got the best beds in the house—they're the best kind for your back," he sighed after a moment. "Well, I don't wanna upset you guys, or embarrass ya," Dad continued, draping his arm over me. "You guys are my right and left wingers, right?" he said in the darkness, echoing his long-time names for me and Jason since Jason was left-handed and me right-handed, so those became the positions we played on Dad's imaginary hockey team, which I always felt a little uneasy about because I failed to take an interest in hockey just as I'd failed to take an interest in Fred Scott's ball mitt, or in any sport, and I felt bad about disappointing him, but still he called us his wingers when he was in a good mood, and as we lay in the darkness his arm hugged me closer to him.

"You guys are my wingers, and you know I love ya—right? You know I'd never let anything bad happen to ya—right? I wish you guys could stay at the age you are now forever," his voice said quietly in the darkness, with a different note in it. "You're my little winger and I'm proud of ya," and he lay there holding me for a while, then got up and sauntered back out to the party.

"What were you doin'?" I heard Mom ask him out there with the other adults.

"I was havin' what you call a father-and-son, man-to-man talk," Dad pronounced with significance.

"Oh, bullshit!" Mom said, laughing.

In the coming week Jason and I had a school holiday on a Monday, the day our dad had off work, and he was going to take us to the secret spot along the lake where he used to swim as a kid, an inlet near the mouth of the river, and he drove us to the beach that was secluded and watched as me and Jason played in the sand and waded into the water. "Nice and sandy along here, eh? No rocks or nothin'!" he said as he watched us. "This is the best part of the beach." He sat on the sand and watched for a while as we played and swam. Then it seemed to get like he was thinking about something else and said to us he was going to go talk to a guy just for a bit at the Ex-Servicemen's Club that was nearby, but he'd be back soon, and don't get into trouble.

We played in our own private bay and could see the big boats and tankers moving to the river beyond. The boats moved through the afternoon and the changes of the sky were mirrored in the lake, and we ran between the excitement of the waves and the pleasures the sand offered, the digging of tunnels and forts through the afternoon to its latter part, when the silence of the shore beyond its murmuring tide and the seagull's cry became more ominous, and the shadows lengthened on the sand dunes, and the air turned cool so we didn't feel much like swimming anymore. My brother and I ended up lying beside each other on the sand as the sky darkened, wondering where Dad was and if he'd forgotten us, shivering in the cooling wind, my arm around my little brother for protection and warmth.

"Have a good swim?" Dad asked as he finally drove back up. "Great beach, huh?" I could see his right eye was squinted up that way and he was talking again as if he held something hot in his mouth. He drove us home as Mom was just getting in from work.

"You guys have a good time swimmin'?" she asked us. "You were out a long time."

Yeah, we did, we said, and Jason added that it started to get a bit too cold to swim near the end and Mom said, "Why didn't you come home, then?" and Jason said we were waiting for Dad to come pick us up, and Mom said, "You mean he wasn't there?" Then turning to Dad she said, "I can't even trust you to take the kids for a day! You can't leave kids like that all day at the beach by themselves!"

"Shit," he said, now laying on the couch in his usual place. "I spent the whole summer in the water when I was a kid—never took my suit off from June to August."

"You don't leave kids that age at the beach by themselves!" Mom screamed. "They could have drowned!" It was clear to me he didn't understand just as he didn't understand why Jason had been embarrassed. It was more often that these misunderstandings happened when his right eye was squinted up, which seemed to happen more often as the subdivision was built around us and landscaping around the new houses caused the ground level to be raised at each side, so that when it rained, our yard was flooded till it was like it was a lake.

At least one time, though, his acting this way was more to do with physical pain than with the townhouses and identical split-level homes being constructed all around us. He came down with an abscessed tooth and had to go to the dentist and get it drained of pus. Off work for the day, he stopped at the club after the dentist with his friend Frank Ostachuk, and they came clattering in the door just after me and my brother came home from school. They sat at the kitchen table drinking and smoking, and I came in marvelling at the strange sight of the men there in the late afternoon and asked my dad how his tooth was.

"How do you think?" he asked as he displayed his swollen cheek for me to see.

Mom came home and said, "I see you guys have been helpin' Dirk forget his tooth," and she started to get dinner and asked Dad if he should be drinking while taking the pills the dentist had given him for his tooth. They started arguing, and Frank Ostachuk came out to the living room where we were watching *The Brady Bunch* and silently smoked his pipe, and I went back to the kitchen because I remembered that tonight was Parents Night at our school, and Mom said, "Oh, that's right," and looked over at Dad and said, "How are you gonna go in the state you're in?"

By this time Dad was holding his head and moaning with real pain, but somehow it seemed warped and deformed by the amount he'd drunk, as if his feelings were passing through a filter that made them bigger but at the same time blurred them, made them crude and block-like and fuzzy, and we had supper, Mom making friendly talk with Frank Ostachuk, and we all ate except Dad, who sat drinking, and after when Frank Ostachuk rejoined my brother and me in the living room while Mom got ready for Parents Night, I crept back to the kitchen to see how Dad was doing just in time to see him standing by the counter and slamming his hand down on it. To my horror he burst into tears, grimacing as he sobbed with a strange, high-pitched sound.

I ran back to Frank Ostachuk who sat smoking his pipe, and hardly able to form the words with my mouth, I said, "Mr. Ostachuk, something's wrong with my dad—he's crying." Not nearly as fast as I wanted, Frank Ostachuk stirred himself and slowly padded out to the kitchen and put his hand on Dad's arm.

"I'm alright, Frank," Dad sobbed. "I'm alright."

Mom came out and said he was in no condition to go to Parents Night, and he said no, no, no, he'll go, he didn't want to let the kids down, and so Frank Ostachuk left and Dad drank more of the drink that wasn't his usual beer, and we went out and got into the car, rumbling through the countryside till we got to the school, unusually alive with golden lights in all the nighttime windows, people visible in the classrooms even from the road, parents standing in the aisles, the cars parked all around the building over the hopscotch and four-square marks on the asphalt.

My brother and I watched Dad not just for the way he was acting but also for the pain the tooth was giving him, the side of his face swollen up as he walked slowly into the school with a sense of being duty bound and grimly living up to his responsibilities, and down the hallway as the parents of various children that he knew from the community or from the barbershop passing by, and him pausing to greet them with an over-friendliness that had his hand leaping up into the air to greet them and his laugh not coming from a real place but from an idea of what he now believed approximated good humour, and I looked from his lopsided grin to their faces to see if they knew, and mostly they bid hello to him in a regular way, and chuckled as he hazarded an irreverent joke as we walked down the hallway of the school, and he now seemed to waver as we walked into Jason's classroom and we spoke to his teacher, her face taking on a solemn cast as Dad greeted her and they talked of Jason's math, and he expounded on the difference between math when he was a kid and math now, and she nodded, and he talked about his tooth and how it was infected and they had to drain the pus, and he swayed on his feet and it struck me that Jason's teacher thought that this was how my dad actually was, that he was mentally slow and had to be patronized and listened to as a courtesy you extend to someone because you are a good person, and it was her job to listen to the concerns of the parents of her students no matter what handicaps they may have, and Dad was telling her about when he was a student and in the midst of one of his most florid pronouncements a little drop of spit came out and landed on the edge of her desk, and though he was unaware of it, I wondered if the teacher saw it, and I looked up to her face and saw it trained upon the tiny bead on the corner of her desk, which she looked at for a moment with no expression, or rather the same expression she had when looking at Dad's face, so that it didn't change as she took her attention from the bead and moved it back up to him as he finished with a joke and she smiled and chuckled briefly to show that she knew it was a joke and then we walked from the classroom down the hall, Dad saying, "She's nice, huh, Jason? Not bad lookin', either!"

We were making our way to my classroom, me dreading Mrs. Winchell for what she might say since she hated me, her doorway appearing with its nameplate where I used to cover some of the letters so it read *Mrs. Hell*, my dad lurching beside me and groaning as he pressed his fingers to his swollen jaw, and me seeing some of my classmates emerging from the room with their parents as we approached, some of the kids smiling at me, and some of the meaner ones who ignored me, and the other ones who smirked derisively at me, but we were all checking out each other's parents, and some of the kids simply stared with wonder at my dad, who moaned a bit from the pain in his tooth as he came into the room, his eye squinted up belligerently as he looked around at the kids' paintings on the walls, and there was Mrs. Winchell with her black helmet-like hair, her tiny eyes behind her glasses and her mask-like face, its muscles frozen, only roused to action by an apparently intermittent electric zap running coldly through it, the wrinkles at the sides of her mouth downturned in blunt disapproval even when she smiled, as she did now, extending her hand to Mom and Dad, smiling a smile that wasn't a smile but only a token signifying she knew that she was supposed to smile.

"Now I know Tim don't have a problem with drawing and art," Dad was saying. "It's those other subjects like math we got to watch him on!" I looked from Dad's careful movements of his mouth which showed that talking for him now was a treacherous exercise akin to maintaining one's balance on an uneven and shifting terrain, and I looked over to Mrs. Winchell watching him, her tiny eyes taking him in behind her glasses like a scientist through a microscope, and as Dad went on, encouraged by the sound of his voice and her interest, his words fell into the rhythm they sometimes did where he pronounced his words as if they were much bigger and more impressive than they actually were, and his hand gestures, similarly encouraged, shot out and presented the propositions he was speaking of with unnecessary and exaggerated drama.

"Now when I was in school they taught long division in a certain way, but now I guess they figured out this different way to do it, they must've figured it out better," and he cocked his head to one side and listened with some severity to her response, the elbow of one arm cradled into his hand as his other hand came up to touch his cheek in a thoughtful manner but also to rest upon the swollenness.

I watched Mrs. Winchell as she tendered her response, answering with what for her was a rising and diligent passion for the subject she excelled in, her voice like a key fitting into a lock, its unmusical stubbornness coming out with a metallic complacency for the fact the rules would never change, and in this inhuman security she staked her claim, and was only too happy to engage in all the conversations in which the only subject was that the rules never changed, and whose conclusions could only be that the rules never changed, and all the while I was glad because she wasn't talking about how I cried because I couldn't understand the math, or how I drew stupid pictures on my notebooks, or how I shouldn't even be in her class and should be in a special school. No, she was happy to talk of how the methods of teaching long division had changed, and as she was doing so she seemed not to notice my dad's screwed-up eye or how his expression was bleared and blurry and out of sync with what they were saying, and she didn't notice how cautiously he was pronouncing his words even as his voice grew louder, and that even with that cautiousness the words came out wrong, or his sentences seemed to be missing words, or his words were missing syllables, like those neon signs where some of the letters are burnt out.

Now he was somehow talking of his abscessed tooth again, and she was nodding and something in her fed on this subject too, the subject of pain and suffering which caused her to narrow her eyes in interest and hasten to his words. "Yes, they can be quite painful, my husband had one of those," she observed with what seemed to be wry satisfaction, and as Dad explained with glazed vividness the procedure of draining the pus, her frozen face was trained on his like an animal on food, and as his acting out the way various dental problems were dealt with attained an energetic theatricality, I realized that his simulations of conversational good cheer that rang so painfully false to me were entirely captivating to Mrs. Winchell as she nodded and waited to share her story of dental woe. She was utterly engaged and looked on my father and his over-the-top gestures with rapt interest and even admiration—in some essential way she connected with my dad in this mood as she connected with little else. She was alive with a respect that even overflowed a bit onto me as we parted and she allowed, with a new tolerance toward me: "Well, Tim's coming along."

We left the classroom and continued down the hall, and my dad's hand went to his swollenness again as he grunted, "Jee-sus *Christ*," and Mom went, "Shhh!" There in front of his office as we filed up the hall was Mr. Gosland, his bald dome under the nighttime fluorescent lights entirely living up to his moniker of Shiner, Shiner, Forty-niner. He spotted us and identified me as his "in-house cartoonist" with a chuckle, and he knew my dad from the old barbershop in Point Edward, and so he invited us all into his office to look at some arrowheads and other archeological artifacts that had been unearthed on his property, proudly displaying the arrowheads and watching my father as he went into a lengthy and slurring explanation of the arrowheads he'd found as a boy.

As I had with the other teachers, I watched Mr. Gosland to see if he knew and it seemed to me he did not, his rust-coloured eyebrows dipping up and down behind the upper frame of his spectacles as he followed Dad's emphatic story, the muscles around his mouth, the movement of his lips beneath the bristles of his red moustache forming a friendly and welcoming expression as he reacted to the twists and turns of Dad's tale, and I thought of how a week before I'd gotten into trouble for pulling Mary Hiemstra's ponytail on the bus to school, how the truth of it was that we were both fighting back and forth, but the grade eights who were assigned to bus patrol, wearing their yellow bands, had decided to take Mary and me to the principal's office, not because what I did was so bad, but because, as I heard the grade eights say as we walked into the school, by taking kids to the principal's office they could get out of French, which they hated, and when we were all in Mr. Gosland's office they stood accusing me, and Mr. Gosland stared sternly at me, and though it was true that I did pull Mary Hiemstra's ponytail, it wasn't the same as the way it was being said, and I knew the real reason we were there was because the grade eights wanted to miss French, but I couldn't say that.

The grade eights looked at me threateningly, and in stifled rage I cried, unable to explain, and Mr. Gosland took my tears as remorse and pulled me to him, his arm around me holding me to his chest, the buttons of his jacket against my face, comforting me in what he thought was my being sorry but he did not understand that my tears were of fury at the injustice of not being heard, just like he didn't understand now: a grinning, willing audience of my dad's warped performance, putting in his own comments about the tribes of Shankton County and reacting to my dad's grandiose speechifying with amiable enthusiasm.

The conversation turned to Mr. Gosland's chipmunk in his terrarium, and Dad looked at the rodent and proclaimed that it reminded him of the rats he and his friends used to go hunting for down by the riverfront. "We'd throw somethin' in there to get 'em movin' around, and we'd go shittin' around…" He paused to lick some excess saliva from his lips and in that strange and awful moment I looked from my father's lips which had just said "shittin'" over to Mr. Gosland's face, which at the pronunciation of that word dropped from its receptive friendly interest into a dismayed frown, his mouth sagging and pulling down the bristles of his moustache, and as I watched, in that brief interval that seemed to last an eternity in which my father had sworn at my public school principal in my public school principal's office, in that disapproving eon in which Mr. Gosland looked with a sad, almost hurt disappointment which almost can't comprehend that such words exist, much less are spoken, I felt an apocalyptic dread flowing across my stomach, until my father continued, correcting himself, saying, "*shootin'* around," at which point Mr. Gosland's features perked up again into happy receptiveness, his face relaxing into its former smiles, having been reassured that all was right with the world.

Out into the car I thought of how Mr. Gosland couldn't tell, and Mrs. Smitchell too, and how they didn't know and would never know, and riding home with Dad holding his swollen jaw in the front seat as Mom drove, groaning a bit since we'd left his painkillers at home, and somehow I thought of this again weeks later when we were supposed to go to the Birdtown Fair. It was the biggest fair for miles around, forty miles away, and we only went to it every so often over the years because of the distance, and my brother and I were excited when our parents said we were going because of that, and looked forward to the Sunday that had been set aside for it coming up, and our excitement only faltered when we woke up that Sunday morning and I padded to our parents' bedroom and saw that my dad hadn't come home the night before.

Now the Sunday was an unhappy one, as we knew better than to ask Mom if we would still be going, and in the bright Sunday morning which seemed to be mocking me with its empty sunniness I sat in a chair by our big front picture window and I looked at the cars passing back and forth on the road before the field of weeds behind which the train tracks with their tower sat, and beyond which the stacks of the refineries soared in their midst, and I wondered if in the cars there were people going to the fair, or to church, and if they were trouble-free and unconcerned, or if, like me, the minutes and hours trudged with leaden weight, and no part of their bodies and thoughts could rest in easeful happiness, and I watched for my dad's car at the furthest periphery of my vision, where the road disappeared behind the newly raised walls of the subdivision's construction, my heart racing when I saw a car that looked like it could be his, with a bad comedown when it turned out that it wasn't, and as the morning passed the promise of the Birdtown Fair moved further and further away, until amazingly, a car that looked like his did come down the road, and unbelievably, the front turning light blinked as it slowly turned into our driveway, slowly, as he always drove slowly when sidling into the driveway to show that however much he drank he was being cautious and careful, or maybe in his state he thought this was how sober people drove, but I found that the slower he drove down the driveway the more trouble he turned out to be, and I sprang from my chair to tell Mom that Dad was home, but she only grunted, and he came in through the kitchen, and yet he seemed to my eye not to be in a bad state, but more tired and rough-voiced, and he sat in a chair he usually didn't sit in in the living room, and he lit a cigarette of the strange brand he never smoked at any other time, and he said, "Geez, that Bill Hornblower," and my mom looking at a copy of *Chatelaine* didn't even look up at him, but he went on, saying, "That goddamn Bill Hornblower—we had a game of poker goin' and he just wouldn't stop! I told him, I says to 'im, 'You can't keep the game goin' just because you're down some money,' and he says, 'No, goddamnit, let's keep playin', I got to at least get some of it back,' and I says, 'Come on, your wife Marlene's gonna be waitin' up for ya, you can't keep her up all night,' and he says, 'No, goddamnit, I got to keep playin.'"

By this time my brother came out and was lying on the floor at my dad's feet looking up at him, and we both listened to his story as Mom sat reading her magazine. "So I says to him after a while, 'You can't keep Marlene up all night waitin' for ya, forget the money and go home,' and he don't answer me at all, so I go across the street to where him and Marlene live, and I says to her, 'I can't get him to go home!' and she's sittin' there just about cryin.' And they got a nice little apartment there overlookin' the lake, and the sun's comin' up—just beautiful—and she says, 'Dirk, he's been this way for thirty years—he goes on a tear and he can't control it—he goes off and it might be for a week, or it might be for a month—never less than a week—and I don't see him, he don't call, nothin'. I can't depend on him for nothin', I can't count on him, nothin' means anything to him except the drinkin' and gamblin'—and there's nothin' I can do about it—and don't you feel bad, Dirk,' she says to me. 'Don't you feel bad that you can't bring him home. What he's got is a sickness—a week, a month, every couple of months, he goes haywire and that's it, and no one can find him, or talk sense to him even if they can find him—so don't *you* feel bad, Dirk, that you can't bring him home, though I appreciate it that you tried.'

"And I'm lookin' at her there in her bathrobe sittin' on her couch, and she looks so frail and sickly, Jesus!" Dad said, taking out another cigarette and lighting it. "You know she had that problem there a year ago, and she says, 'I just give up waiting for him now, he's gonna do what he's gonna do and there ain't nothing I can do about it,' and I say, 'Marlene, Christ, I wish there was something I could do to help ya,' and she says, 'There ain't nothin' anyone can do,' and she just sits there by the window with the sun comin' up over the lake, with her skinny body like there ain't nothin' to her—Jesus!" He grimaced and shook his head as if to drive the image from his memory.

"So," he said with the air of one determined to turn the page to happier themes, "we goin' to the fair?" He looked down at us kids and then over to Mom who was still looking at her magazine, and me and my brother looked over to her too, hoping against hope there was a possibility, since Dad's story held in it his excuse for being out all night, and maybe that would cool the fire of her anger, make it alright for all of us to go to the fair together as a family, and after a moment she put down her magazine and getting up, she said, "The kids and I are going. You can come if you want," and she walked off to the bathroom to get ready.

My brother and I were happy and excited, smiling at each other but we knew not to act too excited in the sombre mood Mom was laying down, and we all went out to the car, and we were surprised when Dad got into the back seat with us instead of sitting in the front passenger seat beside Mom, for though Mom usually did drive as Dad didn't like to drive, he usually sat up beside her, but I figured this was his way to acknowledge that they weren't okay with each other and maybe even too, a way to be contrite and shamefaced, though my brother asked him, "Why aren't ya sittin' in the front, Dad?" and he said, "Well a guy likes to have a change every so often, right, partner?" and then he said to Jason, "Why don't you sit up front today?" and we pulled out into the early Sunday afternoon, motoring out into the countryside to the fair, and nobody talked much, and my dad smoked a cigarette looking out the window at the farms and fields passing by, and since my mom and dad weren't talking to each other my brother and I didn't talk much either, as much not to jinx the outing as anything else, and finally we were at Birdtown, and our car crawled over the soft earth of a field serving as the parking lot for the fair, and we walked in past the livestock all waiting to be judged, and through the buildings with the produce, the plump grapes around which the bees and wasps jiggled, the pumpkins and the watermelon and the honeycomb, the small midway with its gambling and games and Conklin Entertainment rides, the families and the kids so easy to bump into and smear their ice cream, and as my brother and I were treated to some rides and games we still looked over to our mom and dad to see if they were talking all the while, and were heartened when, at a display of aluminum siding, they exchanged some words on the practicality of the product.

But mostly my dad stayed back with me and my brother, even as we got into the car, my dad again climbing into the back seat with me, and we pulled out of the field and headed on the road home, except for one turnoff which would've led us to our house, my mom without explanation took the other way, and my brother and I looked at each other questioningly, and it soon became apparent we were on our way to our grandfather's house, my mom's father, a visit to whom was usually met with complaining and resistance by my dad, but now, since he was in trouble, could only be meekly assented to by him as he rode in the back seat, and we turned down the old gravel road to where my grandfather's farm was, the stones biting and clicking against the car's undercarriage, and we crept down his laneway, and entering by his back door where my grandfather's wife greeted us with, "Well, isn't this a pleasant surprise!" and my grandfather said, "Come in! Come in!" and we were offered food as we were every time we visited, and suddenly, somehow there was supper, and all was well except for the moment my grandfather asked Dad if he'd been out playing golf that weekend and my brother piped up, "No—he was out all night playin' poker!" and my grandfather who'd never wanted Mom to marry Dad in the first place simply stared at Dad and slowly shook his head from side to side.

Getting into the car and heading home, my dad now sat beside my mom in the passenger seat and after a while we could hear their soft talking in the twilight as we motored through the darkened countryside and I noticed my dad stretching his arm along the back of the seat and tentatively touching Mom's shoulder as she drove, and looking around I saw my brother now sleeping beside me in the back seat, and we got home and went in the house. Going to the washroom before I went to bed, I looked through the window beside the toilet into the backyard and saw the reflection of the moon in the water that flooded there from the subdivision being built at a higher level than our yard, and I realized that tomorrow I would have to go to school again and my parents would have to go to work, and though now they had started talking to each other and it would still be a day or so before Mom could laugh at Dad's jokes so that things would be normal again between them, and after that it would only be a matter of time before things—meaning Dad—would go off the rails again, until it exhausted itself and Mom forgave him again, and so on, and in between there was us going to school and them going to work so that we never got to the bottom of anything, so that there was never a real moment, or a place you could sit and know and see and feel why or how you were doing anything.

It was like a week earlier when I got up and said to my mom and dad that I didn't want to go to school anymore because it was boring and we just did the same thing every day and Dad said, "Well geez, don't you think work is boring? Do you think I like to get up and go to work every day? Don't you think it's the same old thing for me every day?"

"Yeah," I said, "but at least you have different customers coming in every day."

"Yeah, but it's the same old thing!" and Mom said, "What do you think you're gonna do when you grow up and have to get a job? Do you think that's not boring? That's the way it is!" and I wondered why we all had to do that, go to school and go to work; it wasn't like we'd all sat down and agreed this was the best way to live life, or some wise person had come up with this great master plan, it was just something that happened, something that came about that nobody had anything to do with, that just gathered and collected and came together, and Dad said, "Geez, well, what're you gonna do, you can't change the world, that's just the way it is—you need money to live, so you gotta work," and looking out the window at the moon on the water, feeling the movement of Monday coming and my mom and dad going to bed with the sense they'd have to get up for work in the morning, I saw that we'd never get it, the cycle would just keep going, there would never be the time to say an honest word, and there would never be a restaurant we opened in the living room of our house, and things would keep on in the direction they were going.

Book Two:

The Bridge

1. Ran Hutchison

TIM WALKED IN BRIGHT MORNING LIGHT THAT WAS ALMOST blinding as it shone off huge drifts of bluish snow. Cars moved at a cautious pace, timidly crunching through the deep whiteness still prevailing against the pavement. He had a difficult time moving, the depth of the snow making him have to lift each foot up to knee-level in order to progress—some of the snow always finding its way into his boot, into the space between his foot and his sock.

It was a twenty-minute walk to his high school. There was a bus service, but since the beginning of his high school days, Tim had preferred to walk or to ride his bike. This was initially because he'd feared being picked on by some of the kids who rode the bus. There was one in particular he'd encountered in the summer before his first year of high school, on the street, who had pointed at Tim and said to his friend, "You see that guy? He's gonna get the shit kicked out of him in high school."

It had been enough to make Tim scared all summer long. He had always been afraid of bullies and it was only in his last year in elementary school that he had finally begun feeling at ease. He was thin, and didn't act in a recognizable male manner, and so he was called the worst and most shameful name any boy could be called: *fag*. He was called this long before he or the hurler of the name had any idea what fags were or what they did. He only knew, as did his accuser, that a fag was unmanly, disgraceful, contemptible and the worst thing that anyone could possibly be.

Tim cut through an empty lot of a housing development near the high school, crunching up the street toward the back gate of the running track. Beyond that and across the parking lot, the crowd of kids stood in black and grey and blue coats, clotted around school doors in a wispy haze of cigarette smoke. Bypassing the mob, he entered through another door, the bells going off as he did so, the halls suddenly filling with teenagers, a blur and murmur of conversation.

He moved through the halls feeling self-conscious. He walked behind others who were popular and were greeted on a regular basis by those who strode toward them. The only people who ever waved to Tim were two girls who had a reputation around the school for being nice, and were known for going to church. He figured they waved out of a sense of pity for him, motivated by their spiritual beliefs.

He entered his English classroom and sat down at his desk. The class was studying *A Portrait of the Artist as a Young Man* by James Joyce. It was a book he had begun reading before school started, over the Labour Day weekend when the Jerry Lewis telethon was on. He had read it while Jerry Lewis brought the numbers up, and he waited for the boy in the book to pick up his brush and start painting. He thought that the word *artist* only ever meant drawing and painting. The idea that someone could be an artist in any field, or by simply having an artistic sensibility, was new to him.

"An artist doesn't care about money," the teacher was saying, after he'd read aloud a section in which Stephen wakes up, puts on a stained shirt, drinks out of a dirty tea cup and cadges some change before he goes out. "Stephen doesn't care that his clothes are dirty. He doesn't care that the dishes aren't washed. He doesn't care that he's broke. He doesn't care about any of that stuff. An artist only ever thinks about art. He doesn't care what you think about him as he's walking down the street in his rags. He's not interested in buying the newest model of car or following the stock market. An artist is concerned with what's in here," the teacher said, tapping his head.

"It's what's in his head that counts, what he feels. He's not concerned with impressing you, living up to your expectations, succeeding on your terms. He's thinking about beauty. Everybody's running around, trying to make money, trying to become secure. An artist couldn't care less. He's always broke. He knows there's no real security anyway. Or maybe the security he wants is the kind money can't buy. He drifts out into the day like a dream—daydreaming—that's what the artist is doing. He is immersed in his dreams of beauty—so immersed that he doesn't see his own poverty. He is above it all. He is an *artist*. Quite a commitment to make.

"How would that be, if I were simply to say one day, 'I'm an artist, and what I'm going to do is to say screw everything, walk out on my family, and go to Paris and write?' Would that be acceptable, would that be right, simply because I've decided I'm an artist?" he asked. "Now then," the teacher observed, "who can tell me why Stephen sorts through the pawn tickets before going out the door?"

Around Tim, several eager arms reached into the air as he gazed out the window and saw a TV repair truck idling at a stoplight, voluminous clouds of pale white exhaust rising like steam behind it, a light snow sifting down in the still mid-morning air.

At the end of the period, borne along by the crowd around him, Tim saw the slight, long-haired figure of Ran Hutchison coming through the clusters of teenagers. As the older boy approached, Tim felt his insides tighten, his heartbeat pounding. The tiny-eyed Ran Hutchison came abreast of him, and as he always did, whispered fiercely: "Fuckin' faggot!"

The summer that began with Tim overhearing he was going to get the shit beat out of him in high school was the summer he had met Ran Hutchison. Somehow, the warning had only made Tim more interested in pushing boundaries, and when he walked into parks that summer with his brother and his cousin, he would often yell insults at the other kids, trying to bait them into fights, and then run off. He often antagonized boys in the neighbourhood into wanting to beat him up, then lived in nauseous fear that they would carry it out.

One day, Tim and his brother and cousin walked past the field behind his father's barbershop where Ran Hutchison was playing baseball with a group of boys and Tim yelled some jeering insults through the fence at them. The baseball players looked over but didn't give chase. When their baseball game finished, the boys leisurely surrounded Tim and his brother and his cousin where they sat on the swings. Most of the boys were older and bigger, but they shoved forth the smaller, skinnier Ran Hutchison.

"Hey, Ran's the same size as that little fag!" one of the boys said.

"He can fight 'im!" said another.

As the larger boys cried, "Come on, Ran, you can take him!" Ran began to affect a wild bravado, and they pushed the two boys close, commanding them to fight. Ran Hutchison began flailing with his fists against Tim's face, the blows coming like white cold blasts. Tim threw his fists into the other boy's face with terrible exhilaration. They fell to the ground grappling, twisted into quick, furious combat as the boys around them cheered and shouted with laughter. Tim's brother Jason ran to their dad's barbershop. "A bunch of kids are beatin' Tim up in the park!" he cried.

Dirk ran with Jason back to the park, jogging across the expanse of field in his wine-coloured barber's uniform, his name sewn in cursive blue letters into the breast pocket. "Hey!" Tim's father shouted, and the crowd of boys parted.

The fight was separated, and Tim was crying. To his horror he looked down and saw his glasses lying on the grass, one of the lenses cracked. His father asked what was going on, and the boys' voices rose as they claimed that Tim had been mouthing off to them. Dirk saw the glasses lying on the grass and bent down to pick them up. "Who's gonna pay for these broken glasses?" he shouted. "Somebody's gonna pay for these broken glasses. Do you know that it's against the law to hit a guy who's wearing glasses?" One of the kids started laughing. "Hey! Don't laugh!" Dirk exclaimed, turning to the boy. "Don't laugh! It's a fact! It's against the law! You can get charged for that!"

"He started it by mouthin' off," said one of the boys, pointing at Tim.

Dirk gave a swift glance at his son. "Well, someone's gonna pay for these glasses. I know your father!" he said, pointing to the boy Tim had fought with. "You're Vic Hutchison's boy, right? He goes by my shop all the time—I'm gonna talk to him about this!"

"C'mon," he said to his son. Dirk's cheeks reddened as he did so, because of all the boys gathered in a crescent around him in the later afternoon sun, he realized Tim was the only one crying. "I want you guys to come back with us to the barbershop," Dirk said to the other boys. "I want to figure out who's gonna pay for these glasses."

They all walked back to the shop. Dirk set to work cutting his customer's hair as the boys bickered about the fight. "You guys started it!" Tim's brother charged.

"You lie like a fish!" another boy retorted. Ran Hutchison looked around the shop, his eyes flashing. A short, compact man in a T-shirt walked by outside the window of the shop, smiling serenely. The kids recognized him as Vic Hutchison, Ran's father. The barber was obliged to step to the door and beckon him in. Returning to his customer, Dirk noted, "Our kids had a bit of a fight, Vic—and my boy's glasses got broke."

"Hm!" Vic Hutchison observed, looking sharply at his son. "Well, now, Dirk," he smiled at Tim's father, "what are we supposed to do about that?"

"He started it!" Jason cried, pointing at Ran.

"Bull!" another boy yelled.

"Kids," Tim's father chuckled, smiling at his customer and shrugging as he clipped his sideburns.

"That kid was shootin' his mouth off!" a boy shouted, pointing at Tim.

"I told 'em, Vic, I told 'em that it's against the law to hit a guy with glasses," Dirk said, gesturing with his comb. "One of 'em gave me a little snicker, but I told 'em—it's against the law."

"Come on, Ran," Vic Hutchison said, opening the door to exit the shop. "Don't see why we should be payin' for glasses somebody broke themselves." As Ran walked alongside his father outside the large window at the front, the other boys following behind, he turned and grinned scornfully at Tim.

"Do you know how much it's gonna cost to get new glasses?" Dirk asked Tim, looking over at him darkly, his scissors clipping softly. This was the beginning of Ran Hutchison.

Tim walked from school at the end of the day, amidst the mass of teenagers. The girls talked among themselves and the boys moved in groups and shouted at each other. There was a barely contained restlessness, the warm Thermos-like halls smelled of breath and sandwiches, and in the parking lot the cars revved up, the yellow school buses forming their regular lineup in the slush, white exhaust foaming in the cold.

Like a large piece of lead slowly lifted from the back of one who has struggled to bear it for too long, a palpable weight lifted from Tim's heart as he approached the battered brown metal swinging doors opening from the school to the white freedom beyond. Released, his heart rejoiced over the sounds of the crackling ice splintering like glass beneath his boots as he walked.

"Do you do art?" a voice asked suddenly at his side. Tim turned. It was the girl who sat in the next row and up a bit in English class. She was new in the school that year, one of a large number of kids who had begun attending Tim's high school since their school had been closed the year before. She shared an allegiance with her fellow students of the old school, and as a group they tended to remain aloof from their schoolmates. She was tiny, with long brown hair falling down her back. Her face was heart-shaped, with high cheekbones. Her nose was small and upturned. She was smiling at him earnestly as she came abreast of him.

"Yeah... I draw," he murmured.

"I thought so," she said. "I saw the way you wrote the title on the front of the essay we handed in last week, and I thought you might do art..." she said trailing off, her voice fading away with a vague hand gesture. He tried to catch her words as they dissipated to a pale whisper, since her voice, like herself, was small, and forced him to bend lower to her to hear it.

"Do you do art?" he asked, thinking that was the right thing to do.

"Yeah," she said. "I draw too." Looking to the street where a city bus had just pulled up at the stop, she added, "There's my bus—gotta go." She began a quick sprint over the snow to the bus. "See you in class on Monday," she called out, her voice now louder, bell-like in the icy breeze.

She took the city bus, he thought as he watched her join the line to board, because she'd transferred from the other school that was further downtown. He trudged on up to the road as the bus merged into the afternoon traffic with a billowing exhale of exhaust. He crossed the road, jogging over the grey flattened slush to mount the dune of plowed snow on the other side and vaulted over. He walked from the road down a curved street on his way to the plaza where his dad's barbershop was and made his way through the sub-division.

Around him were the quiet split-level homes and bungalows of post-war vintage, the burgundy-bricked and aluminum-sided exteriors alike enough to be comforting in their uniformity yet different enough to be distinguished from their brethren. In front of each, the snowcapped arrangement of shrubs or bushes varied, and more rarely, a young fir tree stood sheltering a corner of a yard.

Tim had asked a girl from this neighbourhood out on a date the year before. He'd never had any experience with the opposite sex, and felt badly about this mostly because of the shame: in front of other males—his relatives, his father and his brother—his lack of female companionship and his seeming indifference to it were highly suspect. His abstinence from sports didn't help. He also felt that his slight physique and lack of muscles barred him from having any appeal to girls.

That was certainly the case according to his father and brother, and seemed to be validated by his surroundings. All the guys who had girlfriends were the large jock types. "Hey kid—you work out?" one of his classmates had asked him with a grin when he took his shirt off in the changeroom after gym one afternoon, and all the rest of the guys laughed. When Tim confided in Dirk about the comment, it was adopted as his new catchphrase whenever Tim was seen around the house without his shirt on: "Hey kid—you work out?" So Tim took to wearing long-sleeved shirts and long pants, even through the hottest days of the summer.

He had asked out the girl from the subdivision behind the plaza more from a sense of duty than anything else. He thought he'd seen her looking at him one morning during home room: their eyes met, he'd smiled, and she returned the smile after a moment of looking at him blankly. Tim didn't know whether the smile was a reflex or a sign of encouragement.

He arranged to be near the door when she came out of the school at the end of the day. As she headed home he fell into step beside her. They talked about goings on in their homeroom and in the one course they shared together. As they walked across the asphalt of the schoolyard that stretched to the plaza's parking lot, he suddenly murmured, "Your hand cold?" and took her hand in his and she allowed him to hold it for the rest of the walk. She had blonde, puffy hair, and her face and posture seemed already to have taken on the demeanor of a woman in middle age. He felt the absence of a girlfriend and she seemed like the best bet.

A couple days later he looked up her name in the phonebook and called to ask her on a date from the phone in his parents' bedroom. Her voice was friendly but flat, her words weighted down with a strange listlessness. She agreed to go see a movie, but it was difficult finding the right night to do it. She had lots of tests to do, and a major project to turn in. She was an honours student. A date was finally decided on. She would pick him up in her parents' car. They talked on the phone about school and homework. Her main courses of interest were math, science, chemistry and physics.

Tim was hoping he didn't come off as too weird. He'd chosen a movie with Christopher Reeve playing a priest. He thought that likely there would be little in it that would offend her. The movie was appropriately sombre and pious until it was discovered that a brothel was being run out of the Catholic church, and the screen was emblazoned with scenes featuring naked prostitutes. Tim was nervous and embarrassed, sneaking side glances at his date's face, an unreadable profile.

Her profile was still impassive as she drove him back to his house. He suggested going for something to eat or drink at the mall, but she had to get home early because she had a chemistry exam. There was vague talk of getting together and doing it again. The girl smiled sweetly, reflexively as she said it had been nice.

He got out of the car and walked into his house. "Hey, Tim's home," his brother Jason called out.

"Didja punch her panties?" asked Dirk from the couch.

"Didja get your dick wet?" his brother asked. Dirk and Jason often spoke like this. Tim sometimes joined in, but mostly his brother and father communicated in a language that was a near equal mix of scatology and pornography. At the dinner table, the code flourished into full flower. Instead of saying, "Pass the salt and pepper," it was always, "Pass the salt and pecker." Peanut butter was "penis butter." Ketchup was "cat shit." And mustard was invariably referred to as "mussy turd."

"Hey, Tim punched her panties!" his brother continued.

"Well, don't imagine he'd have too hard a time getting in there once he unleashed that role of tarpaper he's got between his legs," his father observed. Part of a coping mechanism Dirk had for the fact that his eldest son had no interest in sports or virtually any other type of manly behaviour was the idea that this deficiency was compensated for by the fact that Tim had an abnormally large penis.

Dirk began the assertion once Tim hit puberty, often with humour at the incongruity that one so slight and effeminate should be so well-endowed.

Once, a man waiting for a haircut in the barbershop eyed Tim skeptically and grunted to his father, "Your boy play hockey?" Dirk, who in his time had played hockey, baseball, football, golf and pool, who had hunted, swam and boxed, gestured with his scissors and replied, "No not that one, he's not built for fightin'. He's built for lovin.'" He winked, and over the tide of knowing laughter added, "I'm not gettin' out of the shower when he's in the room anymore, no way!"

Tim waited for weeks for an acknowledgment from the girl about their date together. He watched her as she walked through the halls, but the most he got was a polite, weak smile. He tried to follow up on their suggestion of a second date, but exams had started and she was busy studying for them. In his nervous despair he was driven to seek the advice of Dave Finestone, one of the popular and attractive boys at the high school whom Tim knew from elementary school. Dave had always shown acceptance, or at least tolerance, toward him.

"So maybe she's shy," Dave offered, gesturing as they stood where the wire mesh fence at the back of the schoolyard opened onto the weeds of the empty lot by the subdivision. "Some girls are like that. You just have to say to her, 'Cathy, I need to know what you're feelin'.'" With his dimpled features and feathered bangs, Dave Finestone inspired the sighs and longing looks of the girls at the high school—Tim had often noticed girls murmur in the school library as Dave walked by.

"You don't have to be shy about it. Just ask her how she's feelin', what's goin' on," Dave offered. "It's all about confidence, Tim. That's what girls like. You gotta have confidence." As they parted ways, Dave suggested, "You should get in touch with Russ. He's interested in a lotta the same things you are, and he don't have too many friends either. You should give him a call sometime." Dave made this suggestion often. Russ was Dave's younger brother, an introverted, bespectacled loner who was as scrawny and ungainly as Dave was compact and attractive. He had long, thin, white arms with red blotches that looked like burns. Tim knew him resentfully as the boy who had won a cartooning competition he'd entered several years before.

In spite of Dave's advice, Tim was never able to get an acknowledgment from the girl of their first date, much less ask for another one. He would see her in the hallway and she would smile in the same bland, noncommittal way that the religious girls smiled at him, a gesture in the service of niceness. He still prayed each night that he would find a girlfriend, and to that end he would periodically refrain from masturbating for weeks at a time, entertaining the belief that that would bring him one.

Tim's bedroom wall adjoined the living room where his father watched television and it had not been long before that Dirk was moved to observe, as an aside in conversation at the barbershop, "The way this guy goes at it, I'm afraid he's gonna come bustin' through the wall sometimes at night!"

"That's alright, just do it in the shower," his father advised Tim over the wave of laughter. "But don't do it every day—it takes all the good out of ya!"

Tim walked through the snowy park past the bleak empty swing set where he had fought Ran Hutchison, and shivered as he remembered how the very sight of it from the back of his mother's car used to fill him with dread. Rounding the wire mesh fence, he came to the back of the plaza to Dirk's barbershop. Across the massive back wall of the plaza, above the dumpsters and the parked cars, the words THE DOGNOISERS were emblazoned. He never knew the origin of the words, nor did any of the adults he asked.

Tim walked down the plaza to begin his shift at the variety store. He had started working there at the beginning of the school year. The store was owned by the wives of two brothers who worked in the oil refineries. Aside from Tim, it was staffed almost exclusively by women of late middle age. Tim would be paired with one of them on each of his shifts. Each of them complained about the behaviour of the other women as they worked the cash register, sold lottery tickets or doled out penny candy.

At the end of his shift, after Tim had replenished the milk and pop in the coolers at the back of the store, he walked out into the black snowy night, his footprints leaving a fresh trail across the unblemished fluffiness of the parking lot. He walked back across the park and through the yard of the elementary school, the silent chill of the night ringing in his ears and all around him, back before the golden lit windows of the humble suburban bungalows and out to the road that led him home, which curved and glowed with the smearing white glare of steady traffic.

As he walked in the slush at the side of the road he rounded the curve where the fuzzy blast of headlights seemed to come directly toward him in the moment before they swerved to the side, and always Tim imagined the lights continuing toward him, mowing him into oblivion. When they turned he detected disappointment in himself, and at times he imagined jumping into their path, even counting to three in order to egg himself on. He considered this plan and reproached himself for lacking the courage to carry it out. If a car could have obligingly veered off the road and hit him, that would have been okay. But then, being hit by a car was no guarantee of death. It might only leave him paralyzed for life, or in great pain, and both these scenarios would only make worse the misery from which he sought escape. Still, he remained hypnotized by the oncoming headlights of the rushing, hissing traffic as he walked through the black night, the brazen, unyielding beams mesmerizing him with promise and danger.

2. The Clown

"NOBODY IN THIS CLASS DID AS WELL AS THEY SHOULD HAVE on this test," the teacher was saying. "And there's no excuse for it. It was a simple case of lack of preparation." He had just finished laying the marked tests on the desks of his students. "You people want to go on to university next year. Well, I'll tell you, they're not going to be holding your hand and walking you through everything in university. You're going to have to take responsibility for yourself and your choices. You make the choice not to prepare, to go do something else instead, and you're going to fail. Does it matter in the larger scheme of the things, in the long run, if you fail a test?" he asked, outstretching his arms.

"No, of course not. It doesn't matter at all. But it's like a baseball game. It won't matter an iota to the history of the universe if you win or lose a baseball game. But while you're playing the game you can't think that way. When you're in the game you have to believe that nothing in the world is more important than winning that game. Otherwise, you won't win the game. That's the way it is with these tests. A hundred years from now it won't matter in the least whether you passed or failed a single English test. But in order to succeed, you must believe that nothing is more important."

Tim passed through the halls after class, his large binder beneath his arm. If he didn't have a friend or a girlfriend, if he was so disinclined to athletic activity that the teams in gym argued about who had to take him for a player—if his ineptitude at sports was such a wonder that a teacher was prompted to remark, "You don't mind if we laugh at ya, do you, Tim?"—if he had disappointed his father by failing at every male task known, still there was one certainty: he could draw. It could not be denied by anyone who saw his drawings, which had been a source of astonishment to others since he was very young.

He had begun around the age of six. The fluid and evocative lines of the Disney characters seemed magical to him, and he tried to capture them on paper. He worked dedicatedly, practising obsessively, and after a while he was able to reach a level of proficiency, and so attained an ability to create a sort of magic of his own. It allowed him to transport himself out of his time and place for hours. At times he would get so excited by what he was creating that he went into a trance and needed to rhythmically gyrate his fingers in front of his eyes. For the last several years, he had become rather glib about his drawing. It was a reliable way to impress people. There was little doubt in his mind that he would earn his living from cartooning when he grew up. In fact, he could not conceive of being able to bear any occupation other than that of an artist.

Tim walked with a special sense of purpose through the crowds now bottlenecking toward the doors at the end of the school day, for he had been watching the petite girl who had greeted him last week. He knew now that her name was Sherrie, and he had wondered at the back of her head and at her profile—her upturned nose and her cheekbones just visible beyond the brown curtain of her shoulder-length hair—as she sat three seats ahead of him in the next row in their English class.

She had said that she did art herself. She was unlike the other girls. Her compact form was usually in blue jeans, sneakers and sweaters. He had seen her again in the hall and had been too shy to look at her, afraid that she would ignore him like the others did. But he had hazarded a glance at the last moment and found her smiling at him, unreservedly, welcoming, like an unexpected cloud-parting.

He pushed open the brown metal door and crunched across the ice-laden sidewalk. Tim knew that Sherrie would be hurrying to catch the city bus now arriving at the stop to idle for a few minutes in front of the school. His eyes, blinking against the sudden whiteness of the snow, strained to find her figure among the clots of teenagers dispersing across the school's front yard. He saw her moving toward the bus and instantly began jogging to her, jostling against other students at either side. Just before he caught up to her he settled into a casual saunter, trying to keep his shortness of breath out of his voice as he greeted her with a note of surprise.

He made up a reason to be taking the city bus along with her, saying that he was going to the library downtown to research a project. In truth, he planned to ride into the city only to take the next bus back home. Sherrie seemed happy to see him, and as they moved with a knot of teenagers into the bus, finding seats near the back, Tim kept up a nervous babble of conversation, the words spilling out of him with excitement and increasing confidence, almost without his awareness or consent.

Her smile encouraged him, and from time to time she would make a comment but the hum of the bus as it pulled out onto the road and the murmur of the people around them made it harder to hear what she was saying, her voice was so quiet and faint. He bent to hear her words, and when he bent close he was dumbfounded by her eyes and her lips. As stricken as he was by the nearness of her face, he was also carried away by its expression of keen and welcoming interest.

She appeared as surprised and perplexed by the words tumbling from his mouth as he was. With his eyes locked upon hers, Tim was emboldened further in his humorous monologue, his words flying out and tangling in comic rhythm so that other people standing or sitting on the bus turned to look at him and laughed along with the girl as the bus made its way through the slush-filled streets into the small downtown core of the city.

From an early age Tim sought to make people laugh. He took falls and danced around in the manner of the old slapstick films he saw on television. He would spend his recesses at school improvising comedy routines for the laughter of the other boys. Tim's father would become angry about Tim acting stupid in the same way he would become about him "diddling" his fingers in front of his face. All of this troubled and dismayed his parents.

The reasons for their embarrassed discomfort seemed to present themselves most forcefully in a performance he gave at his grade five Christmas assembly. His class, led by a teacher who was a sports enthusiast, was contributing a display of tumbling to the program of musical numbers and skits. They rehearsed on mats in their classroom, and at one point each student was to execute a backwards somersault in succession. The first time Tim tried it, he found himself stuck with his backside in the air, looking up at his teacher and laughing classmates from between his legs.

When his turn in line came around again, he affected more difficulty with the manoeuvre, straining as he tried to complete the somersault to the loud amusement of his audience. The teacher was inspired by this to conceive a new role for Tim within the presentation: whereas the rest of the children would be dressed in identical T-shirts and shorts, he would wear a clown suit and whiteface. As they went through the drill of somersaults and flips, he would incompetently try to do the same—his bungled backwards somersault being the centrepiece of his performance. At the end, when all the rest of the kids had assembled themselves into a pyramid, Tim would run in front of them, shouting, "Merry Christmas, everyone!" causing their structure to collapse.

The audience was more perplexed than amused by the sight of the child in whiteface floundering around in the midst of an otherwise standard display of gymnastics. Unlike the laughter that had greeted Tim's antics in the classroom, the reaction in the auditorium was one of uncomfortable silence. Even Tim's greatest success, his struggling with his legs akimbo in mid-backwards somersault, yielded nothing as he grunted and strained with his buttocks high in the air, despite his best efforts to play up his discomfort.

After he cried "Merry Christmas, everyone!" and brought the pyramid down, he retreated to the wings, fearful of the reaction of his parents on the way home. Backstage, the other kids avoided his gaze. He looked into a mirror and saw the white paint had begun flaking off. Tim may have been anticipating his parents' angry disapproval, but their reaction was graver. In the front seat of the car, as the red tips of their lit cigarettes glowed in the night, they made no mention of his class's presentation or of his role in it. They talked of other affairs in quiet voices.

But as he spoke to Sherrie on the bus, his words hypnotizing himself as they came in a flurry, he looked into her eyes and saw understanding and appreciation. Looking around, he saw the other people on the bus, strangers, looking over at him with interest and amusement; people turning around in their seats to watch him, looking over their shoulders, laughing with surprised delight. His heart raced as he hungrily absorbed their appreciation, and like a dynamo, inspiration surged within him to further feed their interest, exploding his creativity in all directions. The air was suddenly alive in the back of the bus as it made its way through the snow-clogged streets—the silver metal of its interior, its smeared, salt-stained windows and floors were freshly invested with a new significance, a new life. No one experienced this ecstasy of the incomprehensible more than Tim, who had no idea what was going on or what he was saying, but merely experienced it all like a great glowing light.

A young woman passed by the window of Dirk's barbershop, and as was customary, Dirk paused in snipping his customer's hair, his hands poised holding the scissors and the comb as he stood in demonstrative assessment, watching the woman as she walked down the pavement. He shook his head, making a smacking noise with his lips as he turned with an almost pained expression to the rest of the men in the shop. "She's built, that one, eh?"

The other men voicing their approval, he returned to his barbering, noting to his co-worker, "Bet you'd like to get on that, eh Howard?"

Howard clipped at his customer's hair, stating quietly, "Yeah, but I'd rather get off on it." A wave of laughter greeted this remark and even Dirk had to shake his head in surprised amusement.

The door opened and a woman came in with her young son. By unspoken agreement the men stopped their racy banter, and as Tim's father finished with his customer he welcomed the young boy, placing the upholstered cushion he used to elevate children in the chair, snapping his apron and calling out, "You're next, partner!" The boy came fearfully, but Dirk amused him throwing his brush into the air and catching it behind his back. The woman hovered by the chair to calm her child but Dirk soon had him comforted and amused, keeping the boy distracted with funny remarks and questions.

Tim got up from the waiting chair and left, walking down to begin his shift at the variety store. That night, Tim and the customary middle-aged woman he would work his shift with were graced with the presence of one of the sisters who owned the store and her husband who came in periodically to attend to matters. The owner of the variety was a small bird-like woman, her white skin stretched like tissue paper over her angular bones. Her scalp was visible beneath the mesh of her thin, straggly hair, which deposited sprinkles of dandruff on the shoulders of the raggedy sweater she wore. She would frown as she examined the displays of chocolate bars and knick-knacks, her eyes squinting behind the oversized glasses perched on her pointy nose, or she sat in the back doing the books, counting the money.

Once, she asked Tim to make up labels for the bags of jujubes. He added a flourish to the labels, underlining the numbers after the decimal point, which he rendered with a small o. "Do these again," she grunted, bringing back the labels. "These are too fancy. Make 'em so people can read 'em."

Her husband was a bald, pot-bellied man who'd sit in the back paging through magazines while she attended to business. His beak-like nose, as porous and nearly as red as a strawberry, protruded from between the yellow-tinged lenses of his glasses. "C'mere!" he said to Tim when the boy had gone back to the stock room on an errand. The man sat at a desk in the tiny office. Before him was a magazine opened to a centrefold of a naked woman with her legs wide apart. "You like that?" the man asked with a smile, jerking his head in the direction of the magazine. "Whattaya think of that?"

Tim made some uncomfortable, vaguely approving sounds. He acted a bit more embarrassed than he actually was, chuckling as he got out of the stock room, away from the man's keenly searching gaze. The man came up front and took over the cash register for a while, something he did every so often as a lark. When Tim bent down to dole out the penny candy, or when he perched on a stepladder to replenish the cigarettes, the man would often take the opportunity to goose Tim, quickly diving his index finger between Tim's buttocks.

Tim's reaction would be to leap suddenly, with exaggerated surprise in the manner of the slapstick comedians from old films, in the manner he used to entertain his friends in the schoolyard. When Tim would jerk around in faux puzzlement he would see the man grinning and laughing with a keen expression in his eyes. "Gotcha that time, didn't I?" the man would say.

Tim's thoughts were not on these actions, but still vibrated with his encounter with Sherrie on the bus. It was in her eyes and her manner that had so heartened and transformed him. For she was one like him—who drew, who created art—and what he saw was a true knowing of his spirit and an acceptance of it like he had never known before. This had inspired him to be more himself than ever before. He felt he had scored a triumph. As he stacked the milk crates at the back of the variety store he played and replayed their conversation on the bus in his mind. He could hardly believe that the loneliness which had been with him for so long would soon be a thing of the past.

He walked home at the end of his shift, past the giant hydro lines. The skeletal towers holding them aloft seemed bleak and Eiffel-like in the chill night air silhouetted by a silver and icy moon. In his bed that night, Tim refrained from masturbating and prayed, giving thanks for the occurrence on the bus. He offered up some words pleading God for help with Sherrie. He recited again and again in his mind the words he would say to her when they next met, at times diddling as he imagined them. He gritted his teeth especially hard as he put forth to God his desperate appeal. Dropping back from this intensity, he concentrated again on the possible scenarios that might occur the next day, his thoughts growing fainter and further apart as he sank into unknowing.

Tim moved through the crowds in the hallway, his head craning to see beyond the shoulders and heads, searching for Sherrie's form: she told him she'd be coming out of Chemistry at this time. For a moment he grew anxious, fearing maybe that she was absent that day, or had left early. He needed to see her now, when their encounter on the bus was so fresh she wouldn't have forgotten him, now when he had the courage to approach her. Anytime other than now would be too late, he feared, his panic causing his heart to be beat faster, when suddenly she emerged from class. She turned and walked up the hall, her binder under her arm. This caught his attention: all the girls usually carried their binders in front of their chests.

Catching his breath with excitement, he jogged ahead, swerving from side to side to make his way around the other students blocking his way. He came up alongside her and called her name. She looked over, surprised and pleased to see him there. They walked beside each other down the hall. He made some witty remarks and she laughed, the light twinkling in her eyes until she closed them in her mirth, shaking her head in her amusement. They came up to her locker, and as she got out her books for her next class, he chuckled in the wake of a joke and offered, seemingly as an afterthought, an invitation to go see a movie some night.

She turned, her face suddenly serious.

"Oh no," she said quietly, shaking her head. "I have a boyfriend."

He continued to smile and to converse with her. He accompanied her down the hall to her next classroom, still trading observations on their classes, on their art. But as he looked at her face while she spoke, it seemed as though he was watching it recede like the light at the end of a tunnel, or the far-off sky viewed from far within a deep well down which he was falling, falling. He felt his stomach floating as one does when falling, and he tried mightily to pretend he was still in the land of the living as he joked with her, as he said a goodbye to her at the door of her class.

She turned from him and his face fell into an expressionless mask. He walked down the hall like a robot. He was stunned. The floor was swallowing him. Tim moved through crowds of students who were phantoms to him. As he got his coat from his locker and left the school, his eyes smarted and his throat itched. He didn't cry as he walked through the brisk afternoon, for more than sadness he felt dread—the dread of misfortune stalking him like a horde of black clouds moving in from the horizon across a field, throwing down their blankets of darkness as they settled in. He felt the wry twinge within him that answered the clouds and their low rumble: the rueful admission that once again doom had asserted itself, and it was only to be expected.

Tim felt as though he were suffocating. He found himself at home without any memory of walking there, yet every moment weighed as heavy as iron on his heart. Lying down on the couch his father slept on at night, he stared out through the picture window to where cars motored by on the road, and beyond that to the snow-covered, weed-filled vacant lot, and beyond that to the freight trains idling on their tracks in front of the distantly visible towers of the oil refinery. Tim laid on the couch for the several hours leading up to supper. He made a slight attempt to eat with his family, then slouched to his bedroom. "What's the matter with him?" he heard Dirk say.

In the morning he was granted a brief respite: the first second after awaking, in which he was unaware of his situation. The respite then became bitterness when the full force of the realization fell on him, smothering him. He heard the alarm clock buzz in his parents' room, heard Dirk get up and walk into the bathroom and, as he did every morning, cough shreds of mucous for several minutes into the toilet bowl.

Tim walked through the grey morning to school. The day passed in a dull river of sameness. He sat bent over his desk as he had so any times over the past twelve years, crushed by the oppressive monotony that was most of his education. His notebook was opened to a page that had existed in all the notebooks he had possessed through school: one on which he had scribbled over and over with pencil and pen, forming a large black shape, indenting the page with his repeated scribbling until the shape was shiny and the paper was nearly worn through. The shape came to an impossibly sharp point at one end which he imagined to be gouging into his heart, creating the fierce pain he felt there. He sat at his desk, grinding his pencil further and further into the large black shape as his teacher droned on.

After, Tim went to where he knew Sherrie would be as she exited her chemistry class again. He sidled up to her and she was happy to see him once more. He apologized for how he may have come off as weird yesterday. She shrugged, smiling, seeming not to know what he was talking about. "I hope, though, that we can be friends," Tim offered.

"Sure—that would be great," she said.

"Well, I'm not being totally altruistic," he noted, gamely trying to keep up his jocular manner. "Because I like talking with you."

She frowned. "What does altruistic mean?" she asked.

Tim often used words he had read in books that people didn't know the meaning of. Sometimes he didn't know the meanings himself. He'd use them according to what he thought they meant, from the way they sounded, from where they appeared in books he'd read. Sometimes he didn't even know how they were pronounced, since he'd only read them and hadn't heard them spoken. But this time he knew what the word meant. "Just means charity... that I'm not... just being charitable by being friends with you," he explained embarrassedly.

"Oh—great," she said, smiling.

As he parted from her, he walked through the mass of students scrambling to get to their classes. There were the pubescent jocks striding with exaggerated masculinity, their faces besieged by pink welts of acne, their foreheads shining with grease—some of them sporting the preliminary shadows of moustaches on their upper lips. There were the girls in pastel-coloured sweaters, with carefully blow-dried hair curtaining their painstakingly made-up faces like the spumes of an arrested fountain.

There were the others held in contempt by these, the blue-jeaned or leather-jacketed ones called burnouts and stoners, always rushing past to make it to the smoking area. Then there were the ones who were the most disdained—the bespectacled lonely ones, that fat ones and the ugly ones who were accepted neither by the browners or the stoners. They were solitary particles that floated meekly around the periphery of the others, trying not to attract attention.

Tim passed through these crowds dully unaware that he moved unnoticed by the faces around him—even as Ran Hutchison approached him, his slit-like eyes half-hidden by his shoulder-length hair, and hissed furiously, "Fuckin' faggot!" At other times, the feral intensity of Ran Hutchison's anger would cause his heart to race, and he would feel a spiralling, sinking sensation in the pit of his stomach. Even seeing the boy from a distance caused him to fill with anxiety. But now he was removed even from the boy he had dreaded ever since their fight in the park six years before.

Still, he knew the clashing, violent energy could never be completely relegated to the past. It was fresh, ever renewing itself. There was something primitive and deep-rooted in the hatred in Ran

Hutchison's eyes, and was all the more unsettling to Tim because it seemed as though Ran knew something about him, something he himself did not know—or rather did know but didn't dare admit to himself. Behind Ran Hutchison's contempt was a barely restrained, crazed ferocity like that of an animal that can never be trusted not to leap suddenly at your throat.

3. Sherrie

TIM REMAINED A FRIEND TO SHERRIE OVER THE COMING month, contriving to run into her in the halls between classes, or in the library. She always seemed as involved as he was when they would talk together. He became more aware of his appearance, too, noticing that the other students at the school had nicer hairstyles than he did. He came to realize that they showered daily rather than once a week. He began to get up an hour earlier in the morning so he could shower, then blow dry and style his hair. Soon he had a similar hairstyle to the other boys: bangs parted in the middle and feathered to each side.

Sherrie remained mysterious to him. Her silence, and her few and quiet words when she did speak continued to make him lean toward her. He felt an otherworldly quality in the calm, innocent beauty of her face and in the dark pools of her eyes, which some-times flashed with deep meaning then shyly danced away. She never spoke of her boyfriend, and Tim never brought him up. If he never mentioned the boyfriend, she might come to realize how irrelevant he had become to her.

On his own, Tim found out that Bruce Ferguson was twenty years old and worked at the Radio Shack in the mall. He was a man, not a teenager in high school. Tim scoped him out one day and saw that he was tall and stocky, and that to Tim's disgust and dismay, he had a thick black moustache far beyond the dim fuzz that Tim could cultivate. Tim imagined Sherrie kissing that moustache—and eventually imagined scenarios in which Bruce Ferguson died suddenly in a tragic mishap. Each night he would check the obituaries in the local paper to look for Bruce Ferguson's name. If Tim ever heard a friend of Sherrie's mention Bruce Ferguson's name, or even make mention of the fact she had a boyfriend, Tim would stiffen, his stomach would tighten and his smile would freeze on his face. So consumed was Tim with his obsession with Sherrie, he was driven again to seek the advice of Dave Finestone—

"That's always a heart-stopper," Dave remarked after hearing of Sherrie's boyfriend. "Not much you can do about that. It's up to her. You should just do what you're doin', staying a friend, being there for her. If the connection is as close as you say it is, she must feel it too," he continued. "If you like her as a friend, you can always see her at school. And who knows? Maybe someday things will work out." They parted, Dave heading across the vacant lot to the townhouse he lived in. "Hey," Dave called out across the field, "you should think about giving Russ a call. I think you two would really hit it off."

Russ had been transferred to Tim's art class some weeks before and Tim had avoided him since he was perilously close to resembling the outcasts and social pariahs of the school, with his glasses, thin arms, and flaring acne on his forehead and along his jawline. It was only after Tim knew Russ for a while that he began to see a certain noble handsomeness in his features. Russ's high cheekbones and strong chin made his face as angular as his body, and he moved with quick, bird-like grace. Although he was always alone, he possessed a dignity in his solitude; he did not feel ashamed of it, of his otherness, as Tim did. One day Tim saw some students playing with a faucet in the art studio. They put their fingers in the end of it and turned it on so that a stream of water sprayed in Russ's direction. Russ leapt to his feet and turned around to see them suppressing their laughter. "Well," he said quietly, staring them down, "everybody has to have one day in their life that they act like an asshole. I guess this is that day for you guys."

Tim moved from pitying Russ to worrying whether Russ would accept him as a friend. They exchanged some humorous remarks while washing up after art class, and Tim was gratified that Russ reacted to his jokes by bursting into laughter, his eyebrows raised with surprise over his squinted eyes. And Tim laughed in response to Russ's own acidic comments to a degree he had never laughed before. He was inspired and somewhat frightened by Russ's keen intelligence.

As they began walking home together at the end of the day, they would improvise jokes and routines. In the vacant lot where Tim had earlier stood with Russ's brother, Tim and Russ would talk for hours in the dying winter sun, each not wanting to part, their conversation punctuated by convulsive, nearly hysterical laughter. One of the routines they conceived was that of a cafeteria where overfed men stood in place of food, with the names of the meals they had consumed on signs around their necks. As you moved down the line with your tray, you'd be obliged to punch the men in the stomach to receive the food of your choice, which was then vomited onto your plate.

More seriously, Tim shared the ideas he had gotten from Joyce's *A Portrait of the Artist as a Young Man* in English class. He was so inspired by Joyce's conception of the writer as artist that he had begun to move away from thinking of himself as a cartoonist to seeing himself as a writer and beyond that, as an artist whose vision could express itself through any medium. The discipline was unimportant; what was important was the sensibility of the artist no matter what form it took, if it took any form at all. Tim now considered the medium of his drawing to be too limited. To be a cartoonist seemed a cheap ambition. He was now yearning toward a more serious art. In Joyce's work, the idea of *non serviam* came up, which was the protagonist's answer to society's demands on him: "I will not serve." The Latin phrase was taken from Milton's *Paradise Lost*, when Lucifer states that he would rather reign in hell than serve in heaven. Tim and Russ adopted *non serviam* as their credo.

One Saturday, Tim and Russ took the city bus downtown. They walked the main street past the nearly defunct shopping mall, the remains of old independent businesses, the pawn shops and the strip clubs. A brisk wind was blowing in their faces, and across the street was the incline down to the river and the train tracks beside it. They turned and made their way down. On the other side of the river were the buildings of America that seemed to peer intently but with no great interest across at them. Downriver were eighteen chemical plants and two oil refineries that composed the industry of the city.

Tim looked over at his friend as he spoke, the wind blowing back Russ's thick black hair and turning his nose red. Russ's father, an Anglican priest, had died of lung cancer five years before. Russ's mother wished for Russ to follow in his father's footsteps and become a minister. Russ stared ahead up the river as he spoke, with an intensity and seriousness unknown in other boys his age. "I know God's real," he said. "I know Jesus is alive and God's real. I've felt it. But I don't know if I'm the one to go up behind an altar and tell people that. I don't think I have *the calling* like my father had. I saw people all the time in church after my dad died and they'd give this sad smile and say they knew how I felt. But they didn't know how I felt. They didn't have the slightest idea."

As they walked by the docks near the grain elevators and the wind whipped them from down the river, Russ said angrily, "There's like this thick crust of mediocrity over everything. You're put in the position of always having to please the people you respect the least. Having to stay well-liked by all the people you can't stand. This could be Liverpool!" Russ said, waving his arm toward the anonymous-looking apartment building facing the river. "We could be the Beatles. We could be greater than the Beatles! This could be Dublin! We could be Joyce! You talk about James Joyce, about how everyone says he's the greatest writer. Well, I've never written anything, but I say I'm a greater writer than Joyce. I can say that because I have my life to make it true."

Numbness began to creep into Tim's toes as they trudged. "But that's the answer—*non serviam*! Don't even let them have a chance," Russ said. "I don't know about you, but just about everything I've learned in school is crap. It's not supposed to challenge you or educate you. It's supposed to crush you, to keep you down. The purpose is to keep you mediocre—to destroy your individuality. That's all it is…" Russ' peeved, outraged face looked out onto the waves, at snowflakes now slanting down into the green-black depths. He shook his head from side to side and suddenly spat angrily into the river. "*Non serviam*!" he repeated emphatically. "I will not serve!"

Tim had never had a friend whose interests and concerns aligned so closely to his own. Russ's quiet self-confidence and self-respect gave Tim senses of these qualities by osmosis; if Russ was not ashamed of his difference from others, then perhaps Tim could do the same. Russ also drew strength from their friendship; they were becoming like a team who saw the world and were up against it in the same way. As much as Tim felt empowered by his new friendship, he was still distressed about Sherrie: elated by the closeness he felt they shared, yet confounded by the fact they could not be together. He spoke to her every day, watching her eyes for a sign, a flicker of deep, knowing agreement that would bring their union into reality. Compassion, kindness, deep interest and even love was in her eyes, but never the spark that would demolish the false world around them and create the true one—the authentic life they should be living. The closer he got to Sherrie, the longer he knew her, the deeper it pained him. He prayed to God that some way, somehow, Bruce Ferguson could be removed from the picture so that he could be with Sherrie.

Tim began to outline the situation for Russ as they walked along the river. He had never spoken to his new friend about Sherrie, but now he gave some general details, still not mentioning her name. Russ walked quietly along, listening, and remained silent for a time after Tim had stopped speaking. The snow flurries were thickening, swirling in front of their eyes in a feathery blur.

"Ever think of how strange it is that your parents had sex?" Russ asked. "Do you ever walk through the mall and look at all the older couples—and some of the younger ones, too—and think, Those people have sex. Later on tonight they can go into a room, take off their clothes and have sex—and I can't. I look at those people and think about them having sex and it makes me sick because I know it's wasted on them—that I'm a thousand times more sensitive than they could ever be, that I'd appreciate what they have a thousand times more than they could ever dream of."

After a brief pause, Russ declared, "I know I'd be a great lover because I'm so creative. It takes creativity and imagination. When I think of some of those guys you see at school, lumbering around with their girlfriends..." He paused to make an expression of distaste, sticking out his tongue. "That's why you would be a great lover, too," Russ said turning to Tim, fixing his large brown eyes on him. "You're sensitive and creative—that's all it takes. You're the most intelligent and creative person I know."

They were coming to where the banks of the river split apart into the opening of the great lake; where the throat widened and the large, iron, Meccano-like construction arched high above: the bridge over to America. The only notable structure of the area loomed over the river, throwing a band of shadow over its waters, its web-like girders bisecting the sky, its murmur of cars and trucks rustling past each other as they made their way across its span, above the water, between the countries. They stood beneath it, under the giant pillars where cars parked to watch the river. Beyond the bridge was the vast blankness of the lake—the wide, vaulted, unobstructed sky joining with the lake as it merged into the invisible, leaving the ineffectual grasp of the land behind.

"If this girl is as special as you say she is," Russ said, "she's got to see that, sooner or later." He smiled at Tim, the flakes of snow collecting in his black hair. "I'm sure the guy she's with can't be as exceptional as you—it sounds to me like you've got nothing to worry about," he assured Tim. "It's just a matter of time."

Tim woke up and got to school early and as had become customary, searched Sherrie out in the library. As he came through the door he could see her sitting at a table with Mike, her locker-mate and friend from her old school. Tim focused on the back of her head with her light brown hair trailing back over her red sweater and his heart pounded harder. His breath quickened with excitement as he sat down at the table. Tim knew that Sherrie knew he was there, but for a moment she was involved in saying something to her friend. Tim's throat tightened as he waited for her to acknowledge him. As the seconds went by his hopes began falling into the depths of his stomach. Did she not know he was here? Was he of so little significance that his presence didn't register with her?

Suddenly she turned to him, smiling, and he instantly sprang to life. Tim began talking frantically to capture and repay her attention. He looked over at her friend as well, charitably including him in his performance. His eyes darted from Sherrie's face to Mike's at intervals, but the spaces between these intervals grew longer as Tim was unsure of Mike's attention. He could not help but see a trace of mocking skepticism in the other boy's eyes. Tim continued his stream of chatter, fighting to keep Sherrie's attention, but a glance over at Mike shook his focus and he momentarily forgot what he was saying. Mike knew Bruce Ferguson, and Tim had no doubt that his own spellbound obsession with Sherrie was immediately obvious to anyone who saw him in her presence—and he was strangely proud this was the case.

After a moment Mike gathered his books and left the library. Tim and Sherrie were left sitting at the table alone, and Tim was just about to go into another of his story routines when Sherrie smiled gently and said in her quiet voice, "Have you heard of Charitas?"

The word sounded like an exotic chime or a bell. He had never heard it before.

"It's a kind of retreat... a Christian retreat," she explained. "Well, it's not a big heavy evangelical God thing," she continued, rolling her eyes ironically with word *evangelical*. "It's hard to explain."

She sighed, looking down as Tim moved closer to her in order not to miss any of the information. "I mean, it's just a weekend thing. For people our age. It's for people to experience God." She shrugged. "It's something my church does. You know how it says in the Bible, 'Faith, hope and charity, and the greatest of these be charity'? And how charity is supposed to mean love? Well, that's what it's supposed to be about—experiencing *that* kind of love, of all of humanity—that God is supposed to represent."

Tim was dumbfounded by her words. He hadn't heard a person talk like this before and hadn't expected to be having such a conversation with her. Her words came at him and he took them in as best as he was able.

"Anyway, I can give you the information if you're interested," she said, waving her hand as if to dismiss all that she had said.

"So… one of those weekends is coming up?" he asked casually after a moment.

The bell rang and Tim and Sherrie collected their books from the table, heading out of the library. "Yeah… look, sorry, maybe I shouldn't have told you about it," she said. "Sorry if I…" Her words trailed away.

"It's just been a long time since I was at a church," Tim observed.

"They have it in the basement of a church—you stay there for a weekend," said Sherrie. "It's supposed to be amazing… an amazing experience."

"You're going on it?" Tim asked as they made their way through the crush of students rushing to their classes. They were cutting it close.

"Yeah," she said, smiling briefly as she took her leave of him, sprinting up the stairs.

For the rest of the day Tim was dazed, walking through the halls and attending his classes yet removed from it all. He was giddy, heartened by this new unforeseen development, but fearful. He had essentially been invited to spend a weekend with Sherrie—that was the incomprehensible reality. Of course, the weekend was a religious retreat. Yet that also meant it was unlikely Bruce Ferguson would attend.

Tim sat in his drafting class idling and drawing cartoons in his notebook. He felt the urge to diddle and contented himself with wriggling his fingers underneath his drafting table. Affixed to the surface of the table was a perspective drawing he had been working on for several months. Drafting was a course he'd had to take to fill out the number of electives he would need to graduate; he hadn't wanted to take any science, math or gym courses. Every day he came in and pinned the same drawing to his board, but after a certain point he rarely worked on it. He'd write or draw in his notebook instead. The teacher was a white-haired older man who often spent at least part of the class time sleeping at his desk, sometimes drowsing off in mid-sentence. He'd walk through the room every other week, checking the class's drawings, remarking as he looked at Tim's work, "Very good," or alternately, "You need to think about picking up some speed, Tim."

As he passed the hour in class, Tim tried to remember the last time he had been to church. As a child, when his family lived in the old house in the country, they had made some attempts to go to the church his mother's family attended. He remembered a few Sunday school classes from that period, but that was about it. Since then they had attended the church on special occasions to please his grandfather through the years, but these visits grew rare. Tim remembered that walking up the aisle to sit with the old people made him feel as though he was being ushered into a rarefied, holy place, being given a special front-row seat for salvation, somewhere on the fringes of heaven. But his reverent elation lasted only until the sermon began, at which point boredom and discomfort began to take hold, and even Tim's grandfather began snoring, his chin resting on his collar.

He felt some trepidation that the retreat might turn out to be as boring as the church services he remembered. But how could it be boring if he was in such close proximity to Sherrie? Any wariness

Tim might have felt about signing up for something he wasn't sure he believed in was washed away by the fact that there was no way he wasn't going to take advantage of this opportunity to be close to Sherrie. Maybe she had suggested the retreat to him for this very purpose—to deepen their relationship in spite of the fact she had a boyfriend. Perhaps this was like a test, and if he proved himself in it, she would make the decision to leave Bruce Ferguson for him, though Sherrie also certainly seemed sincere about the religiosity of the weekend. In her eyes and her nature, he saw a gentleness that seemed so rare as to be exotic. Her words of love and God now made her she seem like an angel. She was pulling him further into her mystery, and he was following, out of the dead grey world in which he had lived for so long.

"Sounds like a cult to me," Russ declared when they met up outside the side door after school. "I've heard about those weekends—they deprive you of sleep and feed you low-protein food to make your resistance lower—to brainwash you. That's what it is—a brainwash session. It certainly isn't good theology." Russ blinked behind his spectacles. "It's a type of manipulation trying to force people to God when they're in a vulnerable position." He grimaced and shook his head.

"It can't be that bad," Tim ventured. "She said they have it at her church."

Russ smiled wryly. "I don't think anything I say is going to deter you from going to this thing," he observed, "because this girl is going to be in attendance."

Tim looked down, embarrassed and thrilled by his friend's words.

"But I still have to say that this seems like a hokey thing," Russ said. "I mean, God is not a gimmick. This is serious stuff, not something that can be summed up in a group hug."

Tim exchanged goodbyes with his friend as he headed off in the opposite direction, gratified by Russ's understanding, despite his skepticism, of his need to attend the retreat. He walked straight to his job at the variety store, through the subdivision and the long silent park, bracketed at each side by the backyards of the bungalows, their garages and garden sheds, their clothesline poles and birdhouses. Tim took his place behind the counter, at the side of one of the several middle-aged women he worked with.

When Tim had gotten the job the year before, he had taken a long time to master the cash register since math was a struggle for him. Beatrice, the portly woman who had been given the task of training him, would fume with exasperation beside him as he fumbled to make change for customers, her irascibility causing him to lose count and have to start again until she'd shove him aside and take over.

In those early days, a man had come in wearing a bus driver's uniform. A thick thatch of black hair stuck out from beneath his visored cap, and a cigarette jutted from between his lips. He flung a five dollar bill on the counter. "Gimme an Ol' Yeller," the bus driver grunted, his eyes squinting from the smoke of his cigarette.

"What's that?" Tim asked, puzzled.

"An Ol' Yeller! Come on!" the bus driver exclaimed. "Jesus Christ, where'd you get this kid?" the man asked, looking over at Beatrice. "Ol' Yeller!" he shouted. "Sweet Caps!"

"What…" Tim mumbled, looking around.

"Sweet Caporals! Cigarettes! Jesus Christ!"

Tim got the yellow-packaged cigarettes for the man and rang his purchase through.

"Hey! I gave you five dollars!" the bus driver said, holding out the currency Tim placed in his hand. "What's the matter with you? How'd you ever get a job here?"

It took a couple of more tries and some help from Beatrice before the correct change was tendered to the man.

"God*damn!*" the bus driver cursed, tearing out of the store.

The next day the man came back in carrying several empty pop bottles to the back of the store. He came up to the counter and ordered: "Ol' Yeller."

Tim got him the cigarettes and gave him his change.

"Nope," the bus driver said.

Tim was sure that he'd given him the right change.

"I want the deposit on those two bottles I brought in taken off the price," the bus driver said, stabbing his finger in the direction of the back of the store, his cigarette bobbing between his lips as he spoke.

With the new complication Tim took several minutes calculating the change, causing the man to fume. "Aw, come on, dummy! Hurry up!"

From that time on, the bus driver would come in daily, buying his cigarettes and lottery tickets and pop. He would bring in empty bottles almost every day, as well, lifting them up as he came in, taking them to the back of the store. But sometimes it was difficult for Tim to see the number of them to calculate the discount the man would receive on his purchase. The bus driver would stand sighing and seething, always on the verge of losing his temper. It seemed to Tim that the man enjoyed flustering and humiliating him, particularly if there were others waiting at the counter. Tim sometimes suspected that the bus driver planned various combinations of complexity—with the bottle deposits, with lottery tickets—to confuse him. When he looked into the bus driver's eyes he saw a hatred so intense that the bus driver almost seemed to smirk with amusement at it.

Tim's heart would start beating faster when the bus driver entered the store, and when the man came to stand before him, smirking as he anticipated the mistake Tim would inevitably make, Tim would vibrate inside with panic and anger—so that he was more likely to make a mistake. He felt like he was becoming the fool that bus driver willed him to be, for his need to humiliate and abuse.

As time went on, the man began including among his many complaints his annoyance with a sore that festered on his lip, which Tim had noticed. Around Christmas of last year it had appeared, a small red dot on his lower lip, right at the place where he habitually rested his cigarette. It seemed to be a cold sore, but it was a stubborn one. It also appeared painful. "This sonofabitch has been hanging on for a month," he would mutter, pointing at the wound where his lip curled around his cigarette. "Got some ointment from the doctor, put it on, it didn't do a damned thing."

The sore stayed and grew larger. More and more it became the target of the bus driver's anger. Tim would look at it and think, You don't have such a big mouth now, do you? It was as though the anger and hatred Tim felt as a result of the bus driver's abuse, necessarily suppressed, had found expression through the sore blossoming on his lip, red and glistening at its centre, sporting a strange white crust around its circumference.

One night as the bus driver came in, throwing his five dollar bill on the counter and demanding his "Ol' Yeller," Tim saw him wince as he took his cigarette from his lip with the suppurating wound and he saw him shake his head disgustedly, turning to Beatrice, grumbling about the "goddamn thing" and muttering that his doctor now wanted him to "go to London" to have it checked out. "Goin' to London" usually only meant one thing.

As the bus driver picked up his pack of cigarettes and peeled off the cellophane band, he glanced over at Tim, his customary disdain glinting from beneath the heavy lids of his eyes. He replaced his cigarette with a new one and lit it with a match, stalking out of the store as he exhaled a large cloud of smoke which dissipated behind him, the bells on the door jingling as he strode out, Tim watching, awed and ashamed at what his anger had done.

4. Charitas

"WE ARE HERE TO EXPERIENCE GOD. THIS WEEKEND ALL OF us will experience God—you will feel His presence in this basement. God is alive. God is love. And God will make His presence known to us over the next forty-eight hours. God will enter this room and He will enter our lives."

A middle-aged man was speaking in a Scottish brogue. He had a thick, grey moustache and the dark pupils of his eyes glowed soulfully behind the lens of his glasses. He sat on a couch addressing the group of teenagers sitting on the carpet before him. His wife sat beside him, a woman with glasses like his own over sunken eyes, her greying, permed hair encircling her head like a mushroom crown. She sat holding her husband's hand, her other hand holding a cigarette that she periodically brought to her lips. The flames from the myriad candles around the darkened room flickered on the lenses of their glasses.

"We are here to experience the love of God, known as *Charitas*. In the Bible it says, 'Faith, hope and charity, but the greatest of these be charity'—love. The love of God is not the love a mother has for her child nor the love a husband has for his wife, nor even that of a friend for a friend. The love of God is the love God has for all of humanity, simply because of the fact that we are all His children. This is the same love God calls on us to have for each other and for all of humanity—a wide, all-embracing love we experience by knowing we are all God's children and as such we are all brothers and sisters to each other and deserving of love."

Tim had gone to Sherrie the day after she'd told him about the retreat and expressed his interest. She seemed quite pleased, and said she'd bring the forms with her to school the next day. To his puzzlement, Tim had been required to supply an array of personal information, and there was a checklist of objects he was expected to bring to the retreat such as a sleeping bag and a formal suit. They were not allowed to bring a watch or any type of timepiece to the retreat. Tim's mother had also been required to be in touch with the organizers.

"During this weekend, we ask that you call me Father or Dad," the man with the Scottish brogue was saying. "And we ask that you call my wife Emily Mother or Mom. It isn't that we are attempting to replace your real mothers and fathers," the man noted with a slight smile. "Rather, for this weekend, in this basement, we are pleased to be able to fill in those roles for you during what is bound to be a most emotional time. If you like, you can all us Co-Mom and Co-Dad. In addition, there are Charles and Caroline," the man said, indicating a middle-aged married couple on the other side of the room who raised their hands agreeably upon being named.

"For this weekend, they will be known as Co-co Dad Charles and Co-co Mom Caroline. Please don't hesitate to rely upon them as well for any needs you may have over the weekend—they will be most pleased to help you. Perhaps you have heard things about Charitas from friends. Perhaps you have heard things at school or in the newspaper. We ask you to disregard all that you have heard and to simply experience it—to experience the love of God as it will be revealed this weekend. We are all here in this basement for a reason—God has brought us together here to experience His love."

Tim looked around the darkened room at the forms of the other teenagers stretched out on the carpet or seated on cushions. He recognized some of the other kids from the halls at school. There was a banner stretched across the wall that read *Charitas*. He felt ill at ease and stretched to see around the shoulders of those in front of him, looking for Sherrie. He could see her sitting on the carpet looking up at the man who was speaking. He saw her profile, her upturned nose, her eye gleaming in the candle light that outlined her cheekbones and her chin and glowed along the edges of her hair. To Tim she seemed beatific, like a religious icon.

She was so far away from him, though! Tim had accepted that the goal of the weekend was to share a religious experience with the group, not with one person. It had still been difficult during the sign-in not to sidle over to her, not to have his attention entirely drawn to her in the midst of the crowd, rather than trying to manifest a wide, expansive love for all of humanity the retreat seemed to call for.

After the speech from Co-Dad, the group was taken to the gymnasium to play a game of volleyball. The co-parents got the game started and before long the teenagers were playing the game with abandon. The usual hooting and laughing started up. But Tim didn't like sports and always failed to engage in their good-natured rapport. He looked around at the smiling faces and the shouting mouths of the other kids and felt outrageously estranged from them, as though they were a different species. Again, he looked over at Sherrie to see her smiling as she volleyed, and as she burst into laughter while sharing a joke with one of the other teenagers.

After volleyball they moved into another room and began a singalong, with several of the teenagers breaking out guitars and strumming Christian songs mixed with vaguely spiritual works by the Beatles and Cat Stevens. Tim looked around at the singing faces, and saw Sherrie clapping her hands and harmonizing. He tried to join in with abandon, especially on those rare occasions when she met his gaze. At those times he would quickly grin and nod his head in time to the music. But the unnatural-feeling music combined with the volleyball game made him feel as though he'd made a terrible mistake in signing up for the weekend. As the voices around him united in an uptempo melody about "reaching out for

Jesus," he felt desolate and hollow inside, adrift on a voyage he now regretted taking, feeling his familiar life receding like a vanishing shoreline.

Co-Dad addressed the group, coming to sit on the couch before them, rumbling in his thick Scottish brogue. "It's time for an exercise called 'Minus Plus.' Charlie, could we have the blackboard brought in?" Charlie wheeled in a large blackboard. "Now for this," Co-Dad explained as he got to his feet, picking up a piece of chalk from the ledge of the blackboard, "we're going to make a list of all the reasons your parents drive you nuts. I'll write *minus* over here," said Co-Dad, drawing on the board as a murmur of laughter ran through the teenagers. "Yes, God knows there are enough of them. Parents can be a real drag sometimes. Now," he said, turning to face the group, "let's have it. What are the real bummers about your moms and dads?" He looked around at all the faces. "Come on now—no need to be shy. We're going to use this to learn something about ourselves."

"Well," a bushy-haired boy volunteered, "one thing about my mom—she always puts this curfew on me of nine o'clock, and all my friends get to stay out till ten, and that's kind of a drag."

"Alright," Co-Dad said, turning to write on the blackboard. "Curfews." Another boy raised his hand. "Yes, Gus?" Co-Dad asked.

"Well," said Gus, "sometimes my mom puts the juice container back in the fridge with only a few drops left in it, and then I go to get some juice and I take it out of the fridge and there's nothing in it!"

The group burst into laughter as Gus shook his head and looked skyward in exasperation. "It's like—Mom, when you finish the juice can you at least not put it back in the fridge so that people might think there's juice in it when there's not? People like me, maybe?"

"Ah, yes," remarked Co-Dad, chuckling along with the general laughter. He listed it on the board as one of the minuses: *Leaving nearly empty juice container in fridge.*

"Yes, Stacey? Do you have a minus about your parents?"

"Sometimes my mom kind of bothers me a lot about marks," Stacey said.

"Yes! Nagging! Very good!" Co-Dad remarked, writing it down. "That's a big one." The exercise continued. Co-Dad wrote down the various parental gripes on the left side of the blackboard, and when he came to the bottom, he moved to the right and wrote the word *plus*. He then ran through the list of complaints and showed how each minus the teenagers had could be seen as a plus in that the perceived misdeed was actually an expression of love. The parents of the boy who had bemoaned his curfew were guilty of no crime other than a protectiveness motivated by love. The girl whose mother nagged her about her marks was shown that the nagging was an expression of loving concern for her future success. Even Gus's mother, in returning the near-empty juice container to the fridge, was displaying a thriftiness in which her love for him was easily discerned: by ensuring that the last drops of juice weren't wasted, she was saving money to buy more juice for him in the future.

"So we see," explained Co-Dad, gesturing with his piece of chalk, "that many a time when parents do things which upset us or anger us, they do it with the best intentions. *Out of love.* We see that much of what we perceive to be minuses…" here he pointed to the word on the board, "are in actuality pluses, if we can only stop in our anger and think to see the love behind their actions. Now then, everyone stand up," Co-Dad commanded.

The teenagers pulled themselves to their feet.

"I hope we all learned something from that exercise. And since we are all learning together, I invite everyone to turn to the people on either side of you and give them a big Charitas hug. Come on now—we are all part of one family here. We are brothers and sisters in God, and it is time to share the Charitas love that we're feeling," said Co-Dad.

There were murmurs of embarrassment in the group as the teenagers awkwardly hugged each other. Tim found himself between two boys who were short and thin like himself—he quickly, gingerly encircled his arms around each of them in turn. Over the shoulder of one boy he saw a large jock bending to embrace Sherrie. Why on earth couldn't he have been seated next to her at this time? The image of the boy hugging Sherrie seared into Tim's brain.

He knew how irrational it was to be jealous of her when she already had a boyfriend, but somehow that fact made him even more distressed and furious to see her enjoying other people's company—as though they might win what was forbidden to him. There had been times at school when he had even been jealous of her female friends. He coveted every crumb of attention she bestowed. He was still overcome by his thoughts and emotions, his brow furrowed and his fingernails digging into the palms of his clenched-up hands, when Co-Dad called out, "Alright, then! Time for floor hockey!"

The teenagers were corralled back into the auditorium, and before he was fully conscious of it, without realizing what he was doing, Tim was jogging along the floor with a plastic hockey stick someone had shoved into his hand. He tried to play along with the other teenagers, but the running gave him a cramp in his stomach and attempting to be a good sport when he felt annoyed and furious only made him more annoyed and furious. He realized all at once that he had no idea what time it was: there were no watches allowed and all the clocks were covered. He knew it was night, but he didn't know how late it was. Tim began feeling disoriented, light-headed, his scalp prickling weirdly as he ran, brushing his stick along the floor.

Through the rush of running, sliding forms, he followed Sherrie's small body with his eye as it gracefully weaved, as she frequently smiled and laughed, calling out in a communal fashion to the other kids. Tim felt as though he were a ghost, destined only to stand and watch. "What have you led me into?" he asked silently as he hopelessly feigned participation in the game, mournfully peering at her from what seemed an intractable distance. All at once, Sherrie looked at him, eye to eye. Tim's heart stopped. She smiled and jogged over to him. Had she read his thoughts, had she sensed the desperation that was pounding in his temples? She held his glance as she approached him, smiling with the kindness he loved to see in her. "How're you doing?" she asked. "Alright?"

"Oh, yeah!" Tim exclaimed, bobbing his head up and down, smiling with enthusiasm.

"Great!" she responded, holding him in her smile for a moment more before turning and rejoining the game.

Tim returned to the game as well, finding he had more energy to devote to the running and darting, heartened by her attention. After the game it was bedtime, and Tim realized how late it must have been—or early in the morning it was—when he crawled into his sleeping bag on a cot in the auditorium. He immediately felt the weight of exhaustion on him and sank into deep, dreamless sleep.

It seemed as though no time had passed at all when loud music awoke him. The adults were moving through the auditorium waking each teenager up individually. The song that was blaring intoned, "This day was created by the Lord!"

"And here I thought the day was created by Johnny Carson," Tim noted to the boy at the cot beside him.

"What?" the boy asked.

The girls slept in a different area than the boys did, so the first opportunity for Tim to see Sherrie was in the breakfast lineup. When he sighted her sleepily helping herself to some juice, her eyes a bit puffy and hair dishevelled, Tim grew excited. Although many other people were present, it thrilled him that they had slept under the same roof.

After breakfast there was another singing session, then the teenagers were instructed to put on their suits and dresses. They were shepherded out of the basement into a school bus that waited outside. The bus drove them to an old age home several blocks away. The teenagers were separated into groups of three and given room numbers to visit. Tim and his group members were assigned to the small room of an eighty-seven-year-old, short, compact man in a white shirt and grey slacks. His sparse white hair was combed back from his forehead. He was agreeable but not notably excited to have the company of the teenagers. He sat on the edge of his bed and responded to their questions politely but succinctly.

In the long silences between the teenagers' attempts at conversation, the man sat patiently alert, waiting for the next sentence. When they smiled, he did not smile in return but nodded once with great dignity, in acknowledgement of their good wishes. When their assigned twenty minutes had passed and they rose to leave, the man shook their hands in the same affable diffidence with which he had greeted them. As they left his room he laid down on his bed and stared serenely into space.

"Many of these people we visited have no one to come visit them," Co-Dad explained when they returned to the church basement. "Many of them are alone, suffering from ill health and fading from life without anyone who cares. The one thing that unites them is the fact they are at the end of life—not the beginning. They are going where our parents must go and where we all must go."

A screen was set up and a film projector began clicking. The teenagers were shown a film of a middle-aged couple and their son going to visit the elderly, dementia-afflicted patriarch of the family. The film concerned the upcoming transference of the grandfather to an old age home. As the family visited with the old man, flashbacks were shown of the times they enjoyed earlier in life, when the grandfather was still mentally fit and reasonably agile. These memories were starkly contrasted with images of the present, of the old man sitting slack-jawed, feeble and infirm, his family struggling to communicate with him. The family professed their love for him, but his eyes looked through them, staring without recognition. Tim recognized the actors from bit parts on TV shows, and the grandfather in particular he remembered from a hot dog commercial.

The film was over, and some lights came on. The room was still dimly lit as the adults silently made their way about the room, passing out envelopes to the teenagers. Tim watched, puzzled, as teenagers opened their envelopes—many of them being quite moved by the contents. He could see some kids begin to cry. He couldn't remember the last time he had cried, and he feared he might not be able to. How would that go over with Sherrie? he wondered. Perhaps he could pretend, he thought, by licking his fingers and rubbing them by his eyes. As the envelopes were passed out and more teenagers seemed to be sobbing, he wondered what it was that could make them have such an intense reaction.

Tim took the envelope Co-Mom handed to him. He ripped it open and found several letters. He recognized the writing of his mother:

Dear Tim,

This is your mother speaking.
I am proud of you and I love you...

Next with a jolt, he recognized the overly careful, hard-pressed-down script of his dad on the paper beneath at the same time as he took in the first several lines.

Dear Tim,

You are an excellent writer while I am a terrible one, so please excuse my spelling. I love you and am proud of you...

Tears washed the words from his eyes in a rush as he bent over double. He heard himself utter a wail unlike any he had ever known himself to make. He was crying uncontrollably, in great spasms, liquid flowing from his eyes and nostrils.

Suddenly arms were around him, and through his blurred vision in the dim room he could tell that this time it was Sherrie. He locked his arms around her as he melted further into the frightening sorrow that had overtaken him. He had become unmoored from all that previously governed his emotions, flowing further into the awful cleansing truth. Sherrie held him close in the dimness of the church basement, weeping as well, making quiet exclamations of empathy as he shook, shattered and vibrating in her arms.

5. Freedom

TIM WALKED THROUGH THE SNOW IN THE FENCELESS YARD OF one of the subdivision houses. Every morning he took this shortcut, usually running from the road into the backyard and through to the street on the other side. Once the owner of the property shouted from his window telling him not to cut through, but this morning Tim didn't run, for now he didn't care about getting caught cutting through. Usually he would also have been fretting about the time, worrying about being late for school, but today he didn't worry. He strolled blissfully along, unconcerned about all that had troubled him before.

The sun shining brilliantly on the snow seemed to reflect his mood. The rich blue sky above the snow-capped suburban roofs, the band of grey trees on the horizon, were all still, quietly beautiful and as untroubled as he felt inside. He swung his binder under his arm, not quite sure if he had what he needed for school that day. It didn't matter. It would all work out. Life was as pure and simple as the icy air he inhaled and exhaled. He felt a fresh wind blowing inside him, and he felt as though he was being blown by it, walking on air, suspended a foot above the earth.

Tim's heart had opened and God had come into his life. Everything had shifted, and a vast expanse of space and light had been revealed. In the dark room, he had embraced and been embraced by his brothers and sisters. He had felt their love and he had known that love was the truth, the essential heart of everything. He had hugged his friends, the other teenagers of Charitas, the strong and the weak, the thin and the fat—he had hugged them all, with tears streaming from his eyes. He had hugged his co-dad, his arms stretching around the large, sweatered torso. He hugged his co-mom and his co-co mom and co-co dad. Tim knew now that all people were his family, were part of him. He saw that God loved him, that there was nothing to worry about. He felt that he had laid down a huge burden, one he had carried since birth. He had never imagined life without it, but now, without it weighing him down, Tim felt impossibly light, almost in danger of being whisked to the far ends of the universe.

After the crying time, when the adults had moved through the room distributing Kleenex boxes, the teenagers filed out for a meal in the gymnasium. There, by surprise, everyone's parents were waiting. Tim's mom had even brought her older sister, Aunt Maxine. All the teenagers had emotional reunions with their parents, and Tim hugged his mother for the first time in years. "Tim's gonna be a preacher now," said Dirk to Uncle Elmer, stabbing his cigarette in Tim's direction when they got home.

Over the subsequent days, Tim felt the bright, fresh truth on him. He could not remember the last time he had hugged his father or brother or mother but he now hugged them frequently, to their bemusement. When his father lay on the couch at night, Tim would offer to make him a cup of coffee, or volunteer to change the channel on the TV for him. He tried to help his mother more around the house. At the variety store the customers were no longer annoyances but opportunities for him to express the love that God had implanted in his heart. At school, he serenely made his way to his classes; it was no longer a place of stress, heartache and isolation. He didn't worry about his work or his grades. He knew it would all work out. He recognized his Charitas brothers and sisters in the halls and unashamedly hugged them all. His movements were no longer governed by fear.

He hugged Sherrie as well in the halls at school. In that mutual embrace was contained all the intimacy of what they had shared over the weekend. Tim felt joined to her more than ever. When they met each day at school their eyes held each other in total understanding. This sense of being bound to Sherrie by the events of the weekend, of the looming inevitability of their union, was a factor in the new faith he felt. It seemed that true love had come to him and in knowing that love, he was able to believe in *all* love, was able to see the ruling, infinite love of God manifesting Himself everywhere.

In the envelopes the teenagers were given at the retreat were letters from their friends at school as well as from their parents. Tim received a letter from Sherrie—in it she revealed that she was not a first-time Charitas participant. She was one of the helpers, teenagers who had been through the retreat before and were now going through to help other kids have a successful experience. Tim was taken aback by this, but then allowed himself to be moved by the thought that she was so concerned for him as to take a personal interest in his spiritual health. As was the case with all the letters, she expressed the hope that he would come away from the weekend feeling that it was a positive experience.

I hope Charitas hasn't made you too weirded out, she wrote. *For me it really helped me understand about God and love and helped me to see God in people. You are funny but at the same time you are gentle,* following the form of the letters by praising the recipient and encouraging them. *You try not to be sometimes, but you just can't help but show it. I know that if you are not challenged by something you'll get bored and move on. I hope you'll get lots out of the weekend because you're a great guy with lots of potential,* she wrote. *There are a lot of people who care about you very much, and one in particular who loves you.*

Tim could not determine for certain if the beginning letter of *one* in *one in particular who loves you* was a capital *O* or small *o*. It looked a little too big to be a small letter, but he held out hope that all that made it appear large was a sizable loop at the top. As much as he tried to convince himself that Sherrie wasn't talking about Jesus Christ, he could never entirely believe that she was making such an open declaration of her love for him. After all, it wasn't really the place to make such a confession, and she hadn't yet broken off with her boyfriend. He spent many hours studying the size of the *o* trying to ascertain whether it was a small capital *one* or a large small *one*. He peered deep into the grain of the paper and inspected the way the blue ink bled into it.

This was all immaterial, however, in view of the great truth that had been revealed to Tim, and the incredible metamorphosis that had taken place in their relationship. He had achieved an intimacy with Sherrie that would have been unimaginable a week before. He almost felt sorry for her boyfriend—surely her relationship with him now seemed paltry and shallow in comparison. Bruce Ferguson had no idea how limited his time was—for it seemed to Tim that in an essential way, Sherrie already was his girlfriend, and the external recognition of that fact would be merely a tedious formality.

It would all work out, Tim thought as he approached the school, walking through the grey haze of the smoking area to the side door. Before, he would have felt as though his heart was in a steadily tightening vice as he approached this door. He would have been frightened by the sneering faces, the possibility of violence. Now, all the forms around him seemed to flow and dissipate as if composed of mist as he advanced, solid and true with the love he felt inside him. Moving through the halls before, he had suffered as each gaze looked past him; he had walked feeling more alone with every moment. Now he walked through the school with ease, feeling a peaceful equanimity. He made his way to Sherrie's locker and bent to embrace her small, welcoming body. Looking past the strands of her golden hair, he saw the skeptical face of her locker-mate, Mike. Tim was not bothered by this, either. If Mike didn't know now, Tim thought, he soon would. A Biblical passage ran through Tim's head, likely remembered from his Charitas weekend: *He who has ears to hear, let him hear.*

"I'm not really the hugging type," Russ remarked, and neatly side-stepped out of Tim's reach. "I've got to say, though, that your weekend sure seems to have had an effect on you." Russ peered at Tim with surprised, interested eyes. "There's something different about you—in a way, everything's different about you."

They were in art class. Their teacher, Mr. Kosinski, was an artist himself who periodically showed his paintings in galleries around the county. He was a tall, lanky man with a goatee who played in rock bands in the sixties. Since the friendship between Russ and Tim had begun to blossom, the two boys were far more interested in talking and laughing with each other than working on the projects they were supposed to be completing. "Alright guys," Mr. Kosinski would intone, hearing them cackling from across the room, "enough of the funny stuff—you've both got projects to complete."

"Well, that's just it—it opened my eyes," Tim said, still barely believing what had happened to him, barely believing he was saying the words he was saying. "It just opened my eyes—to love," he said, shrugging. "That's what Jesus is about anyway, isn't He? Love."

Russ shook his head, then looked at Tim deep in the eyes again. "Are you serious?" he asked. "I mean, I don't know... I never know when you're joking."

"Of course I'm serious," Tim said and laughed. "You're the guy who was talking about Jesus, right? Well, that's what I learned at this thing—or more than that, *felt.* That beyond all the crap, the real message is love—that that's the only real truth, and that's the only real way to live."

Russ began chuckling, then let out a sharp bark of laughter.

"What's so funny?" Tim asked.

"Nothing!" Russ said, shaking his head again. "It's just that I guess you must be serious, since I've never seen a person change to the degree that you have. It's amazing."

"I certainly feel happier, that's for sure," said Tim.

"It's not just that though," Russ noted, looking at Tim through squinted eyes. "It's something else, something bigger" he said suddenly. "You've lost your fear."

"What's there to be afraid of?" Tim asked matter-of-factly.

Tim's apparent nonchalance set Russ to laughing again.

"Hey, you guys!" said Mr. Kosinski, his goateed face appearing from behind the canvas he was working on. "Keep it down over there!"

At the end of the day, Russ and Tim stood talking where the school fence opened up onto the empty lot by the subdivision, where they daily lingered before parting in their separate directions. "I guess I was unfair to this Charitas thing," Russ noted. "I mean if it's had this effect on you it must be a good thing."

"Well, it just makes everything so clear," Tim tried to explain, gazing off into the frozen sky as though he was trying to define it for himself as well. "It changes you inside because you see what the real truth is. Sure, some parts of it were kind of hokey," Tim allowed. "Needless to say, I hardly think that singing along to Cat Stevens songs was the apex of my spiritual life"—he rolled his eyes—"but you look at the intention of the whole thing, and it's about people accepting each other, loving each other, without all the crap that gets in the way."

"You're just trying to get a hug out of me," Russ joked, chuckling as he pre-emptively shrank back from Tim's touch.

"No—but anyway, you know what I'm saying," said Tim. "There was something else there at work."

"And there was your friend," Russ observed pointedly. "Sherrie."

"Well, yeah," Tim said. "I went on the weekend mostly because of her at the beginning, sure. I wanted to get to know her better. And I did get to know her better. But as time went on, I got to know something else too. I got to know that God is real," Tim explained, still in wonder at his own words and feeling. "And it really feels like I've been set free by that."

Russ stood for several moments in silence, staring down at his feet. He then turned and began walking across the field. He stopped just as he was about to reach the next fence. "Congratulations!" he called back.

Tim cast a glance back at Russ's receding figure as he moved on down the subdivision street that led him to his road. As he kept in his mind the image of Russ shrinking into the snow, Tim began to feel sorry for his friend. After all, Russ had not had his experience at Charitas, nor did Russ have a girlfriend like Sherrie as Tim soon would. Russ always seemed to be trudging through the snow alone—a sad, proud figure.

Though they shared the art class, Russ was a year younger and a grade beneath Tim, as Sherrie was. In spite of his relative youth, Russ's concerns and interests were adult, far more sophisticated than any of his peers including Tim. He shared Tim's tendency to use words he had read in conversation without being entirely clear about either their correct meaning or pronunciation. He was more sophisticated than Tim as well in terms of his sexual experience. He had told Tim about an incident which had occurred when he was at an art camp a few years ago. The week at the camp was the prize Russ had won in a drawing competition.

"The camp itself was no big deal. Just a bunch of art classes up in the woods. It was okay. But there was the one instructor there: she was older, and a big woman. And I knew that she was interested in me. She would always come up and find some way to brush against me. And any time she had an opportunity to meet my eye, she'd really hold my gaze with these significant, meaningful looks, you know. So one night after supper she comes by my table and drops a note: *Slip out after lights out and meet me at the rectory.*

"There was an old rectory they used for an art studio during the day. So I wait till I'm pretty sure everyone else is asleep in the cabin and I slip out. I make my way to the rectory and find the door's unlocked—I go in and feel my way down this pitch-black hall into the main room where the light from the moon's coming in across the floor. I'm there for a minute, then I hear her slip in. We laid down. I think we might have kissed some, but we didn't make out. Her hands were all over me, and she grabbed by hand, opened up her pants, and stuck it down there. I didn't know what she was doing at first, but then I realized that she was masturbating herself with my hand.

"I thought, My fingers are in her vagina right now—she's masturbating herself with my hand. After a while, she started moaning and shaking around, and I thought, She's having an orgasm right now—my fingers have masturbated a woman to orgasm." Tim had observed Russ' abstracted expression as he told the story, his almost clinical relation of the event, and he found another cause to envy his friend: not only had he won the drawing competition, but this victory had allowed him to have a mature sexual experience far beyond the ken of anything Tim had known. If only he had won the competition instead of Russ—as he should have—then perhaps it would have been him instead of Russ masturbating the woman on the floor of the rectory, Tim had thought bitterly.

He didn't think that way now, though, as he walked through the slush at the side of the road. Now that he had been awakened by Charitas, now that he would have Sherrie, he didn't envy Russ anymore. Russ was cold and couldn't connect emotionally. It was all understandable—he was hiding behind the shield of his intellect, using that as something to take pride in. But because of that, Tim thought sadly, Russ would never be able to make the leap of living Jesus's law of loving others as opposed to just talking about it, and he would never know the bond of trust formed by opening up to a girl like Sherrie.

Tim thought back to earlier in the week when he'd introduced Sherrie to Russ. He had walked with her down the hall to the art studio after school was over for the day, knowing Russ would be there working on a painting he was supposed to have finished that week. As they came in, Russ was standing by his painting in discussion with Mr. Kosinski. They both turned and Tim introduced Sherrie to them. There was some awkward conversation and some joking around by Tim and Russ that made everyone laugh. After a moment Tim shepherded Sherrie from the room, saying goodbye as they left the studio.

"Have a good time!" Mr. Kosinski called out as they got to the door. Tim turned to see the teacher smirking as he sat on the table, Russ at his side baring his teeth in mid-laugh. Tim flashed a smile in response to them to show he was undaunted. They could think they were as clever as they liked, but they didn't know the depths of emotion he did.

Tim also had God, he thought, turning from the road into the driveway of his house. The front yard was a huge snow-covered ice rink, the water drained from the elevated yards of the condominiums and subdivision houses at each side frozen solid. He was unashamed to hug his Charitas brothers and sisters in the halls at school, and to offer his embrace to everyone else. At the variety store he would sprint out from behind the counter to hug fellow Charitians when they came in. He saw the derisive expressions on other people's faces, but he didn't care. Hadn't Co-Dad said to not let the Charitas flame die, to carry it out into the world? Tim was glad to be considered a fool for doing that. Why should he worry about the opinions of those who were missing out on the entire point of being alive?

The further Tim got into this new identity, the more beauty he found in Sherrie. She had been attractive to him before, but now he found her heart-shaped face sublime. Her eyes seemed to glow with all the promise of heaven and all the sadness of mortality. She was like a guide to him. As he watched her, he often thought to himself that her looks were angelic, ethereal. She had brought him to this new place, and the quiet fountain of her whispered words and shy grace of her movements continued to nourish him.

One night, Tim was at home doing his homework in the rec room when he heard the doorbell ring and let his father answer it. Dirk came down the hall and said, "There's someone at the door for ya." Tim went to the door and was stunned to find Sherrie there. "I was just in the area," Sherrie smiled. "I thought I'd drop in." Her dad's car was parked in the driveway. Overjoyed and panicked at the same time, Tim ushered her into the next room. They sat on the floor and talked, Tim marvelling all the while that she was sitting on the same carpet he'd walked on, in his house.

They ended up looking at a book of Tim's that was dear to his heart, a large book about Walt Disney filled with art from all of his films. He'd seen it seven years before in the bookstore at the mall; they only had one copy and kept it high on a shelf over the counter. Tim would enter the store and stand staring up at the monstrous book, wondering what unknown treasures and magical wonders it contained. At one point he screwed up the courage to have the man take the book down so he could have a tantalizing look at the pages inside. But he was too timid to ask again, so for the next several months he had to be content with gazing up at it as if in homage, trying to divine the contents behind the exhilarating Mickey Mouse cover. The exorbitant price of the book put it out of Tim's reach, but later a condensed soft cover version was offered for seven dollars.

Tim developed a plan to sell large pictures of cartoon characters—drawn to order—to the other kids at school. He used oversized paper from an old blotter his mom had brought home from work. Although most of the characters requested were not Disney ones but rather contemporary stars such as Hong Kong Phooey, Tim drew and delivered them all, made the required money, and bought the book. A year later, his mother bought him the original, large version of the book for his birthday, and he had been surprised and thrilled. This was the book Tim now pressed into Sherrie's hands. "Here," he said. "You can have this."

"What?" Sherrie demurred. "I can't take this!"

"No, it's alright," Tim said. "I want you to have it."

"No way—that wouldn't be right." In the end, Tim was satisfied with her taking the smaller, softcover version. But it seemed important to him that she take it, that he give it to her—this most sacred object in his life so far. He needed to show her that he would sacrifice his most valued possession for her—for he now looked at her with the same excitement and devotion he once felt while staring up at the Walt Disney book. Even the letters in her name seemed to have significance, in the way they looked on paper, or when he pictured them in his mind. The way her name sounded when he heard a voice—any voice—always sounded beautiful to him and elevated the moment he was in.

"Tim's girlfriend was over last night," Dirk observed to Jason the next day.

"Did he pickle his penis in 'er?" Jason asked.

"I dunno, but it was gettin' pretty quiet in there," Dirk said. "I think he might've been unrolling the tar paper."

The pickle the penis part was one of his father and brother's favourite jokes, as in:

> *How do you pickle a penis?*

> *Put it in cider.*

Tim was further driven to press the book on Sherrie by his need to prove that his love for her was greater than her boyfriend's. Surely Bruce Ferguson must have been faulty at expressing love, so why would she continue in her incomprehensible relationship with him? In Tim's view, there was no way she could refuse his love if she were able to know its immensity. As he saw it, it was his job to demonstrate it in all ways possible, making her shedding of Bruce Ferguson inevitable. By the great light he would shine on her, Tim would make what Ferguson had to offer look so paltry and false that Sherrie would be obligated to drop him purely for the sake of truth.

Tim, with his new outlook of love for all of God's creatures, was distressed that at times he still caught himself wishing for the death of Bruce Ferguson, glancing through the obituaries in search of his name. It wasn't that he wished pain on Ferguson, but it would have been ideal if he had never existed or had never met Sherrie at all. Still, he wasn't as obsessed about Bruce Ferguson being taken out of the picture as he had been before. He had more faith now that his love for Sherrie would come to fruition. It would all work out.

Several days after her visit, Russ invited Tim to a concerto of Vivaldi given by a quartet in a church downtown. Tim mentioned it to Sherrie, who said she also wanted to go. Since she drove, she offered to pick Tim and Russ up in her dad's car. Tim was thrilled by her offer. It seemed to him that this would be their first date. The presence of Russ would offset the uncomfortable fact of Sherrie having a boyfriend; Russ would act as a chaperone of sorts, giving their date the appearance of being above board.

As the day of the concert approached, Tim was feverish with anticipation. He watched out the front window as Sherrie's dad's beat-up brown car pulled into the driveway, her small frame looking even tinier behind the wheel. He sprinted out and jumped in. They drove over to pick up Russ at the townhouse where he lived with his mother and brother. With Tim and Sherrie seated in the front and Russ in the back, they made their way to the concert. "You know, Bach was quite influenced by Vivaldi," Russ noted as they took their seats.

For Tim, the performance of the music was like the rituals of a church service: tolerance of such a formality was a measure of one's virtue. For him, its entire beauty derived from the fact that Sherrie sat beside him. They stopped by a Country Style Donuts shop on the way home, and sat in a booth around a gleaming mahogany table, Tim and Russ on one side, Sherrie on the other. "Tim seems to have had quite a positive experience at Charitas," Russ observed.

"Well, a lot of people have found it really worthwhile," Sherrie said.

"I've certainly had a few reservations about it," Russ said. "But Tim has really been changed by it, for the good, it seems."

Tim smiled in response. "It's surprising to me, too. It's strange that something so simple can turn your whole life upside down,"

Tim said, glancing at Russ and Sherrie in turn. "But then, what else would it be, but simple? The truth is simple."

"Your experience at Charitas was similar?" Russ asked Sherrie.

"Oh yeah," she said, looking down. "It really helped me, helped my faith. Sometimes it's difficult to believe in God's love if you don't really experience it. Charitas is a really great way to do that."

"Experience God's love,'" Russ noted, looking severe behind his spectacles. "What do you mean by that?"

"I can only speak for myself," Sherrie said, somewhat flustered, but intent on explaining. "You just get put in with a lot of people at their most vulnerable, their most emotional. And you are too, of course. Something just happens in the room… it's like you feel God's love at the time when everyone's most honest with them-selves. People talk about God all the time," Sherrie went on in her quiet voice, carefully finding her way. "But in church, or in the way He's used on TV, you don't get the sense that He's an active, living being who's involved in people's lives. It's weird that that's the pic-ture of God most people get. That's what I like about Charitas, that you feel that."

"It is deplorable the way God is used on TV," Russ agreed. "You see these people on there obviously just shilling for money. And then there's the ones who use God as an outlet for all their sexual problems. I saw a woman on TV talking about God's disapproval of immoral practices, and she went on and on listing them: homo-sexuality, adultery, sodomy, bestiality…" As Russ related the list he began breathing heavily, rolling his eyes and fluttering his eyelids to parody the woman's rising excitement over the sins, somehow becoming the woman as he did so.

Tim thought Russ looked rather unsavoury as he contorted his face while nearly feigning orgasm, but Sherrie laughed. At the sound of her laughter, Tim laughed too, pleased that she found his friend funny. The fact was a further bond between them, and he felt as though the laughter and delight were for him as well, reflected like a refracted light off his friend and onto him.

"It's not that church is so bad," Sherrie said. "I've gone to church all my life. It's just that the message can get a little bit lifeless sometimes. The people though, they're great," she stipulated. "They haven't let me down."

Sherrie's mother had gone through a series of breakdowns ten years before. She was unable to take care of herself and so Sherrie had to bathe her and look after her. Her mother was a collector who crammed their house with piles of newspapers and objects of every description. "People seem to have this romantic, exciting vision of being insane," Sherrie noted. "But it isn't romantic at all. It's just hard and frightening."

From time to time Sherrie's mother would disappear, and Sherrie would have to go looking for her. Often she would be in Simpsons-Sears, or in a nearby grocery store, believing she was shopping. "People don't know what to say when they meet my mother," Sherrie said. "But at least at church I can see people trying to be kind, and in some cases trying to help. Out on the street, people are just rude... They just don't want to understand at all."

Russ looked down at the bottle of juice in front of him on the mahogany table. "People don't know what to say," he murmured. "People sure didn't know what to say to me after my father died," he said, staring abstractedly at the bottle. "It was always, 'I know how you feel,' when they obviously didn't have the slightest idea how I felt, or they never would have said it. Or there was, 'Take care of your mother,' and the ever-popular, 'We'll be praying for you.' *We'll be praying for you*," Russ sneered. "Just pray for me! Why do you have to tell me you're praying for me?" he asked. "Or else they stare at you waiting for you to cry and getting all puzzled if you don't.

"That was the deal with me," he continued. "They took me to a psychiatrist because I didn't cry after the death of my father. But my father had gone through such hell over so long a period of time, that when he died I really had no reaction. He'd been sick for so long, and then one day my brother and I were in the basement watching Bugs Bunny and they came down the stairs and told us. We went right back to watching Bugs Bunny, neither of us crying. We really had gone through so much that there was nothing left in us, no tears in us to cry, at least at that time. But I'll never forget that," Russ said, looking across the donut shop. "At the time I was told my father died, I was watching Bugs Bunny."

Tim and Sherrie nodded, Tim thinking that his dad was pretty bad sometimes, but at least wasn't dead or insane. The three teenagers talked in the booth in the golden-lit donut shop into the night, their conversation rising and falling in rhythms of empathy. They seemed to speak from the same understanding, which was the hub that joined them. Tim looked from the face of his love to the face of his best friend, sharing confidences he never thought he could share, hearing confidences he never thought he would hear. Their pain, he saw, was the same as his. And the need for communication, for sharing, was the same as well.

As he spoke, Tim came to the realization that he was speaking the words he truly felt. To that time of his life, he had never dared to speak the words he truly felt. At some point in their talking they became aware of the time and realized five hours had flown by in what had seemed to be only half an hour. It was two a.m. on a school night, and Sherrie drove Tim and Russ home as quickly as she could. Tim exchanged a rushed hug with her before she sped off. When he walked into his house, luckily his mother and father were asleep, his father snoring on the couch.

Tim came into the living room and laid back on the La-Z-Boy recliner. *Entertainment Tonight* was on the television, but Tim was not looking at the screen. He stared off into the distance above the TV, and though it was late he had no desire to sleep. He felt as though he might never sleep again. It was as if he had never talked before, had never known another human being before tonight. He felt alive in every cell of his body, and marvelled at the incredible nature of what he had experienced, replaying it over and over in his head. Not until the light blue of early dawn came through the window did he tire of trying to comprehend the significance of what had occurred.

He fell asleep for a few hours in his clothes before rising to head off to school.

Christmas came in a blur of red, green, blue and white lights as the year accelerated to its end. For children and certainly for many of the adults, Christmas Day was the peak of the year, the summit of the meaning of the year and all the years past. In the weeks preceding, the garlanded displays would appear astride the main street of the city, and the oil refineries and chemical plants would install their yearly light show that families would drive out to admire. A dubious Santa Claus would appear by the Woolco in the mall and in school, earnest children's voices would sing of the difficulties a young married couple had in finding accommodations in Bethlehem two thousand years ago.

People became more buoyant as the day approached with calls of, "Hey, if I don't see you have a Merry Christmas, eh?" echoing through the barbershop and the variety store and on the sidewalk before them. Then suddenly, Christmas Eve came and the world closed in on itself like a flower before bursting open on Christmas Day, radiant even though the sky was grey and frosty, affording all lucky children the most wondrous sight of their lives: silhouettes of toys dimly sighted in the rooms before them as they ran from their beds.

In the weeks before Christmas, Tim went out with his mother to the mall when she went shopping. He bought trinkets, books, stuffed animals and little plaques with inspirational sayings on them from the Hallmark store. His plan was to wrap them up with some streamers and balloons and put them in Sherrie's locker to surprise her on the last day of school before the holiday. He'd gotten her skeptical locker-mate Mike to give him the combination. He'd even purchased some expensive wrapping paper that had her name on it in a multicoloured design. "Don't you think you're going a bit too far with this?" his mother asked. "I don't want you to put all this time and money into this and get your heart broken."

Tim stayed up late in his room wrapping the presents and writing poems to go along with them. He was going to get to school early in the morning to get the gifts into her locker before anyone else arrived. As he put the finishing touch on a colourful flourish he was adding to one of his poems, he looked out the bedroom window and saw his dad's van slowing to turn in the driveway. He could tell by the speed what condition his father was in. Tim rapidly turned off his light and scrambled into bed, hoping his father hadn't seen the light suddenly go off.

After a moment, he heard Dirk enter at the back door, brushing against the walls on each side of the hall as he made his way through the house. Tim's door swung open and the silhouette of his father stood in the hallway light.

"Bull*shit!*" Dirk sneered, his shadow swaying, affirming he'd seen the light go out. "Do you wanna fight with me?" he asked.

"No," said Tim, lying in the darkness.

"Cause you know I'll win—*right?*" the shadow in the door reasoned. "Right?"

"Right," said Tim.

The shadow stood swaying irresolutely for a moment, then turned and ambled out to the living room, mumbling to itself.

6. Winter

THE NEXT MORNING TIM GOT TO THE SCHOOL EARLY AND crammed the presents he'd purchased for Sherrie into her locker. He stuffed in the balloons and streamers as well. He imagined the surprise when Sherrie would open her locker and the brightly wrapped gifts tumbled out with the streamers and balloons. He was excited additionally that other people would see the spectacle and would know his love for her.

Later in the day he strode past her in anticipation, both of them rushing to classes, and she called out to him, "Thank you, thank you!" her smile bright and wide as she shook her head in disbelief at his efforts. Later she thanked him in more detail: "I really appreciate all the presents," Sherrie said quietly as they talked in the library. "But I'm just a bit freaked out."

He watched her as she looked down to the side contemplatively. He was touched by her gentle thoughtfulness.

"I mean… you go to all this trouble," she said. "And sometimes I think you have an idea of me that isn't really who I am. That you may not be seeing me."

"I can see you," Tim offered, feeling the smile on his lips as he spoke, which seemed to always be there when he was in her presence. "I can see that you're someone who's as beautiful on the inside as you are on the outside."

Sherrie rolled her eyes, then looked away. Tim told himself he saw a blush along her dimpled cheeks. "This is too much," she said.

"I don't think I can be what you want me to be."

In Tim's eyes she was already everything he could ever want her to be. He was just about to tell her that when the bell rang and they had to move on to their next class. They made their way out into the hall.

"Thanks again," Sherrie said, smiling. She extended her arms, and he bent to embrace her.

"Hey—break it up," a passing teacher shouted, half in jest, and several heads turned in the crowd to see them hugging. They released each other, Tim embarrassed and thrilled.

For Christmas Eve, Russ asked Tim to attend the service at the church he went to with his mother. Tim agreed and soon after, Russ's mother invited Tim's mother as well. Tim and his mother drove over to Russ's house and they all set off from there in Russ's mother's car. Russ's mother was a proud minister's widow, a petite middle-aged woman whose eyes glittered gaily behind her spectacles. She was the type of person that Tim's mother Mona easily interacted with, and with whom she was an upbeat fountain of kindness. She acted with Russ's mother the same way she might towards an older person, even though both women were the same age: Mona was pleasant and attentive, her voice rising at the end of her phrases, pitched a little higher than her everyday tone.

They all made their way into the church and were seated for the service. Russ admired the minister because he often worked quotations from writers like Albert Camus into his sermons, but Tim felt the service was like every other church service he had attended, something to be tolerated rather than experienced. At the point when the parishioners were called up the aisle to receive communion, Russ and his mother went up, but Tim and his mother stayed seated in their pew.

"Were you disappointed in me?" Russ whispered to Tim when they were on their way out.

"No—by what?" Tim asked, not understanding.

"For going up there," Russ said, jerking his head back in the direction of the altar. "You know. *Non serviam.*"

"Oh—no," Tim shrugged, but inwardly he was elated that Russ cared so much about his opinion.

On Christmas Day, Tim and his family made their pilgrimage to his grandfather's farmhouse. They drove through the bright day, the snowy fields at each side glistening, the white clouds stretched out thinly above them. The road ran parallel to the train tracks, the same tracks that connected to the railyard across the field from Tim's house. As Tim and his family entered the small town fifteen miles from their home, they turned onto its main street and drove over the tracks at the crossing bisecting the community. Continuing out of the town, they turned off onto a gravel road that ran parallel to the tracks on the other side; the tracks ran through the back acreage of Tim's grandfather's farm, through the fields that seemed to stretch forever.

As they pulled up before the farmhouse, Tim's mother stubbing out her cigarette and unwrapping her gum, Tim looked out and saw all the other cars parked along the long driveway that led to the house and continued out to the barn. In years past he would have felt the familiar pangs of trepidation as he contemplated entering the house, but these were lessened by his new spiritual outlook.

"Well, hello, hello!" his grandfather called from the top of the stairs, and they made their way into the overheated kitchen. There were pots and pans simmering on all the elements on the stove, the smell of the roast in the oven hung heavy in the air, and his grandfather's wife Penny was darting this way and that, attending to everyone's needs. Tim and his brother stood for a moment in awkward small talk with their cousins. They could no longer relate so easily as they grew older, and their amiable banter hardly covered the widening gulf of encroaching adulthood. As his father made his way into the sunporch to lie down and go to sleep, Tim moved out into the front room, where his uncles sat on the couch and on kitchen chairs brought in to accommodate them.

They were all farmers in their late fifties, and all sported generous stomachs; they spoke in gruff, amiable exhalations of breath, invariably offering the greeting, "G'day!" Much of their talk centred on food—whether they would help themselves to another cookie, or a piece of Penny's special "sea foam candy" that was in dishes all around the room, or how large their respective stomachs were in comparison to last year. Later, they'd tease each other about going back for seconds after dinner.

Over the last several years Tim had been embarrassed before these men, ever since the oldest of the uncles had offered him a job on his farm. When Tim was thirteen, Uncle Jim needed labourers to pick up the stones in the newly turned-over fields. It was considered a rite of passage for a young male in the country to put in some good, honest manual labour in the outdoors. Tim was driven to the farm and began working with some other hired hands, walking behind his uncle as he drove his tractor, pulling along a wagon. Tim and the others trudged across the field in the broiling heat, picking up stones—some of them as heavy as bowling balls—and heaving them onto the wagon. From time to time Uncle Jim would point out some of the rocks they missed from his vantage point up on the tractor seat.

Unlike the other workers, Tim lived with his uncle while they did the job. He slept in a spare bedroom on the second floor of the old wooden farmhouse, and in the mornings, after a generous breakfast with his uncle and aunt, he went to join the other workers where they waited beneath a giant oak tree beside the house. At eight in the morning the sun would be sending down fierce blankets of heat, which would only increase through the day. At lunch, if they were close enough to return to the house, Tim would eat there with his uncle while the workers ate beneath the tree.

Two days after the work began, the weekend came and Tim was driven back into town. On Sunday night he called the farm and told his aunt he wouldn't be coming back. He was more than glad to get back to his usual summer routine of watching television all day. Still, there was the uncomfortable sense he'd failed yet another test of masculinity, which only increased when Uncle Jim stopped for a haircut at Dirk's barbershop and tersely commented to his father, "You can tell Tim that I was very disappointed in him."

After that, he was ashamed in the presence of his uncles. He was thin and more interested in reading books than playing sports, and now he had the nerve to be lazy as well. He realized that, having failed to pass the test of honest labour, to them he was not and could never be *a man*. But now emboldened by the Charitas love that had been implanted in him, he walked up to each of them in turn and embraced them, to their considerable surprise. Later, the card tables were pulled out and the games began. After that the meal was served, Dirk awaking in time to partake. All the aunts made sure that everyone got enough to eat, and then helped wash up as Penny went out to tend the chickens. Several of the cousins who had their own cars ambled up to the old man in his easy chair and said, "Thanks, Gramps, but we have to be goin', makin' our rounds, got to go over to Cathy's folks' place now."

The old man looked up, grasping their hands, and said, "Well, thanks for comin', and have a happy new year." The early hours of night greyed the snows outside, and a blast of frigid air came up the stairs with each departing guest, still felt as their cheery goodbyes faded beyond the door. The sons and daughters drank their coffee and helped themselves to another of the treats Penny was making the rounds with. Tim was passing by his grandfather's chair when the old man called out, "And how is Jason today?"

Tim stopped and came to his grandfather's side. "Tim," he said.

The old man reached out and grasped Tim's hand tightly. "Or Tim, rather," he said, grimacing as he closed his eyes. "How's Tim today?"

"Good," said Tim.

"Well, that's good," his grandfather noted, shaking the grasped hand with each of his words. "That's good," he said. "That's good."

It was a characteristic of his speech in recent years to repeat the last phrase of a sentence several times, as if the machinery of his mind, once brought laboriously into motion, couldn't be stopped cleanly and had to idle slowly back into inaction. "It's pretty calm today," he would say. "Pretty calm," he would repeat, and then a minute later he would whisper, "Pretty calm," as if furnishing his own echo. Penny approached him and whispered something into his ear, and Tim's grandfather looked up at his wife and nodded. The old man turned back to Tim. "How's school goin'?"

"Good," Tim answered, looking down into his grandfather's pale blue eyes. Penny was now going about the house, delivering a wrapped package to each of her husband's children. The middle-aged men and women looked at the presents puzzledly—their father had never taken the trouble to give them each personal Christmas presents at these gatherings before.

They opened the wrappings and found themselves looking at newly printed black and white photographs of their mother who had died forty years before. An uncomfortable silence settled on the gathering, in the kitchen, in the front room, on the sunporch. They were confused and taken aback by the gift—it would be several moments before the general banter would begin again. In the midst of it all was the man who was the cause of the silence and discomfort, the cause of the gathering itself, who sat grasping Tim's hand tighter in the final moments before relinquishing it, shaking it for emphasis with each word he spoke.

"Take care," he said. "Take care." And a moment later: "Take care."

As the city had expanded from its nucleus around the river over the past twenty-five years, and an area of postwar bungalows had been added onto the outskirts of the original downtown core of wooden houses, so another zone of split-level homes was added to this, stretching out across the farmer's fields and the wastelands to the east of the city. The new communities were planned and landscaped with curling streets and cul-de-sacs and parks and parkettes for young families; they supported, like a host body a parasite, shopping malls and supermarkets that were worked so ingeniously into the neighbourhoods that they seemed to be connected to the homes and condominiums—to the degree that it was hard to be sure whether the massive stores were there to serve the homeowners or vice versa.

The houses shared a commonality of appearance that was comforting, if not sedative, to their owners as they drove home down the gently curling streets after a long hard day of work, but that was comical to the farmers of the outlying area as they had watched the homes being built. "Geez, livin' there, you could come home drunk one night and end up goin' to bed in the wrong house!" was a recurring observation. The external similarities were not the only ones shared by the homes, for inside there were certain aesthetic codes which were adopted and shared, too. Chief among these was the furnishing of the basements, the walls of which were always covered in dark brown wood panelling. Any sports trophies won by members of the home would be displayed here, and in some houses a pool table or ping pong table, a dart board or an extra television set was present, for this was known as "the rec room."

Tim became familiar with the rec rooms across the city through the aspect of the Charitas program where participants held parties at their homes for their fellow brothers and sisters. The teenagers would gather on the shag carpet of the basements as guitars were brought out and Cat Stevens songs were played. The purpose of these gatherings was to engage in fellowship, but also to plan for the next Charitas weekend.

For Tim these parties were happy occasions, for he had never had a large, ready-made group of friends before. He would enter these homes through a side door, padding down the carpeted stairs to where the teens had gathered, and immediately the hugging would begin. Other teenagers who he might have before regarded as his enemies, or as so inferior to him as to be beneath acknowledgement, were now his brothers and sisters. He would hug them, male and female, his arms wrapping around the differently shaped bodies, their different smells intermingling in his nostrils.

Even more important to this camaraderie was the opportunity to spend time with Sherrie. She was always present at these parties, and Tim would gravitate to her, despite his best intentions to remain in the flow of the more general Charitas love. Still, she didn't seem to mind his close proximity, and in Tim's mind he felt as though their fellow attendees already looked at them as a couple. They had gone out on several more outings with Russ, Sherrie picking up the two boys in her dad's oversized car. Tim continued to tell himself that these excursions were dates, chaperoned by his friend. Sherrie must have thought of them like that as well; she had turned down Tim's original offer to go out because she had a boyfriend, but Russ's presence on their outings made them more acceptable, safer.

"I don't know if your friend Russ likes me," Sherrie observed to Tim one day at school.

"Sure he likes you," Tim smiled. He knew that Russ could appear judgemental and remote.

"How do you know?" she asked. "Did he say so?"

"Well, yeah," Tim offered. "He said he thought you were special."

"Oh, *special*," Sherrie said, rolling her eyes, imbuing the word with its most negative meanings.

In fact, Russ had told Tim that Sherrie was special the day after their long talk at Country Style Donuts, and he had meant it sincerely. But he said he also had reservations about her. "She seems a bit sappy sometimes," Russ noted as he walked beside Russ on their way home from school.

"What do you mean?" Tim asked.

"Well, like when we were going to see that play the other day," Russ said. "She said, 'Maybe we'll be able to learn something from this play and apply it to our lives.' That's kind of sappy."

"Isn't that the point, though?" Tim asked defensively. "When you go see a play or a movie or anything—to learn something about yourself and apply it to your life?"

"No, actually," Russ stated. "I don't think that's the point at all. I don't think that Shakespeare sat down to teach anyone anything.

Inevitably people can learn something if they wish," he allowed, "because it's great art and it has those depths. But to see art as something to learn from, like in some self-improvement exercise...

"It's just typical of this bland, mediocre mindset," Russ said, spitting out his words as if to expel their taste from his mouth as quickly as possible. "Everything has to have some purpose, serve some practical end. Nothing can be art for art's sake. And if you look at the purpose closely," he observed sardonically, "you'll find it always has more than a little to do with money."

"I don't think she's talking about money," Tim said as they walked past a gas station. "She's just saying that, well, with anything in life, you can take from it and apply it to your own situation."

"Yeah, yeah," said Russ. "What she said is trite—and you know it's trite. You're just defending her because you're interested in her, and I can understand that. But don't pretend that what she said has value on any level at all." Russ chuckled, shaking his head. "Anyhow, what's going on with her?" he asked, turning to Tim suddenly and meeting his eyes. "Has she talked to you about her intention toward you and her boyfriend or what?"

Tim looked away, pretending to take interest in a cloud formation over the weed-filled vacant lot at their side. His throat tightened as it always did at the mention or thought of Bruce Ferguson. In his mind, Sherrie and himself were already joined, destined to live into old age together.

In reality, Sherrie had a boyfriend, a person Tim would hear about when friends of Sherrie's walked up and asked her about him, but whose name and existence were otherwise never mentioned— which allowed Tim, in the minutes he shared with her, to pretend Bruce never existed. But if Sherrie never brought up Bruce during their time together, she also never broke up with him. This reality gnawed at Tim behind his smile, even in his most spiritual Charitas moments. As the days went by, he found himself increasingly challenged to maintain the same upbeat outlook.

"Well," he said, "no. She hasn't talked about it... and hasn't broken up with him." It was painful for him to utter the words. "I don't get it, really. It seems we share so much—but then that Bruce Ferguson guy, maybe because he's older, makes her feel more secure given her home life... Maybe it's hard to make the change."

"Yeah, I've talked to Bruce," Russ remarked offhandedly. "He's not that thrilling of a guy."

Tim felt as though his soul had frozen. "You've talked to him?" he asked disbelievingly.

"Yeah, he works at Radio Shack in the mall, right?" Russ said. "I went in there and talked to him... asked him some questions about stereo speakers."

Tim was mortified. It had been a steady matter of principle on his part never to speak of Bruce Ferguson. To consider exchanging words with him was beyond comprehension. Tim felt somehow that it would have violated the possibility of his ever having a relationship with Sherrie if he were to speak to Bruce Ferguson. When he went to the mall he went to great lengths to avoid passing by the Radio Shack where Ferguson worked, and if he had to, he would avert his eyes so his gaze wouldn't fall on him by mistake.

Tim thought back to the one time he had steeled himself to see what Sherrie's boyfriend looked like. He stood in the food court across from the store and saw the stocky fellow waiting on a customer, smiling affably, his white teeth flashing from time to time beneath his thick black moustache. The moustache seemed to bespeak adulthood and manliness beyond anything Tim had to offer—it was mind-boggling for Tim to imagine Sherrie's tiny, delicate body being embraced by the large, cumbersome body he saw before him. He had seethed, the image of Bruce Ferguson seeming to jab into his eyes as he watched him in the mall. He felt like an assassin.

"He's not that interesting," noted Russ as the two boys stopped off at a small donut shop in the strip mall not far from Tim's house. They sat down together at a table.

"I guess he must have something," Tim allowed weakly.

"No," said Russ. "He's just a run-of-the-mill guy." Russ shrugged. "There's a thousand other guys just like him out there. But there's not a thousand other guys like you," Russ noted as he sipped his glass of Coke.

"Well," said Tim looking down, cheered by his friend's words, "but I don't know how much good it does me."

"Sherrie's hemmed in," Russ ventured. "She's like a lot of people—she'd like to be doing something different, living in a different way. But she's stuck. That's what I see. So she stays with this amiable, dull guy, hoping for the best because she simply hasn't got the guts to make a move. But so what? A lot of people are like that. Sure doesn't make her unique," Russ said, looking around the small donut shop. "People are led around and crushed by fear and guilt and cowardice. They end up trapped in lives they don't want, then whine about how they never got a chance, never had a choice.

"The farce of it all!" Russ proclaimed, gazing bitterly into his glass of Coke. "It's pathetic. What pathetic specimens human beings are!" he said as if talking to himself. "Everybody watching the same television shows, talking about the same television shows, wearing the same clothes, thinking the same thoughts. Old, borrowed ideas, old borrowed dreams and old, borrowed lives.

"You know, Jesus said, 'You are the salt of the earth, but if you should lose your savour, you aren't really good for anything except to be thrown on the dust heap,'" a sudden blaze in his eyes. "That's what people miss—that it's a real sin to lose your savour, to not be authentic in this life. It's a sin to give your life over to the forces of mediocrity. Jesus said that anyone of us could do the very same things He did—and greater... But anyway," Russ observed, calming down into a resigned disgust. "This town is just a sinkhole of mediocrity. You must be glad you'll be getting out of it."

This statement took Tim aback. After a moment he realized that Russ was referring to the fact this was Tim's last year in school, and after that he was expected to go on to university.

"I mean, I imagine you'll choose to go somewhere far from here," Russ had noted. "I can't imagine that you want to stay around this place."

Tim was in grade thirteen, the year that students completed only if they were planning on pursuing higher education. He had thought of quitting school the year before but he'd had no real idea of what he wanted to do. He'd toyed with the idea of going to an animation college but had never gotten around to applying. So he had gone back to school to avoid going to work, and now that he was halfway through his final year, the question of what he was going to do with his life was staring him down again.

He had the marks necessary to qualify for colleges and universities, but he had no idea what he wanted to study. He knew that in order to get a degree he'd have to take courses he wasn't particularly interested in, which was not very appealing. He would never hold a job, he told himself, that required a degree. The idea of attending university was attractive to his parents, for no one in his family had attended before, but for Tim the value of the idea wholly resided in the fact that it was something to do and a way to avoid working.

As much as he could tear his mind away from his dilemma with Sherrie—for it was that which absorbed all his attention—Tim's view of his future was nonchalant. In fact, when things worked out with Sherrie the way he expected them to, he told himself, he likely wouldn't go to university at all. Beyond this, he was of the opinion that whatever he did was of little consequence—he was an artist in the Joycean sense, as embodied by Stephen Daedalus in *A Portrait of the Artist as Young Man*, and his purpose was to find the best form through which to express his sensibility. At one time he had drawn, and now he was interested in writing. Perhaps he would perform. At one point as a kid he had a magic act he put on, with a banner that read, *The Great Tim-tini*. Maybe he would do something in that line, he thought.

One thing was for sure, Tim would not be a professor or a teacher or a scholar. To him, these were lower types who lived lives of emasculated boredom. He felt as though he had something more to give to the world, and he needed time, perhaps a lifetime, to bring it out of himself. He wanted to express the pure, illuminating beauty that struck him in the works of Van Gogh, in the writing of Joyce. Tim dared to entertain such hopes for himself, and in this sense the call he felt to be an artist was as irresistible and grave as the call some feel to become preachers and prophets. He also decided he would never use his artistic gift for such prosaic acts as teaching, or prostitute it for money. It would be far better to work menially for a living, or in an area utterly unrelated to art, than to sully and devalue it for such purposes.

Tim's convictions were strengthened and augmented by his new Charitas view of seeing a world of love and truth that existed behind the world he knew. He felt connected to humanity in a manner he had not been before, and Christ's exhortations from the Sermon on the Mount reverberated with Tim's vision of his road as an artist. He would do sacred work beyond the institutions, work schedules and sensationalist hum of society. Such work could take a lifetime to achieve and may not serve humanity's purpose until a lifetime after that; it transcended the concepts of time and space.

As a child, Tim had never wanted to grow up, so miserable and harsh the adult world seemed to him. Existence seemed such a painful thing for most of the adults he observed that he wondered why they bothered. Now he saw that the adult world was not only constricted, brutal and tragic, but was actually sheer madness. The Charitas weekend had shown Tim possibilities he had not known existed before, a hint that life was more than toil and pain. His sense that there was a higher love derived in great measure from Sherrie but beyond her, the spiritual experience she had led him to had freed him further from the monetary concerns and harsh punishments the world threatened him with.

In his freedom, Tim grew more detached and flippant about his schoolwork. He arrived one day at a course he was taking in Canadian literature to find the class was doing a test on a book he had neglected to read. He sat down in front of the test, panicked for a moment, but then relaxed as he saw what he had to do. He answered the questions as though they were about a book he wanted to read, or imagined he had read. He went through the test, writing in answers, sometimes essay-length ones. <u>What is the symbolic significance of the fence post?</u> *The fencepost signifies the dreams and the aspirations of the entire family, now shadowed by encroaching mortality.* <u>Why did Jim slaughter the calf?</u> *Jim slaughtered the calf because of his long-held feelings of hostility for his father.*

Tim missed his next class because of a doctor's appointment, but some of the other students came up to him in the hall and told him they'd spent the entire period going through his test, laughing at it, the teacher polling the class as to whether Tim deserved a passing grade for his ingenuity. Some of the students were in favour of it, while others were opposed, since he obviously hadn't read the book and prepared for the test as they had. The teacher stated that she was giving him a fifty percent grade in view of the writing ability he displayed. Several of the students thought he should get a better grade, one girl noting that Tim deserved something more for his creativity alone.

"Talent and creativity are wonderful," the teacher observed. She was a middle-aged woman who wore stylish glasses that she often took off, placing the end of one of the arms in her mouth with an air of quietly amused sophistication. She had no children of her own and was fond of stating that she looked on all of her students as her children. "But this wasn't a creative writing exercise. It was a test on a book most of you have read. Tim took it as an opportunity to display his talent, and I'll give him a pass this time, but he shouldn't be rewarded for it beyond that."

7. Roberta Cameron

SHERRIE'S FACE HELD ENDLESS INTEREST FOR TIM, SINCE beside the beauty he found there, he read her eyes, the curl of her lips, for clues as to what she was thinking. Her personality for him was like an object sighted in night that can only be defined by the outline around it. She had a particular smell which became identified with her in his mind, an acrid but not unpleasant odour he couldn't recall ever smelling before. When they walked through the halls talking, Tim's head would bob up and down, swooping in again and again to hear her words as they emanated from her small frame. He was always performing, trying to win her over and away from the clutches of Bruce Ferguson.

One day between classes they talked about the movie *Flashdance* that had just come out. "Do you want to see it? I was thinking about seeing it this weekend," Sherrie asked.

A tenuous excitement took hold of Tim. "Sure, yeah," he said. "That'd be great."

"Saturday night?" she said.

"That'd be great," Tim said, hoping he was hearing her quiet voice correctly.

They exchanged a hug and Tim watched as Sherrie moved through the crowds of teenagers. "I'll talk to you on Saturday!" she called back over her shoulder.

So this is the way it happens. This is the way it works, he thought, when a girl makes the decision to take a relationship to another level. She had asked him out to a movie, without mentioning Russ or any of the Charitas crew. For the first time they would be alone on a date. It seemed so logical, such a matter-of-fact thing to happen after all the intimacies they had already enjoyed, but to Tim it was the crossing of a major frontier.

He traded off his shift at the variety store on Saturday night, and all day Saturday he stayed around the house, waiting for her call. He showered and shaved carefully so as not to cut himself. As the day progressed into the afternoon he began to get nervous, and as suppertime came he realized they wouldn't be going to the seven o'clock show. But at eight the phone rang and he leapt on it. "I'll be by in about twenty minutes to pick you up," said Sherrie. "I've just got to stop by and get Barb and Mike, too. You know Barb and Mike?"

He knew them. Barb had been her best friend at her old school, and Mike was her locker-mate. "Yeah," said Tim.

"Okay, I'll see you then," she said. And then: "Are you alright?"

"Yeah," he said.

"Oh," she said. "It just seems all of a sudden your voice is different. Like there's something wrong."

"No," said Tim, pulling his tone up into the higher register of his cheerful, entertaining self. "Nothing's wrong. What could be wrong?"

"Okay, good," she said. "I'll see you soon."

Tim placed the receiver in its holder and sprinted to the washroom. He stood over the toilet and gagged, not sure if he really felt the physical impulse to gag, but needing to do it nonetheless, needing to react in the most radical, unequivocal manner. He convulsed and was able to retch up a small amount of orange-brown fluid into the toilet bowl.

Tim accompanied Sherrie and her friends to the movie, noting that Sherrie seemed more outgoing when she was with Barb than she ordinarily was. He felt estranged from the friends and their shared history, and as they laughed and joked it seemed to him as though they treated him like an elderly or handicapped person they had agreed to

tolerate out of kindness. They were glad to bring him into their camaraderie for a while, but he could never be a part of their lives in a real,
substantial way.

When he looked at Sherrie her eyes seemed different, never
seeming to focus on him or to acknowledge the significance of what
had passed between them, as though it had all been a dream he
dreamed alone. When she dropped him off that night it was though
he was being shut into a tomb. For the rest of the weekend he was in
grief, with a pain in his stomach that wouldn't let up. Years before,
he used to pray that no one threatened him at school the day before
a weekend so that he wouldn't have to spend the two days in anxious depression dreading the Monday to come. Now he would have
gladly traded this new anguish for all of the misery and pain he'd
endured as a result of being tormented by bullies as a child. At least
he had been able to hide from bullies, or to run away from them.
What he felt now seemed strong enough to kill him.

"You're the most sensitive person in the world," Russ noted solemnly, reacting to the gagging story Tim told him in art class. "And
it seems to me she doesn't know what she wants."

"I wasn't too impressed with her friend, either," Tim said, trying
to wrench some dignity from his suffering through anger. "Sherrie
seemed to become a different person when she was with her."

"Maybe she just isn't what you think she is," Russ offered matter-
of-factly. "Maybe she's just a normal, run-of-the-mill person."

"Not all the things she says are ordinary," Tim countered, feeling
a fierce desire to defend her. "And the experience at Charitas certainly wasn't ordinary."

"Yeah, but let's face it," said Russ. "There may be some good
things about Charitas, but it isn't an intellectual triumph. It's hokey."

"Well, I'd still recommend it," Tim said, remembering that he'd
been asked to recruit people for the next retreat. He'd often thought
that Charitas was just what Russ needed to get in touch with his
emotions, to actually feel the love of God instead of talking about
it all the time.

"Hey, you guys," said Mr. Kosinski, his severe, goateed face appearing around the side of his canvas. "Maybe you should get back to work?"

Disregarding Mr. Kosinski entirely, Russ exclaimed suddenly as if remembering something, "Oh hey! Do you really feel that writing about yourself is like trying to nail Jell-O to a tree?" He gave a wide grin.

Tim looked at him, puzzled. "How do you know I wrote that?" he asked.

"My English teacher read it to the class." Russ chuckled. "He got it from your teacher in the staff room. He even printed it up and put it on the bulletin board for everyone to read."

"I didn't know that," said Tim, flattered that his work had been appreciated. He had used a self-interview form from Truman Capote's *Music for Chameleons*. And the quote about nailing Jell-O to a tree was taken from Dick Cavett's autobiography.

"Yeah—he said it was a perfect example of autobiographical writing," Russ said, beaming at his friend. "So," he laughed, "do you still hide in your room whenever people come over to your house?"

Tim wondered if he should feel violated that the teacher had photocopied and read out loud his piece of writing, especially when it was so personal in nature. But he really couldn't feel anything but proud and pleased that his writing was being recognized, and he was thrilled it was being shared with others. He was also glad that Russ's teacher found it so good when his own teacher had only appreciated it moderately.

A couple days later, Tim was surprised by a girl coming up to him in the hall and telling him how much his piece of writing meant to her. Roberta Cameron had large blue eyes and a generous mouth. She was fourteen years old, in grade nine, and the younger sister of a girl Tim knew from Charitas. She that said she wrote, too, and her favourite author was Richard Bach, the author of *Jonathan Livingston Seagull*. She looked at the world with the wide, welcoming eyes of one who had little reason to distrust life and her fellow humans. Her words were spoken with the ease of one who had never known of a reason not to be honest.

Roberta Cameron began to leave samples of her writing and notes in Tim's locker. The subject of many of her writings was a spirituality that depended greatly on, and had a remarkable amount of faith in, the good intentions of humanity. There was serenity at the heart of her work that was even reflected in her handwriting: the blue lines were pressed lightly against the page, and they looped and curled with easy, imperturbable grace. After a while, the samples of writing fell off and the notes increased. Roberta showed little shyness in letting her feelings for Tim be known. Tim was flattered by her attention, and in his frustration with Sherrie he basked in it. He told Roberta of his hopes for Sherrie, but she was still glad to make herself available as he waited to see what Sherrie would decide. She began to call the house, and her notes to him were always signed, *Always on my mind.*

Roberta's open-hearted youth stopped Tim from having romantic thoughts about her because she seemed like a child to him. Her unguarded adoration for him was also difficult to accept because it made the contrast with Sherrie all the more obvious. Where Sherrie was mysterious, Roberta was forthright, and Tim was not attracted to Roberta's acceptance of him. As his hopes for Sherrie had begun to fade, however, he wondered if he was taking Roberta's love too lightly.

On a day off school, Tim invited Roberta to come with him across the river to America where his mother had worked as a secretary for a real estate company for twenty years. Roberta and Tim walked around the city in the snow, feeling in a hundred inexplicable ways the unique American flavour of the place in contrast to their home only miles away. One of Tim's ritual stops on every to the city was at a new building on the banks of the river, in which he could take the elevator up to an unoccupied floor and look out the window down onto the flowing grey river and across to Canada on the other side of it. He took the elevator with Roberta and gazed out with her on the snowstorm turning the wind white, the flakes madly swirling in the air high above the rushing waters. Roberta turned to him suddenly, her eyes seeming larger and bluer than ever. "You're a beautiful person," she blurted.

Suddenly Tim felt the flesh of her lips on his. He looked at her eyelids closed and placid as he felt her moving her mouth against his. He noted the way the pale sunlight was glittering on her eyelashes. They embraced, their bulky winter coats prohibiting any sensual realization from the act. He felt her move her tongue in his mouth, puzzled that he didn't seem to be feeling the way he was supposed to feel. They broke from the kiss and Roberta looked down to the side, suddenly shy. "We can go further," she whispered. "I did with my last boyfriend…"

Panic-stricken, Tim assured her that wouldn't be necessary. What would they do if someone came up suddenly in the elevator, he wondered. He was frightened and guilty at being so close to betraying his love for Sherrie. Such an act would disqualify him forever from attaining his union with her, and to even allow himself to be in the position where such a thing might be possible was a grave infraction of loyalty. He moved quickly from Roberta's welcoming arms, overcome with remorse for Sherrie, for Roberta, for himself.

Mona drove them back over the bridge at the end of the day, and when they dropped Roberta off, Tim got out to embrace her and to exchange another kiss. "Is that the girl who calls the house all the time?" Mona asked after he got back in the car.

He told her it was.

"Are you going out with her now?" she asked.

"No."

Tim's mother thought for a moment as she drove, then said, "You're doing the same to her as what Sherrie's doing to you." Tim looked over at Mona, noting that she looked older than the mental picture he had of her. He thought about the way he pictured people in his mind when he thought of them, and the way it was when sometimes he saw someone he hadn't seen for a while, and they had altered so much he'd have to change his mental picture of them. His mother had not greatly changed, but she had subtly, slightly become different somehow since the last time he'd updated his mental picture of her—the last time he'd consciously thought of her.

In the last several months, Tim realized, he'd been out of the house more than ever in his life up to that time—with his Charitas friends, with Russ and Sherrie, with his variety store job. His brother Jason had begun breaking away from the family a few years earlier, spending most of his time with his girlfriend. Now Tim was moving on, too. In the past he had spent more time with his mother than he did with any other person. For several years they had a membership to a classic films series at the library and would go to the monthly screenings together. From an early age he had read her the stories and comic books he wrote. Now he was leaving her on her own.

When Tim thought of his mother he often thought of a moment at his uncle Jim's house during a holiday gathering years ago. When drinking, Dirk often ruined get-togethers, and on this occasion had started an ugly scene with two of his brothers-in-law. In the aftermath, Tim saw his mother slip from the basement where the party was and he thought to go and comfort her for the embarrassment they both felt. He found her alone in the living room upstairs. She was sitting on the couch, looking at the Christmas cards displayed there. Tim stood at the doorway and asked her if she was alright and she answered in her upbeat voice, pitched in a higher tone, smiling as she said she was fine, nothing was wrong, just looking at Christmas cards.

Tim looked over at Mona as she looked out from behind her sunglasses, smoking a cigarette as she drove. She had travelled back and forth to work for twenty years. As a boy he had asked her why she had to work and she always said, "Well, if I didn't, there'd be a lot of things you'd be doing without." He saw now that it provided an escape, or at least a balance for her. As they turned into the driveway,

Tim thought of his mother in terms of a new aloneness—she was being left to while away the long Sunday afternoons, the long nights alone. Tim vowed to be kinder to her, and also decided to make it clear to Roberta Cameron that he would wait for Sherrie.

For several days Tim had not seen Russ at school. One afternoon on the way home he met up with Russ's brother Dave in the empty lot he cut through. "He won't go to school." Dave shrugged. "Says that he's finished. My mom's worried about it. Maybe you can talk to him."

That night Tim phoned Russ's house. "Where've you been?" Tim asked.

"I'm educating myself," Russ explained. "I can't seem to get the education I want at school, so I've made the decision to do it myself."

"But you won't get any credit for doing it," Tim said. "All you're going to do is flunk out."

"Well, every course of action has liabilities" Russ noted. "And for me, the benefits in this case outweigh the liabilities."

At school the next morning, Sherrie asked Tim, "So what's up with Russ? I haven't seen him around lately."

Tim told her of the phone call and concluded, "He seems to think he can get a better education at home than what he's getting at school."

Sherrie frowned, look off into the distance. "That's weird," she said. "It's like he's basically just dropping out of life."

"Maybe we should go by and see him," Tim suggested, eagerly taking advantage of her interest to come up with a reason to spend more time with her. "We could see what he's up to."

At lunch they walked out the back doors and across the field to the opening in the wire mesh fence that led to the empty lot bordering the subdivision. They made their way past the bungalows whose black roofs were beginning to assert themselves through the melting snow. They turned off onto the street of the identical townhouses all joined to one another like a string of paper dolls. Russ and his mother and brother had lived in one for the last five years since his father had died. Before that they had lived on the outskirts of the city in the parish of the church where his father had ministered. Tim and Sherrie came to the door and rang the bell. They waited for several minutes, then Tim pressed the button again.

Suddenly the door flew open. "Ah, the search and rescue team has arrived!" Russ exclaimed.

"What's been happening?" Tim asked.

"Just what I told you on the phone," Russ said, looking over the heads of Tim and Sherrie and gazing out into the street. "It's gotten warmer," he observed, breathing in the air. "I haven't been outdoors for a while."

"Can we come in?" Tim asked.

"Sure!" Russ obliged, stepping back from the door and lifting his arm in welcome. "Don't have anything to serve you for lunch, I'm afraid." Then as if struck by sudden thought he asked, "You didn't bring anything, did you?"

"No," said Tim.

"Oh well, I haven't been eating that much recently. I'll just wait until supper," Russ said. "Be sure and take off your boots, that's an expensive broadloom we've just had installed."

"Really?" asked Sherrie.

"No," Russ said.

They made their way down to the partially finished basement. There were some barbells and other pieces of weightlifting equip- ment on the carpet that Tim imagined were remnants of an attempt by Russ to augment his skinny physique. The three teenagers sat in old overstuffed chairs. Russ pulled a record out of its sleeve and put it on a turntable. The sprightly melodies of Vivaldi began reverberat- ing in the musty basement air. Russ leaned forward, his hand cover- ing his eyes visor-like as he sat, apparently in deep thought. Sherrie looked uncomfortably over at Tim who took this as a cue to try and engage Russ.

"So what's the deal?" he asked.

Russ pulled his hand from his eyes and smiled at Tim as if seeing him there for the first time. He leaned his sweater-clad, angular body back in his chair. "Deal?" asked Russ. "The deal is that there is no deal. The deal is that I've rejected the deal I've been offered. Unfortunately no one has seen fit to offer me another deal."

"Well, what is it?" Tim asked. "You just got tired of school, then?" He felt as though he was the bland defender of ordinary, insipid existence.

"Tired?" Russ asked. "No, I wouldn't say I was tired of school. Horrified, mortified, repulsed, repelled? Yes." As he spoke, the overhead light glared on the lenses of his glasses, so that only a white brightness was shining where his eyes were supposed to be. "Nauseated, sickened, appalled? Yes," Russ asserted. "But no, I wouldn't say that I was tired, particularly. Come on, guys, you know how it is," he said, waving his hand. "It's a slaughterhouse. The only difference is, more lives are ended in high school than in any slaughterhouse."

"Sometimes you have to do things you don't want to do in order to do things you do want to do," Sherrie suggested.

"That's just it," Russ noted, pointing his finger at Sherrie. "I categorically reject the premise of your argument. Because first of all, I don't believe that one gets to do what one wants by doing things one doesn't want to do. To me, that's backward logic that doesn't make a grain of sense."

Tim noted that Sherrie frowned at having her premise so roundly rejected.

"Secondly," Russ continued, "who says I want to do anything?" He relaxed back into his chair and turned his head in the direction of the strains of Vivaldi. He paused as if to savour the genius of the music. "Why should I have to do anything?" he asked. "Who says I have to do anything? What is this business of everybody having to do something all the time?"

"Well, you want to be an artist, don't you?" Tim said. "You want to create, right? That's something."

"Not necessarily," Russ countered. "Who says you have to create to be an artist? Aren't the things the artist creates simply the evidence of an artistic mindset? So why not just have the artistic mindset and call it a day?

"What do we take from the works of Shakespeare?" he argued. "We know that he was a gifted, wise, intelligent, sensitive genius. Fine—I'm cutting to the chase. Instead of creating works so that hundreds of years after my death people will talk about what a wise, intelligent genius I was, I'll just settle for the fact that *I* know I'm a wise, intelligent, sensitive genius and be done with it."

Having delivered this statement, Russ settled back in his chair and folded his arms over his chest. "Of course, I'm sure you're not suggesting that to be an artist you have to be good in school," Russ added, looking pointedly over at Tim. "*Non serviam* and all that!"

"The idea, though," Sherrie offered in her quiet voice, "is that by sharing your gift with others, like Shakespeare, you're helping humanity, performing a service for it."

"Humanity, schmumanity," Russ scoffed, waving his hand. "Humanity doesn't deserve my gift. What good did Shakespeare do for humanity? Give it something to entertain itself with between butchering excursions? I mean, how can you sit there and say that humanity has been bettered by Shakespeare or any of the so-called great artists? Has it stopped society from killing little children? Has it stopped society from herding kids into classrooms and destroying their spirits and turning them into a bunch of dead-asses for the sake of the almighty dollar?

"Also, sorry to inform you," he continued, "but most of our fellow humans care more about procuring a six-pack of beer than the collected works of William Shakespeare. And further to that, they care even more about winning the lottery or amassing a bundle of loot through some other means.

"Truth be told," he said, "that's what the whole process of school is about. Everybody's just going and getting their credits to get a diploma and get a job. They're not being stimulated or educated in any real sense. They're just grinding through to make money. They don't care what they're learning, and the teachers don't care what they're teaching. It's all about money on both sides—just like everything else in this stupid society."

"I guess that's the thing, though," Tim noted lamely. "Everybody has to do something to make a living."

"Yeah," said Russ. "Well, maybe being a minister is the thing, then," he observed wryly. "Just have to do a sermon once a week, you get a place to live, nothing too strenuous..." His face clouded over and he stared down at the carpet as if something there was causing him dismay.

"Well, if you wanted to become a minister, you'd have to get a high school diploma to do that," Tim reasoned cautiously after a moment. He looked over at Sherrie, who nodded in agreement.

"Hmm, yeah, I suppose you're right," Russ mused. "My dad had to go to Bible college. Isn't it interesting," he asked, "that Jesus Christ Himself didn't have a high school diploma, but you have to have one to be one of His representatives, to speak in His name?"

At that moment the phone rang and Russ glanced over at it as if weighing its claim on him. He shrugged his shoulders and picked it up. "Hello? No, Russ... No. Okay, I'll tell her when she comes in, then. Okay. Bye." Russ replaced the receiver and sat staring down at the floor in silence. Then slowly his shoulders began bobbing up and down, and he raised his head in a quiet laughter that worked its way into a loud bark.

"What's the joke?" Tim asked gamely.

"The guy on the phone!" Russ spluttered between gasps of laughter. "He said, 'Hello, Gus?' and I said 'No—Russ!'" He dissolved further into delighted barking.

Tim and Sherrie started laughing along at the silliness of the exchange, but they were also carried away by Russ's mirth. He was kicking his legs and rocking in his chair. As the laughter continued, Russ leaned forward, and Tim could see that Russ's face bore a grimace of anguish. His own laughter stopped. He looked over at Sherrie and saw that she was still laughing along.

"Well, anyway," Russ stated, suddenly sober. "This has been fun, guys, but I've got to get back to work, and I know you do, too." He looked away, and Tim thought that he could see him blinking tears away behind his glasses. Russ led his two friends up the basement stairs and to the front door of the townhouse. They told him that they hoped they'd see him again. Russ shrugged. Tim and Sherrie walked from the townhouse down the street filled with huge puddles where the snow was melting. "Back to work!" Russ called out to them. "Crack those books! Happy hunting!" They looked back to see him bent with laughter in his doorway. "Adios! Sayonara!"

As they continued through the empty lot out back of the school, Tim looked over at Sherrie and saw her disturbed frown. "What's he going to do now?" she asked after several moments in silence.

"I don't know," Tim said, glad that the situation had furnished a problem that bound him and Sherrie together in concern, though he was still disquieted by Russ's behaviour. Was Russ right? Should he drop out of school, too? "He'll be back, I'll bet—he's just going through something," Tim assured her.

Sherrie frowned, looking straight ahead as she walked. "Have you encouraged him about going on Charitas?" she asked.

"Oh, yeah," Tim said, nodding. "But he's skeptical about those things."

"Well, I think it would do him a lot of good," Sherrie said as they entered the school. The bell was ringing and teenagers on each side of them were hurrying to their classes. Tim and Sherrie had discussed Russ attending Charitas many times before. They wanted their friend to experience what they had experienced, and they felt that the retreat would open Russ's heart, free him from the isolation he so obviously felt.

Tim and Sherrie were both helping to plan the next Charitas weekend, which was to take place on Easter. Tim was glad to be involved chiefly for the extra time it gave him to spend with Sherrie. His mother would usually drive him to the planning meetings at people's houses or at the church, but after a while he made the acquaintance of Eric Dunphy, a tall, thin fellow with a lantern jaw, glasses and a peaked cap he invariably wore.

During the prayer at each meeting, Eric Dunphy sat with his head bowed and his hands outstretched before him with upraised palms as though he was balancing tea saucers on them. Eric had a small car in which he began to give Tim rides to the meetings. Much of Eric's talk involved the amazing connection to God that his mother had. Eric would marvel at his mother's ability to pray to God for just about anything and find that her prayers were answered.

"Our church group was going on a skiing weekend," Eric related, motoring along in his car. "For a week before that there hadn't been any snow and so Mom prayed for some for us. Comes the day of the trip—still no snow. We set off anyway. Then that night we get a blizzard that lasts three days! We're snowed in! It's like, okay Mom! We got it! That's enough!" he exclaimed, shaking his head, watching the road. "Enough with the snow already!"

Eric seemed to speak with an English accent, though as far as Tim knew, neither Eric nor his parents had been born in England. His other topic of conversation involved various girls he was involved with in the Charitas group. He spoke of all of them as though they were erotic temptresses, though Tim thought them rather ordinary when he met them.

"Now Emily," Eric would relate, "she does the flirt-flirt-flirt, and last week she gave me a hug that basically knocked my socks off! I said, 'Emily, what are you doing to me, you know I'm with Paige!' She said, 'Eric, when I saw that skinny body of yours I just knew it needed a hug!' Good Lord!" Eric exclaimed, shaking his head, his jaw protruding prow-like ahead of him as he steered the car. "I said to God, you know, just basically, 'What do You want me to do here? You're giving me these two different girls and You're tearing me in half!" He shook his head again. "And that Emily has got such a cute face on her!"

Tim was emboldened to tell Eric of his dilemma with Sherrie. Eric listened with rapt concentration, nodding his head and interjecting with empathetic *hmms* and grunts.

"Well, it seems to me that this Bruce fellow, whatever his name is, is on the way out and doesn't know it yet," Eric pronounced after due consideration. "I mean you talk about the connection you guys have, and wow, if half of what you say is true, then it sounds like God really wants you two guys to be together! I mean, God's really talking to you here!"

Eric pulled his car into Tim's driveway and they sat talking for a while in the night as the lights of the cars streamed by out on the road. "It sounds like God's got a lot to say to Sherrie, here, in particular," Eric continued, eyebrows arching with significance from behind his spectacles. "It sounds like He's telling her to wake up and smell the coffee! Are you talking to God about this?" asked Tim quietly. "Are you praying to Him about this every night?"

Tim answered that he was.

"Then that's all you can do," Eric intoned solemnly, his eyes glowing darkly in the dimness as he stared at Tim intently. The silver cross around his neck shone in the light from his dashboard. "You know that God only gives three answers: *Yes, No,* or *Not right now.*"

Tim was tempted to ask Eric to have his mother pray for him but thought better of it. Eric threw his arms open wide and the two boys embraced each other before Tim got out of the car and strode into his house.

Tim often wondered what God intended for Sherrie and himself. It had gotten to the point where his devotion to her had become a stale joke to disinterested observers. Tim had noted Sherrie's locker-mate Mike looking skeptically at him when he would wait for her by her locker. One morning, a classmate jokingly put his arm briefly around Sherrie when they were fooling around in the hall. "Hey, I'm getting a little bit possessive, here!" Tim said lightly.

"Oh, come on, Tim," remarked the classmate, rolling his eyes. "Give us a break!"

Tim felt humiliated by the boy's scorn. His cheeks felt as though they were on fire with shame. But at the same time, he felt a fierce pride at being humiliated for his love for Sherrie. He was glad to be a fool for her. It was a self-evident fact to him that she was the most beautiful and desirable girl in the world, as well as having the most wonderful personality. The real question, as he saw it, was why weren't others falling over themselves to be near her as he was? Obviously their sensibilities weren't as finely honed as his, he decided.

Tim's unrest wasn't eased by the poems Sherrie suddenly began bringing to school, saying that someone had mailed them to her anonymously. Tim looked at the poems and recognized that they were by e.e. cummings, though the real author had not been credited. He also saw that they had been written with pen and ink in a painstaking calligraphic style that he had seen in Eric's notebook during Charitas planning sessions. "I think these are from Eric Dunphy," he said to Sherrie.

"Why would he be sending me poems?" Sherrie asked.

As Eric was drove Tim home after the next planning meeting, Tim asked him about the poems.

"What type of poems were they?" Eric asked.

"They didn't credit the author, but they're e.e. cummings poems," Tim said.

"Ah! e.e. cummings!" Eric noted, smiling enigmatically.

"You were hoping to pass them off as your own?" Tim asked.

"Now, now," Eric chuckled as he drove through the early evening, "don't go thinking I have some sort of thing for Sherrie simply because I've sent her a few poems. I've sent poems to quite a few girls, Tim, and it's simply as a tribute to them and their femininity and their beauty that I do it... rather like giving them flowers."

"A person usually doesn't give flowers to a girl unless he has some idea about getting together with her," Tim reasoned.

"Well, Tim, in olden days, in the days of chivalry, gentlemen often gave flowers to women in pure tribute to their beauty, without any other designs in mind," Eric explained, turning to face him as they pulled in the driveway. "I consider myself a gentleman of that old school, offering verse and flowers to rare specimens of woman-kind." Eric grinned proudly at Tim, his protruding jaw and the visor of his cap forming a concavity between them in which the rest of his face reposed. "The thing is," he said, laying his hand on Tim's shoulder, "is have you been continuing to pray to God about Sherrie?"

"Yeah," Tim said.

"Well then you have nothing to worry about," Eric assured. "If God wants you and Sherrie to be together, then there's nothing He won't do to make it happen. Sometimes you just have to *let go and let God.*"

At the next meeting Tim noticed Eric and Sherrie talking animatedly in a corner. Eric was gesticulating, twisting his long, thin body as he told a story, and Sherrie was laughing. Tim thought he saw the same glitter of surprised delight that he had seen in her eyes on the bus the first time she and Tim had talked, and which he saw more rarely now. He felt his heartbeat accelerate and his throat tighten. It was one thing that she hadn't felt moved enough to leave her boyfriend for him, but it was another for her to be so obviously impressed by someone like Eric Dunphy, whom he tolerated only for the rides home. Later, Tim approached Sherrie. "You were talking a lot to Eric," he remarked.

"Yeah," said Sherrie, chuckling at the memory of the encounter. "Funny guy," she said. "Strange guy."

"Was he telling you about his mom's connection to God?" Tim asked. "Or was he telling you about his harem of Charitas girls? Or maybe he was passing off more e.e. cummings poems as his own?" He spoke these last words in a rush and betrayed himself.

The amusement disappeared from Sherrie's eyes and she frowned. "Can I be blunt?" she asked.

"Yeah."

"I think the reason you don't like me talking to Eric is because you're jealous," she stated, then turned on her heel to join the others.

It was time for the prayer that concluded each planning meeting. As Co-Dad led the group, they prayed for help in the planning and for a successful weekend. Tim looked around at all the bowed heads, and at Eric praying with his palms outstretched before him, and he felt a helpless, irresolute anger. It seemed as though everyone else was calm, reasonable and ready to surrender all to God. It was only he who was not at rest, he who felt as though he was frantically coming apart at the seams. They were all at one in their spirituality and he did not belong here just as he did not belong anywhere. For a moment he hated their placidity, their self-righteousness. He hated Eric Dunphy, he hated Sherrie and he hated himself. But then he felt ashamed of his bitterness and dark thoughts, and bowed his head and closed his eyes tighter, trying to allow Co-Dad's lulling Scottish brogue to take him down the river of loving surrender and acceptance.

8. Spring

RUSS RETURNED TO SCHOOL ONE MORNING AS THOUGH NOTH-
ing had happened. He and his mother had to have a meeting with
the principal in order to arrange a way for him to catch up on what
he had missed. He walked through the halls with a new diligence,
carrying his binder under his arm. Along with his new attitude, Russ
had an announcement to make to his friends. "To the great happiness of my mother—and yourselves as well, I'm sure—I've decided
to attend Charitas."

Tim and Sherrie embraced each other in the school hall, Sherrie
leaping up and down with happiness. Tim was pleased that Russ had
put aside his skepticism to take a chance with Charitas. "Well," said
Russ, "I thought if it had such a good impact on you, there must be
something to it."

As the weekend approached, however, Tim noticed another
name on the list of attendees at one of the planning meetings: Bruce
Ferguson.

"It makes sense, after all," Eric Dunphy observed on one of their
drives home. "I mean, if she's still going out with the guy, then she'd
want him to experience something that's been important to her."

"Yeah," said Tim, "but that just means their relationship isn't falling off, that she wants to share this with him."

"Hmm," Eric meditated, studying the road before him. "There's a
chance, too, though," he speculated, "that this is sort of a test for old
Bruce—to see if he's capable of opening his heart to God and letting

Him come in. What is it that this Bruce fellow does?" Eric asked.
"Does he go to school?"

"No, he's older... twenty or something," Tim muttered. He
didn't like talking about Sherrie's boyfriend. "He works at Radio
Shack at the mall."

"Radio Shack!" Eric repeated. "Doesn't sound too promising,
does it? Of course, we can never know about these things, but really,
this might work out to your advantage. We'll see if old Bruce is up to
the challenge of Charitas. Maybe this is the last chance she's giving
him before she throws him over for you!"

"You think so?" Tim asked despairingly.

"Well, I don't know, of course," Eric admitted. "But one thing
I do know is that I wouldn't put it past her to arrange such a test.
The female can be a very calculating species, Tim," Eric chuckled,
raising his forefinger. "She has her ways of choosing who she'll pair
off with. Make no mistake: it's the female who decides, every time!
She points her finger and chooses and we're done for! We don't have
any say in it at all!

"But who can say? We really can't say at all," Eric mused, looking out poetically at the stars shining over the shadowed fields they
passed. "There is a reason God is bringing you all together—perhaps
to reach a new understanding. Undoubtedly, what He has planned is
greater than anything you or I could imagine."

Tim didn't want God to bring him and Bruce Ferguson together.
Tim wanted God to banish Bruce Ferguson from the earth so that
he could be together with Sherrie. As much as he believed in the rev-
elation that had come to him through Charitas, he was not prepared
to accept that one he regarded as his arch-enemy was a brother of
Charitas love. He regarded Bruce Ferguson, and somehow needed
to regard him, as a malevolent force with whom there could be no
truce, not even one imposed by Jesus Christ.

As the weekend approached, the past Charitas alumni were
asked to write "friend letters" to be received by the new attendees.
Tim wrote to Russ, calling him his best friend, saying that he hoped

the weekend would be the miracle for him that it had been for himself. He praised Russ's intelligence and talent, and said he hoped the experience would deepen their friendship, a friendship he said he expected would last for the rest of their lives. Tim wrote Bruce Ferguson as well, but instead of a letter he composed a poem and didn't sign it:

> *A challenge is offered, you step from the wings,*
> *From a life and a world of the past.*
> *Suddenly you see and you feel many things.*
> *Has the true way of love come at last?*
>
> *A wondrous flower you hold in your hand.*
> *Do you have what it takes, do you know*
> *How to feed it and water it, do you understand*
> *All it needs to survive and to grow?*
>
> *A new sun is rising, a new day is here.*
> *Can you rise and be born again too?*
> *Out of the past and its boredom and fear,*
> *The only real answer and question is you.*

Tim enjoyed the manner in which the last line put it to the reader with a sudden jab. He imagined Bruce Ferguson reading it, his eyes following the words along to the end, when the challenging tone would cause his thick eyebrows to furrow, and a frown would form beneath his large black moustache. He gave it to Eric to read, who handed it back to him, nodding his head and raising his eyebrows above his spectacles. "Interesting," he said.

The weekend came and Tim helped out on the main floor of the church while the retreat went on below. He heard the singing and remembered his own experience. With the other Charitas alumni, he helped prepare meals and got various activities ready for the attendees. He waited with apprehension as the weekend came to its end. He heard the strains of Bette Midler singing "The Rose" in the gymnasium. He knew that the time had come when the attendees were emerging to find their parents gathered there. He stood outside the doors with Sherrie and heard the emotional reunions the teenagers were having with their parents.

Then the doors were opened to them, and Sherrie sprinted ahead as Tim peered into the dim room. He saw Russ bending to embrace his mother, then turning toward Tim. Russ started walking, his eyes gleaming, and he broke into a jog as he came nearer across the gym floor. Tim rushed to him, and for the first time the two boys embraced, the candles in the room throwing black and red shadows all around them, Russ throwing his arms around Tim and squeezing him tightly. "Thank you," Russ whispered in Tim's ear.

Tim looked across the gym, and saw Sherrie coming into Bruce Ferguson's embrace. Looking almost twice her height, Bruce bent to her, his large dark eyes glowing happily in the shadows, his bright teeth flashing beneath his black moustache. As much as Tim was able to see Sherrie's face, it seemed that she was blissfully smiling, her eyes closed. He quickly averted his eyes from the sight of their hug, as though he feared he might turn to stone from looking at it. He closed his eyes as Russ hugged him, feeling the strange sensation of Russ's thin body against his.

"Would you believe it? I've got a job!" Eric Dunphy was saying. "At the Shell station on Oxnard! Mom prayed for me to get a job, and two days later what happens? We stop to get gas on the way back from church and the guy's complaining that he lost his employee the day before and he had to go through the hassle of getting a new one. Well! Talk about getting it on a silver platter with a bow on it!" Eric drove his small car along the road that followed the river south of the city. Beside him, Sherrie sat in the passenger seat and Russ and Tim sat in the back. The four teenagers had gotten together once before since the latest Charitas weekend, both times at Eric's invitation. He was glad to pick up his friends and take them for rides along the river.

"But that's the way it is," Eric said, "she merely has to pray for it, and God complies. I don't know if that's called a gift or what."

Tim looked over to see that Russ's brow was creased as he frowned with distaste. Russ had been affected by the retreat less than Tim, but believed the cumulative effect to be good and worthwhile. Like Tim, Russ had been changed by the weekend. He was calmer now, less close to hysteria and the slightest bit more forgiving of his fellow humans.

"But do you really think that God reached forth His hand past all the starving children, all the war-torn countries, and arranged for you to get a job at a gas station, simply because your mom prayed for it?" Russ asked Eric.

From the front seat Eric darted his head back for a moment in Russ's direction. "Hmm!" said Eric. "Interesting question!"

Outside, the sun was shining brightly and most of the snow had melted away. The river was a band of flowing blue, and across the water were the docks and factories of America. They had driven past the oil refineries and chemical plants and were now following the river down in the direction of the town where Eric lived.

"It's that whole question of whether we believe in an interventionist or non-interventionist God," Russ postulated. "Whether we think that God takes an active hand in our lives or not ..."

"Well, I think obviously that God takes an active hand in our lives!" Eric exclaimed. "I mean, I've seen it too many times to doubt it!"

"Does God give you what you want when you pray to Him?" Russ asked.

"Well, no. Not all the time, anyway," Eric chuckled. "But if you don't think God takes an active hand in your life, what is it that you pray for?" he asked, twisting his neck around to glance at Russ.

"I'm not sure that we should be praying for things," Russ noted. "I'm not sure if we should be giving God a shopping list. I'm wondering if we shouldn't pray to connect ourselves with Him, to ask Him what He wants us to do—instead of telling Him what to do—and to gather strength and faith to live by His word as we know it from the Bible."

"Mm-hmm! That's right!" Eric agreed, lightly tapping his fist on the steering wheel. "You know, it's funny," he said, addressing Sherrie beside him, "I have Catholic friends, and this whole business of being saved simply by one's faith in Jesus alone is nutty to them. They believe one also must perform good works. But of course we say, 'Not by works alone!' Then there are the Pentecostals and the Anglicans—all these different types and ways of worshipping God. It can make a person loony at times!" He smiled whimsically over at her, his eyes twinkling.

"Yeah, I wonder what people think who don't know Christianity all that well," Sherrie responded. "It's a religion, but it's like there's all these other religions inside it."

"Hmm! Interesting!" Eric said. "Well, all I know is that I got a new job at a gas station!" he smiled, looking over at Sherrie. "And I'm quite content to believe that the strength of my mother's faith got that job for me. You know, I've really been meditating on the idea that if you believe something is real, it's real for you," he continued. "Sort of like when Jesus said that if you had faith the size of a mustard seed you could move mountains. I'm sure you believe in that," he said to Russ, looking at him in the rear-view mirror.

Eric pulled the car into one of the parks that lined the river. There was a fierce, cold wind as they got out. They walked across the grass and sat beneath a tree. "I don't know how much more of this guy I can take," Russ whispered to Tim.

No sooner had they sat down than Eric exclaimed, "Well! Who's up for a walk along the river?" None of the others wanted to move. Eric leapt to his feet and strode off with long ostentatious strides. The three friends sat in silence for a while after Eric left.

"Is he always like this?" Russ eventually remarked.

Tim and Sherrie laughed, Tim enjoying, as always, Sherrie's face as she laughed, her bright, innocent eyes and her mouth opening with surprised delight, showing her teeth. There was a slight blush to her cheeks, as though she was embarrassed to laugh and was trying to resist it. But her eyes closed with her merriment, showing that mirth had won out.

Looking beyond her, Tim saw a sight that he pointed out to his friends and which caused them all to laugh longer. For down by the river, Eric was pacing, apparently immersed in meditation. But he was walking along a ledge hidden on the other side of the bank, so it appeared to them as if he was striding on the river's surface.

The snow had melted and the ice rink that had filled the back and front yards of Tim's house snow became a lake whose shimmering surface reflected the newly blue skies. A fresh breeze was blowing, and Tim now often rode his bicycle to school and home from his job at the variety store in the evenings. There was respite at the store between the customers voicing their displeasure with the coldness and snow of winter ("Supposed to get another three inches tomorrow night! Jesus Christ!") and griping about the blazing temperatures of summer (the ever-popular, "Hot enough for ya?") because spring offered comparatively little to take offence at. The students at school, intoxicated by the new temperatures, began the steadily accelerating tumble toward the end of spring and the rebirth promised by its first green stirrings—the moment when the school doors opened and closed behind them for the final time. It seemed that no light ever shone with such embracing warmth, no air ever blew with such a cleansing, liberating breeze as those which prevailed on the walk across the schoolyard on the final day of school.

For every year of Tim's school career, he had begun anticipating that last day from the beginning of spring, while trying not to long for it too much and thereby make the wait unbearable. This year he regarded it with anxious helplessness. He knew that for each day that went by that Sherrie didn't leave Bruce Ferguson for him, the less likely it was to happen. He also knew that if it didn't happen by the end of the school year, it was likely to never happen at all. Tim walked to school each day with a restless stomach and returned each night with grave depression.

He saw Sherrie just as much or more than he ever had, yet she was receding from him in an imperceptible yet undeniable manner. Or was it that time was running out that made him feel this way? The more she slid away, the more panicked he became, and more manic in his attempts to bring her back. He felt now that when he confided in people about his hopes for Sherrie, they were visibly allowing themselves to tolerate him. There came into their eyes the glint that occurs when a listener disbelieves the words being heard, and hazards to convey a hint of doubt to see if the speaker is aware enough to pick it up: the sort of look often given to delusionals and drunks. His absorption had to some degree soured his friendship with Russ and his other new relationships within Charitas.

Tim often still saw Sherrie, with Eric Dunphy and other Charitas friends, and with Russ. He thought of the changes the past month had brought as he rode his bicycle along the road's muddy shoulder, leaving a weaving snake of a trail past the drainage ditch and the high-tension hydro lines. Tim had been shocked when Sherrie had come to school one morning with her golden tresses gone, now sporting a pixie-ish cut that brought out her almond-shaped eyes and her cheekbones. "I just felt like getting my hair out of the way," she'd said, shrugging.

"You know what they say when a woman changes her hairstyle!" Eric Dunphy remarked when Tim told him. "It means she wants to change her life! This could be very good news for you, Tim!"

Shortly after, Tim had gone with Eric and some other Charitas friends to pick Sherrie up at her house. She never wanted anyone to come into her house because of the clutter her mother collected. She came out the door and in a burst of excitement leapt over the railing of the porch. She landed awkwardly, and her ankle caused her pain for the rest of the night. The next day a sprain was diagnosed and she came to school with a cast and crutches.

For Tim, this offered an opportunity to shower more adoration and devotion on her. He made himself available to carry her books between periods all day, with the result that he was late for his own classes. When she had to go up stairs, he carried her crutches along with the books beside her as she carefully hopped up, step by step. Passing teachers would smile at Tim's devotion.

"You really don't have to do this," she said as she struggled up the stairs.

"I want to do it," Tim said. "Why not? Who else is going to do it?"

"Well, I could find some other way," Sherrie reasoned, shaking her head. "It doesn't have to be you all the time."

"I'm the one that's here," Tim said, trying to affect an easy smile despite the fact that her words made him feel foolish and hurt.

"Hi, Tim," a voice said at his side. Tim turned and saw the wide smile and bright eyes of Roberta Cameron. He smiled in return, and exchanged some light, joking words with the girl. She laughed delightedly, said hello to Sherrie and in parting with Tim, she said she hoped she'd see him soon. Tim continued up the stairs, his arms full of Sherrie's crutches and books, waiting patiently as she gingerly hopped from step to step. Roberta Cameron remained at the foot of the stairs, gazing up at him with unembarrassed adoration.

"I sure do impress those grade nines," Tim remarked to Sherrie, who laughed with great amusement.

After a time, the sprain healed and Tim felt a sense of loss that Sherrie no longer needed the help he had been giving her. As the good weather increased, Sherrie would sometimes drive Tim and Russ to the large park at the north of the city in her dad's old car. The park, given to the city by a wealthy benefactor early in the century, stretched along the shores of the vast lake. Glimpses of the immeasurable water's surface flashed between the trees as they walked across the expanse of green. Tim and Sherrie bantered about school and about Eric Dunphy and others in Charitas, Tim, as always, keeping things light and entertaining. At times his efforts were rewarded by Sherrie's laughter and at others she merely smiled, and he resolved to double his efforts the next time.

Russ strode beside them, dour and scowling, and after an interval he turned to them and asked, "Is that all we're going to talk about? Diarrhea?"

Tim and Sherrie looked at each other, Sherrie raising her eyebrows.

"It just seems to me that we spend an awful lot of time talking about diarrhea," Russ remarked.

The three friends walked along the tree line before the lake. Beyond the weeds and the carpet of dead leaves from before winter, the sandy beach began, the spaces between the foliage affording a view of exotic-seeming dunes. At length, Tim spoke of Eric Dunphy's attempt, the last time he spoke to him, to read a Christian subtext into the lyrics of ABBA songs.

"Mm-hmm," Russ said, with a sharp nod as if to certify the vindication of a belief within him. "More diarrhea."

Tim looked over at him, his eyes smarting with annoyance. "What do you want to talk about?" he asked.

Russ looked down at Sherrie as he walked beside her. "So Sherrie, how's Bruce?" he asked.

Tim beheld the blandly smiling profile of his friend with shock and disbelief. Never before had any of the three of them mentioned the name of her boyfriend during one of their gatherings. It was as though Russ, in one sentence spoken as casually as if it were the most commonplace of phrases, had torn the very fabric of life itself. In the instant the words left Russ's lips, Tim saw Sherrie's consciousness recoil and find its place again. He saw anger and a determined challenge come to her eyes as they met Russ's.

"He's fine," she replied, her voice straining for the nonchalance of Russ's query. Tim's gaze left Sherrie's face and followed a seagull swooping out into the impossibly pure emptiness of the air over the lake.

"That's good to hear," Russ noted, soberly looking before him as he hiked along. "And you, Tim. You must be starting to plan what university you'll be going to in the fall. That must be exciting, to be on the verge of finishing high school."

Tim looked at his friend, puzzled and lost. Russ's words and manner were pulling the earth from beneath his feet, but he was bound to hold on, to refuse to give ground.

"Yeah," said Tim. "I'm supposed to go to university, but I'm not sure if I've got the credits to graduate. Hopefully, I'll get a passing mark in the home ec course I'm taking." He had needed to take elective courses such as home economics and drafting in order to get the proper amount of credits, bypassing such dreaded subjects as math and chemistry. "It seems weird that my whole life and future is based on home ec, but if I don't get it, I guess I can pick it up in summer school. I'm not that worried anyway because I don't have any big plan about university. I'd go if I was able to, but I don't see the point of getting a degree. I don't see myself ever working at a job that would require a degree, and to get one you have to waste time taking all these courses I'm not interested in.

"What I want to do," he continued, regaining confidence as he spoke, "is be an artist, and hopefully I can make my living by that. Sometimes I wonder, though, if I've got the talent or the ability to make people understand what I'm trying to say."

"Oh, come on now," Russ smirked. "Is this supposed to be like the story you told us about James Joyce last week, how James Joyce used to confess his self-doubts to Samuel Beckett on a regular basis, and Beckett would bolster him up, assuring him that he was the greatest of all time? Is that what this is supposed to be?" asked Russ. "Is that who you're supposed to be now? James Joyce? And is that what we're supposed to do, reassure you of how great you are?"

Tim laughed and felt his face grow hot as a spasm of anger twisted in his abdomen. They walked through a tangle of trees and bushes by the lake and passed an old bandstand. Their expressions and demeanour now suggested that they had just left a funeral.

They walked past the baseball diamonds and the picnic tables and large sheltered gazebos where Tim's mother's family had held their reunions every summer when he was a boy. They passed the large rusted swing sets with the fabric seats, and the few words they exchanged were forced and false, quick desperate diversions from the silence that engulfed them.

They got into Sherrie's dad's car and drove into the city through the late afternoon traffic commencing its industrious flow. Tim was due to begin his shift as the variety store soon, so Sherrie let him off at the plaza. He had a few extra minutes to spare, so he walked down the sidewalk to his dad's barbershop. He pulled the door open and walked in; his father was standing in his wine-coloured uniform as he trimmed the hair of his customer, his hands upraised almost as if in a boxer's stance, one hand holding the comb through which he sifted the hair, the scissors in the other, moving in to cut the isolated strands with a steady, musical clipping sound.

Dirk spoke in a low murmur to his customer, who wore a sheet of the same colour as Tim's dad's jacket. Dirk departed from the customer at intervals to grab his electric clipper from the counter, or to get his brush, or to pick up his cigarette from the ashtray and take a drag. At these times he would meet his customer's eyes in the mirror, continuing their conversation. At the chair beside him was his partner Howard, quietly working away on his customer's hair as the radio softly played a Charlie Rich song.

Tim sat in one of the waiting chairs beside the table that was covered with *Maclean's* magazines. The floor was speckled with clots of brown and black hair, showing that the shop had enjoyed a rush of business earlier in the day. The door opened and another man came in and sat down, opening a newspaper in front of him. Dirk finished with his customer, pulling off the sheet and flourishing it with his usual snap. The man paid up and Tim's father counted out his change to him, pulling bills from the money-clipped wad he extracted from his pocket. As the customer left, Dirk called out to the man with the newspaper down the wall from Tim: "You're next, Pete."

The man looked over to Tim, gesturing, asking as hundreds of customers had before, "Isn't this fellow before me?"

"No, that's my boy," said Dirk. "He's just hangin' around."

"Oh," said the man, laying his newspaper down and proceeding to the barber chair. "How many kids you got, Dirk?"

"Two," said Dirk, fastening the sheet around the man's throat. "This one's the oldest."

"That right?"

"He supposed to be going to university this year," Dirk said, beginning to comb the man's hair. "But he's all messed up with a girl right now, so he says he don't know if he wants to go. Lovesick," Dirk chuckled.

"Well, they'll do that to ya, that's for sure," said the man in the chair. "You start to realize you gotta spend half your life tryin' to work it out."

"Yeah," Howard observed suavely in his whisper-like voice, starting up his electric clipper, "or tryin' to work it in." The shop was filled with the surprised laughter of the men. The sun was shining its retiring rays of light to glimmer around the edges of the car dealership sign across the road, on the windshields of the cars in the parking lot and through the big plate-glass window across the hair-covered floor of the shop. Tim looked at the time, got up from his chair and walked from the talcum and witch hazel–smelling place down the sidewalk to the variety store.

He entered and quietly took his place beside the middle-aged woman behind the counter, starting in to serve customers without thought, letting second nature take over. The procession of lottery-ticket choosers, cigarette buyers, and pop-and-Popsicle purchasers passed before him. After an hour or so, a man wearing a sweater over a T-shirt came in. He wore a baseball hat and sunglasses. His clothes hung loosely on him, and his mouth seemed wrenched to one side, the flesh pale and strangely textured.

"Ol' Yeller," the man said.

Tim started, then saw that he should have known by the shape of his nose, even by the outline of the eyes he could now see through the tint of the sunglasses, and in which he told himself he could see the same spark of contempt which had always been there in the past.

"The goddamn things have done this to me," the bus driver said, speaking to the middle-aged woman at Tim's side. "What the hell else can they do?"

Tim had heard of the diagnosis of the sore on the bus driver's lip, had known of the surgery and of the chemotherapy, had heard of his long recovery. He now saw the bus driver's shrunken, old-man physique, and his face so drawn and distorted as to be almost unrecognizable.

"They took the skin off my ass," the bus driver was rasping to the middle-aged woman, "and they put it here!" He pointed to his mouth. "And these goddamned chemo treatments don't let me keep nothin' down. I lost thirty pounds, for Christ's sake!" He shook his head in disgust as he tore the cellophane band from his cigarettes.

Tim couldn't be sure, but he felt as though the bus driver's eyes behind the tinted glasses had now wandered from the middle-aged woman over to him, and he anxiously searched himself for the response such a movement seemed to demand. Still uncertain that the shadows behind the glasses were fixed on him, Tim dared to speak to the bus driver anyway, hazarding what he hoped was an empathetic expression as he looked into the sunglasses and murmured, indicating the entire predicament with a vague gesture, "Sorry."

"Yeah," the bus driver snorted. "Me too."

9. Yearbook

IT SEEMED AS THOUGH EVER SINCE THE DAY AT THE LAKESIDE park everything was different—as though all that Tim had known of life for the past seven months receded and stayed distant. As the school year drained down to its close, he felt estranged from the excitement and concern of his fellow students as he walked the halls. It was the time of the impending pressure of exams and the opening vista of adulthood, but Tim felt none of it. He was in limbo, neither anticipating nor worrying, but in a continual posture of dread-saturated waiting.

The final exams of the year were upon them, and Tim's classmates had entered an austere period of solemn studying. Sherrie, too, was busy studying—or at least that's what Tim told himself, for as the remaining days of school elapsed it seemed as though she had disappeared from the halls. He tried to pass her locker several times a day, but she was never there, nor in any of the other places they once met up at. He asked her locker-mate Mike where she was, but he didn't seem to know. Everybody was buckling down in order to guarantee their futures, but Tim was unable to take any of it seriously. None of it meant anything, as far as he could see, if he didn't have Sherrie.

Walking down the hall at school one day, Tim saw a poster for a play the drama club was putting on at lunchtime. It was *The Zoo Story* by Edward Albee. He was stunned to see that Ran Hutchison was listed as one of the actors. Seeing the name, he realized he had not thought of Ran Hutchison for months, and had not been greeted by Ran Hutchison hissing "Fuckin' faggot!" at him for some time. He marvelled that this individual who had been such a negative focal point of his life, who had caused him no end of anxiety and fear, could've faded from his consciousness so easily.

At lunchtime, Tim went to the drama room. He took a seat in a far corner, hoping to avoid the slight chance that Hutchison might see him in the audience. The play, a product of the sixties, concerned an upwardly mobile, conservative man on a park bench being confronted by a half-deranged, hippie-esque street person who challenged the dishonesty of the conformist's way of life. The truth-telling outsider rants at some length, and the play concludes with the frightened, conventional man accidentally stabbing him. Ran Hutchison, with his small, slit-like eyes and the bangs of blond hair dipping over them, played the demonic iconoclast, a role calling for all the sense of viciousness and menace that Tim had seen in him.

But it was plain from the first moments he stepped on stage that Ran Hutchison was not alive with fury in his art in the way he had been in life. He moved uncertainly, spoke his lines hesitantly—too quietly—and couldn't bring forth the rage that the role required. It seemed to Tim that he had been like the man sitting on the park bench, trying to hold onto some shred of normalcy while Ran Hutchison had hissed in his face every day that no matter how much he felt he could belong, he would always be a "fucking faggot," a boy crying to his father over his broken glasses in the park. Now the tableau had been transmuted into art, and Hutchison was an uneasy, fumbling amateur with no stage presence—trying, like Tim, to be an artist and failing in the most ignominious manner.

The anxiety Tim had once felt at the mere thought of Hutchison was now replaced by discomfort, for now Tim felt embarrassment for the other boy. It was as though through acting, Ran Hutchison had been revealed to be a small, thin, tremulous boy lacking the audacity to channel his pain into his art. His eyes, once so feral and angry, merely looked frightened. After the play, Tim happened to pass by where Ran Hutchison was standing by his locker. In the past, he would have looked around to find somewhere to duck into before Hutchison sighted him. Tim walked up to his former nemesis and with a generosity born of pity said, "Good job, Ran."

"Thanks," muttered Ran, looking down. Tim reeled within, thinking how shocking this diminishment of his former demon would have been to him if only it hadn't happened of its own accord, unbeknownst to him, months before.

Later Tim ran into Mike in the library and asked, "What's happening with Sherrie? I haven't seen her in a week."

"You'll have to ask her," Mike said in his customary deadpan manner.

"What's going on with her?" Tim asked, his plaintiveness betraying him. "Why hasn't she been around?"

Mike sighed. His eyes looked away, then came back to the business at hand. "Sherrie's fighting a losing battle with herself," he stated.

"What does that mean?" Tim asked. But Mike wouldn't say anything more, and his expressionless features gave no indication as to whether the situation was good for Tim or bad for him.

Classes had ended and the week of exams had begun. Tim dutifully studied, but he felt as though he was sleepwalking, walking through a strange, out-of-kilter simulation of existence.

"You must be happy!" Roberta Cameron called to Tim when he came out of the school after an exam one day.

"Why?" Tim asked her, her smile warming him in his turmoil.

"I heard Sherrie broke up with her boyfriend," Roberta volunteered. "Oh... didn't you know?"

Tim was perplexed. Of course, Roberta only heard it—she could be wrong—but it definitely felt as though something was in the air. Could it be true? What did it mean? Was it possible? That night instead of studying, Tim began writing a letter to Sherrie. It was by turns whimsical and philosophical, recounting their months of friendship and ending with the assertion that they would be friends forever, and that he hoped they could form a lifetime partnership.

The spiritual pontification and the expressions of devotion now seemed false and unconvincing to him, so that he couldn't sign the letter. He put it in his desk drawer. The next day he was to go over to Russ's house to study for a history course they shared together. He rode his bike over through the bright, warm day, one of the first that signalled summer's displacement of the spring. The two boys carried their books upstairs to the bedroom Russ shared with his brother. They talked and joked around in their usual manner for a while.

After holding off for a time, Tim ventured, "Hey, have you heard anything from Sherrie? I haven't seen her for like a week. And someone told me that she broke off with Bruce!"

Russ was balancing his stockinged feet on one of the barbells Tim had noticed in the basement a few months ago, and was steadying himself against the upper mattress on the set of bunkbeds in the room. "Sherrie broke off with Bruce," he said, looking Tim in the eye, "to go out with me."

Tim looked away from Russ and stood staring at the floor for several minutes.

"You okay?" Russ asked.

Tim said he was, and Russ asked him if he wanted to study. They sat down and opened their books, looking at the questions they needed to ask each other. It was quickly evident that Tim could not take in the meaning of the words. "You want to not bother?" Russ asked.

"No... I'm going to go," Tim said, rising to his feet.

Russ walked Tim downstairs to the front door. He opened the door for Tim, then turned to him, holding out his arms. "How about a hug?" he asked. In best Charitas fashion, Tim threw his arms around him, holding him close for a long moment before walking out.

People who have nearly drowned speak of seeing their lives pass before their eyes. Tim felt as though he was drowning, and his life and the world were distorting and receding behind a watery veil like the sky glimpsed by one being pulled by invisible tentacles into the deep. He walked through the bright afternoon, the leaves shining as they flickered, casting dancing coins of sunshine and his eyes blinked actively, seeing nothing.

He passed through the yard he cut through to get to the main road from Russ's subdivision, not fearing anyone would catch him, striding slowly, methodically, as if trying not to disturb something fragile inside him. He had forgotten that he'd left his bicycle at Russ's townhouse, forgotten that he'd ridden his bicycle there at all. He trudged along the side of the road, the cars whisking past, the multicoloured triangular flags on the sign in front of the gas station whipping and snapping smartly in the warm wind. He came up over the crest of the railroad crossing until he could see the tops of the trees in his front yard billowing over the roofs of the condominiums before it.

So that was the way it was. Russ had won the drawing competition, he had attended the art camp and had the sexual experience with the woman there, and now he was Sherrie's boyfriend, the one that Sherrie had at long last broken off with Bruce Ferguson for. It was all so logical that Tim could not believe he had never suspected it before, never discerned the pattern of a submerged temple beneath the sand. Russ was and had always been a part of the majority who did things like win competitions, have sexual experiences and attract the love and devotion of like-minded females. Tim could never expect to participate in such essential endeavours. He was and would always be an observer, a ghost in a world of actual, tactile, active individuals. He was unloved and unlovable, good for a laugh, perhaps, but unworthy and undeserving of ever being taken seriously as a human being, ever being considered a suitable partner. He had been a fool to ever hope otherwise.

Had I known it all along? he asked himself. Had the signs been there every step of the way and he had ignored them, pretended they weren't there? Tim's throat ached as he stared, dumbfounded, searching the gravel at his feet as if to find the answer there. Everything around him was glinting, impermeable, impassive, like the shocking truth delivered as simple fact; life was merciless and oblique, it offered nothing to him but the glib refusal of his dreams, and he cursed himself for thinking that he could ever have a part in it.

To think of their shared conspiracy against him, which was a simple knowing that excluded him, induced a nauseating vertigo within him and seemed to pull him back from life like the centrifugal gravity created by the spinning cylindrical rooms at amusement parks. His agony was only mediated by the extent of his shock, for he still could not entirely believe it, still thought that perhaps in a moment he would awake to a world in which those incomprehensible words had never been spoken. Yet he knew, deep within the sinking pit of his being, that it was true. It made perfect sense, he realized as he walked down the laneway of his house, that this outcome was consistent with everything else in his life up to that time. Tim would stay unattached and untouched, cloistered with the eunuchs, the undesirables, the beings that the eyes of the world passed over with so little interest that they might as well have been invisible. As he could never be a man according to the dictates of his father and his uncles, so he now saw that he would also never be a human deserving the designation of friend or lover to his peers. How stupid and blind he had been.

Tim walked through the empty house, through the kitchen and down the hall, his history book in his hand. He went to his room and closed the door behind him as if shutting himself into a cell. He dropped his book on the floor and lay on his bed, staring at the ceiling, allowing reality to sink into all parts of his body, trying to absorb what could never be absorbed. An instinct of self-preservation let the truth come to him incrementally, like the steady drip of an intravenous device. The shadows lengthened in the room, and soon the day grew dim outside the sheer curtains covering the window. Soon the room was dark, and the lights and flames of the oil refineries sent their orange shimmering reflections against the wall. The trains coupling and uncoupling in the railyard across the field crashed and rumbled and shook the windows with their booming thunder.

There was darkness, and then somehow his room was bright again, the walls shining with a light as gold as honey. The bedroom door was open and his mother stood there, dressed for work. Her mouth was moving but Tim couldn't understand the words she was saying. He blinked as he stared at her and the full force of reality came down on him again, plastering him to the bed. "I said, aren't you supposed to be getting your yearbooks today?" she asked, her voice rising angrily. "Why don't you answer me?"

Tim turned away from her to face the wall. She banged her hand in frustration against the door. "Hey! We paid ten dollars for that yearbook! So get up out of bed and get down there to the school and pick it up!"

Tim had the dim memory that this morning was when the yearbooks were to be picked up. To brave the horror of seeing his fellow students was inconceivable, even if he had been physically capable of making it to the school. "Leave me alone," he groaned.

"I won't leave you alone!" she snapped. "We paid good money for it, so you'll get your lazy ass out of bed and pick it up."

"No," he murmured.

"Why?" she demanded, her puzzlement almost overcoming her anger.

"Because Sherrie's going out with Russ now!" he shouted back.

His mother stood at the door irresolutely for a moment then turned and walked down the hall, through the kitchen, out to her car and drove to work. On the way, she stopped by the school and picked up the yearbook.

Later in the day, the phone rang and Tim lay in bed listening to it. It continued with shrill insistence for some time until he finally got up and padded down the hall to pick it up.

"Hello."

"Hi." It was Mona, calling from work.

There was a silence, and then she said quietly, "I just wanted to say that I think it's really awful what Russ and Sherrie did to you." Tim muttered some sort of response, and after he replaced the phone on its hook he began to cry.

For several days Tim stayed in his room and around the house, leaving only to work his shifts in the variety store. He was silent and fragile, like the invalid survivor of a devastating accident. At times he went out into the front yard and sat in the grass under a tree for hours. One night he grew agitated and called Russ. Russ's mother answered: "No, Russ isn't in right now, but I'll have him call you when he comes in." That night and the next night, Russ didn't call back so Tim angrily called him, asking why he hadn't gotten back to him.

"I did," Russ said. "But your mother said you were sleeping. She must have forgot to tell you."

"I guess I must've been sleeping a lot lately," Tim observed.

"What do you mean by that?"

"With all that's gone on," Tim said. "I must've been sleeping not to see it all."

"We didn't go behind your back," Russ stated.

"It sure seemed like it," Tim said. "I had no idea. It was a complete shock."

"We didn't go behind your back," Russ repeated in the same tone and intonation. So flatly was the statement reaffirmed that there seemed little left in the conversation to say, and it ended shortly after.

After spring had steadily loosened and broken the frozen grip of the preceding five months, summer always came in brazenly and ferociously, blasting its oven-like heat in temperatures as extreme as the most frigid depths of winter had been. The sweat-inducing glare asserted itself in the last days of school and prevailed over the next two months. People flocked to the lake and the river, drawn to the water and the breeze that blew over it. In Tim's house, an electric fan stood at the end of the hallway, rotating between the doors of Tim's bedroom and those of his parents and his brother.

Through the summer, Tim retreated further into his world of books, spending virtually all the time he wasn't at the variety store in his room reading. Every week, his mother drove him downtown to the public library, and he came out the door with a pile of books against his chest. He would read them hungrily all the way home, and after they had parked in the driveway and his mother went in the house, Tim would remain in the car reading. The idle machine was the perfect sanctuary in which to disappear into an imagined world, halfway between the library and his home, free of the interruptions and stresses of the latter, suspended in space and time until the shadows grew long on the gravel outside and one of the family came out to call him in for supper.

One night, Tim's father noticed something missing in the garage as he came in the door. "Where's your bicycle?" Dirk asked.

"I left it over at Russ's," Tim said.

"What'd you do that for?" his father asked.

Tim shrugged.

"When are you go gonna get it and bring it back?" Dirk asked with puzzled irritation.

"I don't know," said Tim, looking down at his food

"We paid good money for that bike. You'd better go over there and bring it back," his father ordered.

Several days later at supper, Dirk asked again, "You go get that bike yet?"

"No."

"When are you gonna get it?" Dirk asked, his voice rising. "Why'd we go spend money on a bike if you're gonna leave it in some guy's garage?" he argued, gesturing with his upraised palm, fingers splayed. "Go and bring it back here!"

"No!" Tim was on his feet and screaming. "I'm not going to go get it!"

As Tim hurtled down the hall, he heard Dirk ask his mother, "What'd I say wrong now?"

It was mainly due to the good-heartedness of the teacher of Tim's home ec class that Tim was able to collect the necessary credits to qualify for university. It was fairly obvious that Tim was not interested in the class, spending most of his time in it drawing cartoons. When a major project was assigned, he used all the time allotted for research to achieve precisely nothing, and when it came time to make his presentation, he asked to be excused so he could retrieve his notes from his locker, at which time he went out and walked the halls aimlessly, the class waiting patiently for him to return. When he came back, he put on the most ridiculous, improvised pageant of nonsense possible. But in the end, the teacher gave him the passing mark he needed, seeing that there were times when removing the impediments to future happiness for what she thought of as a unique, confused boy was more important than protecting the integrity of home economics.

Tim had been accepted to several universities and chose one in a large metropolitan city four hours to the east. A grant was tendered by the government to help pay for his education there, though his parents and many of his relatives felt that he could get just as good an education at the local community college. Tim told the variety store that he'd be quitting at the end of the summer, and as the weeks went by, the significance of his departure began to loom before him. He had begun to talk to Russ on the phone occasionally and confided some apprehension at leaving everything he knew to go to a place so far away.

"I think you've gone as far as you can go with your family," Russ remarked.

Tim avoided the shopping mall and anywhere else he thought he might meet people from school or from Charitas. It had been so apparent to so many of them what his passionate dream had been, that to see them when they knew of its grotesque failure would have been unendurable. He could not have withstood their pity or their scorn. One exception was Eric Dunphy, who insistently called the house to fill Tim's ears with the same clucking chatter as before. Tim began to look on Eric's ramblings as a diversion, and his gangly friend began picking him up in his car from time to time.

"Did your dad tell you I came by the other day?" he asked Tim once. "He came to the door to tell me you weren't home. I guess he'd been brushing in his teeth, for his toothbrush was in his mouth and foam was dripping from his lips." He'd start chirping away in his strange quasi-English accent about his favourite subject—the various females he had on the string.

"Well, there's Bernice, and isn't she the coy one, always asking me out for ice cream after choir practice, but God there's Angela too, and the way she hugged me after prayer meeting—well—I was seeing stars, let me tell you…"

Eric's family had a small motorboat in which he'd use to take trips up and down the river and around the small islands in the midst of the rushing current. He took Tim out in the boat several times to go swimming. One afternoon Eric picked Tim up in his car to drive aimlessly around the city, keeping up his endless monologue. "I took Russ and Sherrie out in the motorboat one day last week," he noted, almost as an afterthought. "I dropped them off on one of those islands and went off for a while. I came by to pick them up later but they were… well, let's just say it didn't look like they wanted to be disturbed."

He chuckled. "Oh, look, there's the hydro building," he said, pointing out the window. "My mom'll kill me if I don't take care of this bill while I'm here." Eric pulled his car to the side of the road. "Wait a minute, I'll be right back," he said, slamming his door and sprinting to the building. Tim sat in the hot car as the sun glared in through the windshield. He watched the people walking past in the late afternoon down the undistinguished street. After a while it seemed to Tim as though he had waited a long time. He waited for some time after that, then he opened the door, got out of the car and walked home.

One day as Tim was waiting for his mother to drive him to the library, he was surprised to have his father volunteer to give him a ride instead. Dirk was going to the Ex-Servicemen's Club and it was on the way. As they drove into the city, Tim watched his father from the corner of his eye and saw him turn his head slightly from side to side, sighing heavily through his nostrils at intervals and making periodic clicking noises with his lips, as if he were about to speak. Tim watched these motions with rising dread, for he knew they were the signs that his father was about to say something significant to him and was rehearsing it in his mind.

It took Dirk until they were within five minutes of the library to dart his head forward suddenly as if to shake the words from his mouth, make the clicking sound with his lips for the final time and turn to fix his eyes on Tim: "So, you're still hurtin' pretty bad about that girl, huh?"

"Yeah, I guess so," said Tim.

His father nodded his head with a grave frown. "Well, I'll tell ya somethin' I learned," he said, poking his finger and narrowing his eyes as if giving out a piece of confidential information, "and that's ya can't let 'em get to ya. You gotta be *cool*. Back when I was single, I had this one, and one night she says she wants to break up, and I said, 'You wanna break up, let's break up,' and hey, she was really built, no foolin'," he confided. "So I said, 'Alright baby! See ya later! Bye!'" Dirk waved his hand and assumed an expression of kingly indifference.

"Then she comes to me a couple of months later and what does she say? She says, 'We gotta problem—I think I might be pregnant.' *Oh shit*, I'm thinking." He bowed his head and shook it. "'Will you come with me to the doctor?' she says." They arrived outside the library and Dirk brought the car to a stop, turning to face Tim in his seat. "We go to the doctor—they didn't have none of them home pregnancy tests like now," he explained. "And the doctor says, 'Yeah, you're pregnant, three months gone.'

"Well, shit… We walk out of there and out to my car. She's crying and she says to me, 'What're we gonna do?' I says, 'What're *we* gonna do? Whaddaya mean what're *we* gonna do? Look at your calendar, baby!' I says to her," said Dirk, leaning forward and grinning with triumphant vehemence. "'That can't be mine—we weren't foolin' around three months ago—I know right when we broke up…'" he said, emphasizing each word with a jab of his forefinger, "'and that was two weeks before three months ago! So don't ask me what *we're* gonna do,' I told her, and I opened the car door for her. 'It ain't my problem!'

"'So long,' I told her," he said, waving his hand again, and smirking with satisfied vengeance. "'See ya later!' See, that's what I mean," said Tim's father, a vague gesture of his hand indicating how easily his hypothesis had been proven. "You can't let 'em get to ya. You gotta be *cool*."

With time, Tim was able to bear his days without entertaining thoughts of his own destruction—or rather these thoughts lessened to the rate of prior to Russ and Sherrie's union. There was a definite point several weeks into the summer, though exactly when was unclear, when existence crept back into the realm of the bearable, and his voice and spirit returned, both changed.

As the summer wore on, Russ and Sherrie even came over to visit his home one afternoon. Tim still looked on Sherrie's small, childlike body and her high-cheekboned face with adoration. She sat in an easy chair in the living room that swivelled from side to side, and Tim would always remember how Russ, sitting in the chair beside her, kept his stockinged toes on the side of her chair, spinning it from side to side with a sort of playful, easy propriety that Tim knew to be so far beyond himself that it didn't even make sense to envy it.

The visit had in part come about because Tim had written a novel over the summer about a dystopian world in which to safeguard humanity from war, people were denied the ability to gather into countries or to unite in any form at all. The mad dictator left over from the society that had existed before laughed at the vain spectacle of the people from atop a hill of broken glass. A young teacher, however, was moved to teach his students about connection and intimacy in violation of the laws of the global state, and in the end was martyred for his efforts, as the old mad dictator laughed. Tim had given it to Russ to read and with Tim's permission, he gave it to Sherrie. She had sent a note expressing appreciation for his work, which opened the channels between them again. *I really liked it!* she'd written. *I could see you in every one of the characters.*

"I'm not really a fan of stuff that tries hard to be profound," was Russ's verdict.

Finally, Tim's last day at the variety store came, and it was time to leave. At one time, the trains leaving for the large metropolitan city ran four or five times a day. Now, after budget cuts to the rail system, you could only leave before dawn or in the early evening. The night before his early departure, Tim's mother helped him pack. They should have been sleeping but there was still so much to do, and at eleven the phone rang. It was Sherrie.

"Russ told me you were leaving tomorrow, and I realized *oh my God, he's leaving for good tomorrow!* I'm gonna miss you!"

Tim was thrilled and charmed by her voice all over again, and although he knew it made no sense, he felt the old flood of warmth across his chest to think that she had called him.

"I don't think it really struck me till just tonight that you were leaving!" she exclaimed.

Mona approached Tim. "Who's that on the phone? You can't talk all night! We've got a lot to do! Your train leaves in the morning!"

Tim put his hand over the mouthpiece. "Shut up!" he shouted at her.

The warm, calming tones of Sherrie's voice continued to flow into his ear. They talked for some time more, despite his mother fuming and pacing as she smoked her cigarette. Sherrie reiterated how much she would miss him, how she couldn't believe he wouldn't be around anymore. "You have a really nice voice," she said suddenly. "Did I ever tell you that before? No? I just realized it now. You have a really nice voice."

Mona, Dirk and Tim pulled out into the dark with several suitcases in the back seat and a large cloth bag containing clothes in the trunk. The bag was a linen sack from a company that used to supply the barbershop. Tim's mother blacked out the name of the company on the sack with a magic marker so the company wouldn't see it and want it back. They drove through the quiet streets over to the train station. The night before, Dirk asked Tim to sit in the living room while he watched *The Rockford Files*, giving him the rundown on the plot so far. As Tim was heading to bed he heard a sobbing coming from his brother's bedroom and Tim went in and asked what was wrong. "Well, it's kinda sad you're leavin' tomorrow, ain't it?" Jason had asked.

They came to the station all lit up with golden lights and entered, squinting at the other sleepy-eyed travellers blinking in the harsh fluorescent glare, and soon they were moving with them out to where the train stood, black and majestic in the dim light. They were in the line, moving to the ticket-taker when Tim said to his mother, "Thank you."

His mother said, "Oh, you're welcome," with tears in her eyes.

Dirk said, "Remember pal, you can come back anytime you want. Anytime you want, just get on the train."

Tim sat and watched his parents out the window as they slowly moved from view like small, shrinking figures on an unrolling scroll passing by as the train lurched into motion, gliding smoothly, slowly down the tracks from the station, picking up speed. The pitch black had lessened to grey, and the backs of garages, garbage bins and junkyards fluttered past in dim sepia. The humble houses on the outskirts of the city passed by, the occasional lit window signifying those making coffee before heading off to work, and then there was a lumberyard and some industrial buildings. The bleak wastelands and the sparse cars on the parallel road kept pace then floated back as the train's speed grew and for the briefest moment Tim's house was visible between a car dealership and a sheet metal place.

Back it was spun, spiralling into the past, and pressing his forehead to the window glass, Tim could see the sun rising in the east, bleeding light across the black sky, ragged patches of red slashing out above the rapidly passing fields, the crossings, the barns and hydro towers. As the train charged through the small town, it sounded its baying whistle, roaring its bellow across the countryside. Soon Tim's eyes were smarting as the sun took its final dominion, glaring with prickly, white rays that bristled on the madly passing leaves of the field, the train speeding through the back acreage of his grandfather's farm as it bellowed again and flew in the direction of the sun.

PHOTO CREDIT: Ava Harness

About the Author

KYP HARNESS IS AN ACCLAIMED SINGER-SONGWRITER WHO
has released over two hundred songs on thirteen independent
recordings. Ron Sexsmith calls his work "every bit as powerful as
the best Dylan, Cohen and Lennon combined." His debut, *Wigford
Rememberies*, won the 2017 ReLit Award for Best Novel. He is the
creator of the webcomic *Mortimer the Slug*. He lives in Toronto.